N. H. (Nathan Henry) Chamberlain

The Autobiography of a New England Farm-house

A Book

N. H. (Nathan Henry) Chamberlain

The Autobiography of a New England Farm-house
A Book

ISBN/EAN: 9783337009748

Printed in Europe, USA, Canada, Australia, Japan

Cover: Foto ©Andreas Hilbeck / pixelio.de

More available books at **www.hansebooks.com**

THE AUTOBIOGRAPHY

OF A

New England Farm-House.

A BOOK.

BY

N. H. CHAMBERLAIN.

NEW YORK:

CARLETON, PUBLISHER, 413 BROADWAY.

MDCCCLXV.

To

HENRY WADSWORTH LONGFELLOW,

Poet-Laureate in the loves of many peoples: whose verse is the voice of the tenderness and sadness of hearts throughout the ages, and whose life hath been the gentle echo of his verse: who himself, taught by solemn things, hath spoke to others of those solemn mysteries of life which are to Faith but shadows of the Divinity: to the master of the Mediæval lore and to the Author of a lore that illustrates a new republic: to the teacher of Beautiful Arts, well-remembered of many in our University who have since attained to the sacred heraldry of martyrdom for Father-land in our latest struggle for human privilege, and of others who must henceforth cherish, both for dead and living, the memories of sunnier days: to the man above the poet and to the poet among men, this book is (by permission) respectfully inscribed.

CONTENTS.

THE AUTOBIOGRAPHY

OF A

NEW ENGLAND FARM-HOUSE.

CHAPTER I.

THE SEA.

A PURITAN house of long ago beside the sea. It is eventide. It is also the latter spring-time. Around are the fresh fields, and the new leaves on the old trees. Beyond is the sea, girt here with granite rocks, and silent. Over all the shadows of the night are spreading, and peace under the night. On the house-steps stand two lovers watching the sea, while one by one the stars shine through the night to look at them, — the silence of the spring upon their lips, its hope within their hearts, until the gathering darkness shuts out the sea and leaves them quite alone. For those who love, with clasped hands standing still together, the universe has neither night nor loneliness. Two happy hearts under the night lifted themselves up toward the future. It seemed a sunny day without a cloud fading into the evening red at nightfall. Love spoke in them the same old prophecy of Peace.   And the Love above our love?   Prophesied nothing; only prepared the future in a love for all lovers, which the serene stars in spring-nights dimly express.   Two lovers by the sea under the night.   An accident?   No! A Providence.

So many years come between us and them that we can hardly hear the few brief words at parting.

"So then, you sail to-morrow, Mary?" said the young man, as they came to the hall-door, through which the cheerful light was streaming out upon the trees.

"Yes, dear Henry, and you will join us next week, and then" ——

"Oh, Mr. Henry!" cried a little blue-eyed boy some four years old, maybe, who came running out of the nursery, where they thought him a prisoner for the night, and whose fair, fresh face, so like the young girl's, betokened him as near of kin to her; "are you going away without kissing me?"

The young man bent down over the boy and kissed him.

"Good-by, Mary, till we meet again."

"Good-by, Sir Harry."

And the young girl, patting the little soft-haired head nestling so close to her, watched her lover's manly form as it disappeared among the trees, thinking of the to-morrow.   Alas! the to-morrow came to him with clouds, and its night was starless, and its darkness ran on with him through many years. How cruel is the sea ! It casts its salt spray over many hearts, and the flowers wither. Yet the sea is His also. Let us bow reverently before the Will that rules it.

CHAPTER II.

SANDOWNE.

SANDOWNE is a village of the Puritans. It dates back its birth into the ancient family of towns two hundred years ago. One summer-day some stern-visaged men wandered away from a clump of log-cabins into the wilderness. They had matchlock in hand and sword on hip, as they waded in the sand and forced their way through the brushwood that beset the Indian trail they followed. They were dusty and tired as they chose their night's camping-ground by the side of a clear pond, and tethered their brutes in the long coarse grass of the upland meadow. They were also grimly set upon the errand that brought them here, and lifted up their hearts at nightfall with an invincible faith in Him who they doubted not would cherish them in their new home with the old blessings. Prayer and work joined themselves together when the new town was born that time. The wanderers went no further on that road. They are all asleep now in Sandowne churchyard, at least all of them that sleeps at all, and they have to-day the prayer without the labor. One cannot well avoid a certain

ecclesiastical phraseology in speaking of this town
nativity, for it had certain subtle connections with
another Hebrew Nativity we all have heard of, and
its grim necessity, or fate, severer than any school-
men or stoics dream of, lay enshrined in the dead
centuries. For men in all building, whether of
towns or nations, are very much like children
stringing beads on threads; for though these last
seem filmy and gossamer, like all the others, the
threads that run back through deeds in time are
woven by more pitiless than Parcæ's fingers, and
the texture is of iron. This Puritan village, if one
only knew it, sprang out of the Pentateuch of
Moses, and had its houses built by the Decalogue
of desert wanderers in Palestine some forty centuries back, and wrote with its rude cabins on the
bosom of the Great Mother, under the shadows of
old forests, the Will of God, as interpreted by those
impassioned Saxon hearts, afire of the seventeenth
century, whom men carelessly enough nowadays call
the Puritans.

In the old times the houses of the village gathered themselves around this pond where the Puritans had first encamped. But now they straggled
in a double line along each side of the county road,
of all sorts, shapes, and colors, in the rugged democracy and independence of the true Puritan spirit.
They were not masterpieces of any art known to
the ancients or the moderns. The outposts of this
Saxon village reached all ways. In a winter's

morning thin columns of gray smoke, far off across fields, and up among the hills, and out from under the forest, warned one how the fire had been lighted on the hearths of solitary homes, where life under the shadow of the old hills is as fresh and buoyant as in great cities or ancient realms. It should have been said that Sandowne lies in an amphitheatre of hills, whose summits were swept into arcs of circles by sea-waves centuries ago, and which reach back in under the woods, with sand ravines, worn out by the winter rains, as they slope gently down around the town, which looks across several miles of marsh-land towards the beach and sea. The boast of the townsfolk is San-downe beach. It throws out from the broad pastures its indefinite range of white sand-hills, with irregular black patches of dwarfed trees crawling up their barren sides ; now narrowing itself between the marsh and sea, as if half-conquered of that eager enemy, and then suddenly thrusting out right and left, in inextricable confusion, sand hillocks and tumuli of sea-shells that guard between them green hollows where the beach-grasses thrive ; wasting, drifting sands under the shrubs, — three leagues of sand fortressing that Nature has thrown up against the sea. Thanks to the north wind, that blew in without let or hindrance across the beach, the sea had a very bad temper hereabouts. The fortress was reached only by a long journey across fields, or a voyage in a very broad-backed scow down the black winding creek, that crept, like a great serpent, through the green marsh-sedges, over the marshes, and left a slimy track behind. It was, therefore, a very lonely place. Tradition invested it with a certain mystery and also sanctity. To believe the old folks, strange affairs had been transacted among its sand-hills. It had its Niebelungen lay, or legend, like many another and grander realm, made up of facts that all the townsfolk believed, and somebody, perhaps, had somehow dreamed. To the Sandowner it was as true as Holy Writ, — and he was a sad infidel that doubted it. This story was generally told of winter nights, when the hoarse storm outside drove the Sandowne children closer round the wood-fire on the hearth, and an elder smoked his pipe in the chimney-corner and recalled the past. The heroes of the Sandowne story were knights of a most infamous heraldry, who sailed upon the king's seas without a clearance, and carried cargoes bought on easy terms from ill-starred mariners who never reported back the bargain to their owners. It was said that, in the olden times, beautiful women in tears, and even little children playing around huts built among its sand-hills, had been more than once seen by some adventurous townsman who had crawled through the beach-grass and brushwood to get a nearer view of the visitors whose fires had been observed blazing up at nightfall, across the marshes, in the years when that Lord High Admiral, Robert Kidd, followed his ghastly commerce and buried his ill-gotten gold in secret. There were reputed to be fabulous treasures buried in the beach sands somewhere, and many had dug for the pirate's gold. Only once had there been success. It was notorious that old Bill Swain, great-grandfather of the Sandowne Swains, spent a week at the beach once, returning at night, when no one knew it, and afterward, upon occasion, brought out sundry gold pieces of quaint coinage, which the wise in such matters said came from the Spanish main. In consequence of Bill's researches, he became suddenly rich, though he had been a vagabond all his life before, and has a laudatory monument in the churchyard that proves him to have been very much more than a common saint, as is the wont of graveyard lore in other places than Sandowne.

At the time when our story begins, Sandowne was a serene and somewhat stupid village, for whom the universe was contained between its hills and sea. Its white houses, with their huge front-yards and brass knockers, weekly scoured by the Sandowne matrons, each with the aspiration to eclipse her neighbors in this elaborate toilette of the front-door, the elms and sycamores and locust-trees overshadowing them, while the lilacs clustered under their windows, — its little village store, the bema and forum of Sandowne politics, — its gray, weather-stained meeting-house on the hill above these homes, — are still remembered by those who knew it then. Its ancient rusticity and homeliness have long since passed away. A railroad awoke it, and cursed it, as old-time folks think, with the new progress. But before the new learning, the stage-coach, brilliant with yellow paint and varnished leather, came down once a week from the metropolis, dashing, with its four red horses, along the main street, by little gaping urchins and old men who sat in doorways, up to the postmaster's house, and the heart of Sandowne vibrated with the vibrations of its wheels. Once a week came a few straggling newspapers, to be quarrelled over by the grocery politicians who defended diverse statesmanships, according to their party bent, with the subtlest mental acumen and the most recondite historical lore. The Great Republic owes many things to its groceries. They refine its politics. Sandowne had schools, where, periodically, wandering schoolmasters taught children, vagabond from long vacation, their elements, and learning was absorbed through the pores, in a medley of physical and mental training, by birch and ferule. It had also gospel ministrations; it had gossips; it had weddings, and christenings, and tea-drinkings, and *buryings, like the rest of the world, though it was pervaded by a chronic sleepiness; and tidings of the world without, — of change, of calamity, of battle, of revolution, — crept feebly over its hill-ridge, and the town, as has been hinted, lay silent in its sheltered nook, calm, thoughtless, and asleep.

Below the outside, however, the Sandowne life had many sober elements. It brought out comedy and tragedy on this humble stage, for the sake at least of the one great Spectator of all our acting, and never quite forgot its essential methods in the old town. It was a narrow life indeed, but gaining a certain intensity from narrowness, as rivers, like the Rhine at Bingen, gain from their nearing shores their fleetness. A Sandowner's field of vision was microscopic, but he managed to see very clearly all which was in that. He illustrated in his town-life, under his hills, certain great laws of life that have swept over empires and left ruins often, because they were not heeded; for life had put him, as it puts every man, on his probation, and he had failed to use its gifts, and had, therefore, mentally and morally come to harm. A single fact explains. He was an inveterate gossip. He sank down to a gossip, because, under his town temptations, he would not rise up to be a man, and live like a man upon those great, immutable truths in life that make all disciples men; and as his soul must live on something, he had tried to make it live on the bargains, the alliances, the necrologies of Sandowne, until all his ways had a kind of meddlesome frivolity and childishness about them, and he became a gossip. The narrowness of that made him illiberal and ill-humored in all his judgments of town affairs. It seemed to be his destiny that what another man liked should be to him " the abomination of desola-

tion " spoken of by the Prophet. It was sufficient
to enlist his sympathy against any plan that another
man proposed it. In town matters he cancelled his
neighbor with himself, and felt a sort of instinct to
write as he was able, under every additional sum
of town industry or improvement, zero. He had
not broadened his life with the world's life, and had
become a dwarf. His very feuds were dwarfed, as
could be seen in the quarrels that raged amongst
the Sandowners. One year it was about the rela-
tive sailing powers of two sloops that plied between
the coast towns, and neighborhoods were bitterly
divided on that issue. Then it was about two rival
stage-lines, and next about two peddlers; while
cranberry bogs and conversations, wood-lots and
drift-wood, or an occasional wreck alongshore, the
new minister or the old hearse-house (so strangely
were things jumbled together in the village consciousness), furnished motive-power to the angry
tongues that confused and vexed the town. In his
judgments, the Sandowner was more infallible than
the Pope, as narrow men always are, and had the
best opinion of his own quality and moment to the
universe in general. So magnificent a thing is
Sandowne assurance that it would have excited no
wonder in one if, at any time during the last forty
years, the town-surveyor had undertaken to survey
the pasturage and salt-marshes of the moon, and
the Sandowners had with equal gravity set themselves to quarrel about the distribution of the lots.

Sandowne had also its hierarchies and aristocracies, as well as many a grander realm, though according to the laws of its own narrowness and lack. · No doubt Liberty, Equality, Fraternity, are pleasant words to talk about; but give man or woman or His Satanic Majesty three weeks in any clump of houses of any township, and in that time they will furnish you with a full-fledged aristocracy. The supposition is not meant as satire upon the thing itself, of whose quality one is not called upon just here to judge. Your little boy will wear his paper crown garnished with the gilt stars his sister cuts out for him with her scissors, and strut about as happy as a king. Why laugh then if certain Sandowners wear the paper crown of a cheap royalty, and hold out the sceptre graciously for some poor Esther or Mordecai of us meek citizens to touch? Human nature, when it will not be itself, burlesques itself, and village aristocracies are not, to say the least, sublime. The Sandowne comedy of Family plays out its harmless play, impervious, in its triple armor of self-complacency, to any sarcasm. Let the historian, given to verities, tell how it came out of a pine wood-lot, or a successful voyage after codfish to Newfoundland, or a keg of New England rum, or a calico dress left in a wigwam for the chief's squaw, as purchase-money in a thieving bargain, by which these dusky forest-kings sold their fathers' graves for nought, — or even out of less cleanly fountains. Me, shall no power on earth force to disturb its great serenity. Let us robe it, all unconscious that it needs a covering, with the mantle of silence, and leave it in the choicest company, — itself.

I might be rightly charged with defamation by the Sandowners did I not hasten to say that there were quite other elements in the town-life than those just mentioned. That it is a Puritan town proves so much ; and in Sandowne there were souls with transmitted Puritan instincts in them, oftener women than men, in whom the austere Puritanism gave out a certain intensity and fire of living, and kindled life into true saintly zeal and aspiration ; whose thoughts went over the hills into the world, and traversed the world of time and wrestled with the problems thereof, and added, as they were able, to their Here their Heretofore, that they might lift their Hereafter nearer the stars and heaven! In the town-clerk's records one may find only traces of a life commonplace and dreary. But hereabouts has been quite another life, which for two hundred years or more loved and sorrowed, gained and lost, hoped and feared, had children and friends, and visible fortunes of many sorts, and, above all, those solemn aspirations which come sooner or later to every man of us, though it has only left faint record of itself in field and churchyard, and its legends lie open towards God rather than men.

Sandowne has changed from long ago. A new life is in its streets and at its heart ; but a pilgrim within its borders last spring-time found its mill-pond, where the Puritans halted, as young as ever, only a little darker from the *débris* the streams bring down from the hills to it; with the old willows bending over it, and the rushes flourishing in quiet nooks of it; and the graveyard overgrown with brambles, and its gravestones reeling about with very age, covered with curt mosses hard at work in smoothing over the sharp, chiselled letters, as though they were anxious to have the world forget there was anybody who had laid for so many years so still there; while its horizontal tomb-stones laid on decaying masonry, through whose crannies the adventurous school-boy looks, dreading to find a skeleton beneath, have fallen down in divers angles of decay. Outside the graveyard stand the older houses of the settlers, whose doors have opened so often to let pass a lodger who never bestowed the simple courtesy of good-by on any as he departed, nor returned again to reclaim the room he left, though the door stood open in many a day while the sunlight and spring-light entered at will, and the angels of life and death had often crossed the threshold. The boys who sat fishing lazily by the mill in the soft spring sunshine, as even their betters, the Sandowne elders, who happen to be tenants at will just now in the old borough, had no thought of the historic drama of Sandowne life which had been played through before their day. Nature, too, is always intrusting

our feverish, wayward human lives to the two great
silences of time and change. She will never will-
ingly tell any Sandowner anything of what seems
to me so sacred, unless he demand it of her in certain wise, manly ways she is never quite able to
resist. But you ask, reader, why I have troubled
you to hear so much about this town that Nature
long since laid aside as vanished. Simply because
there is not yet silence for you and me, and I trust
we shall learn something of our to-day from their
yesterday.

CHAPTER III.

A HERO.

IT was an afternoon of one of those spring days, wherein no doubt many of my readers gathered as children the early violets which hide themselves away from the frost in the gray mosses of sunny hill-sides (may they long be as blue to them as then), when the Sandowne stage, that carried in its rough leather mail-bag the outside world into the very heart (I mean the village store) of Sandowne, halted as it reached the summit of the western hill-ridge which looked down on the village. The halt was made, not that the great lobster-faced driver, (they called him " Lobster Bill,") wrapped to-day in his huge, shaggy, many-caped coat, secured tightly about the throat with a very large " comforter," might air his æsthetics in a fresh criticism of the landscape before him, but for the more homely purpose of " lettin' the horses catch their breath a second," as he said. The passenger, however, who sat beside him on the box, seemed otherwise inclined, for after watching for some time the scene, he exclaimed with some enthusiasm, " The old place is always beautiful ! " The driver, possibly thinking himself addressed, answered laconically, as out of his stomach, " Sandowne 'll beat all the world for salt-grass, I calc'late."   At the risk of hindering the government mail-coach, let us keep it here until we can observe a little more closely the passenger at the side of " Lobster Bill." Him we shall leave to his horses and his hay, having written his own epitaph for us, as does many another man we meet, in the short Beotian epigram he has ejected down before us ; but as we shall have much to do with the other, asking pardon of the gentle reader for putting a hero upon no better pedestal than a stage-coach, we give him speedy introduction.

Arthur Bassett happens to be the son of an old Sandowne family, and is going back to look about him on the homestead which has but just fallen to him, as next of kin to the late master of Bassett Farm, and possibly to spend the summer there.   In a history of such plebeian fashions as ours, it would be quite out of place to produce so aristocratic a thing as a genealogical tree, since it is the hereditary policy of all republics to forget how a man was born in observing how he lives.   It may, however, conciliate the interest of some readers towards our hero, — especially of those so urgent of family as to hold that globules of true nobility may be detected in the globules of arterial blood, — to frankly say, that, besides tracing back their pedigree, like all good Christians, to Adam, the Bassett

family were especially proud to find the name of
their founder in the list of the knights who came in
with William Conqueror, and to recall the honorable fortunes of that Kentish branch, whose youngest son, impelled by the old Norse instinct of voyaging, came early in the seventeenth century to the
New England settlements and built himself a house
in Sandowne.   For the rest, Arthur Bassett was
born rich, has lived poor, and now, in the swift
changes of our transatlantic life, is again heir to an
estate. His father he has never known ; his mother,
who struggled for him in childhood, ceased from
her labors some ten years since, before the cloud
was lifted from Arthur, and when her motherly
prophecy of her son's success was as yet her only
solace.   Arthur himself, with his Anglo-Saxon apt-
ness, and compelled to it by a certain grim necessity
of poverty, has put his hand to several tasks : has
cut wood in the winter forests ; has mown in hay
harvests ; has been a raftsman on the river ; a
schoolmaster in many a rough field requiring human
culture ; and being called to something higher by
somewhat that men call instinct, aspiration, genius,
but which is the very voice of God in a soul, has
fought his way against all odds through the University at K ——.   To-day he is a graduate and
twenty-two ; not a handsome fellow, but a tall, thin,
athletic, quick-motioned Saxon, with a clear gray
eye, and features that have a certain delicacy of intellectual expression in them, whereby one recognizes

under all disguises, the devotee of severe, pure studies ; a man of strong will and sensibility, as you may see from the tremulous compression of the lips as he stops speaking, and looks one straight in the eye, with a certain eager honesty of face, which means both force and truth ; so over-ready with his opinions sometimes that you might mistake for arrogance what is only the inner fealty of the man to truth ; uncomfortably proud, perhaps, as poor men of genius always are when they measure the world by worth ; and the world's children of quite another lineage from theirs, in self-defence, measure themselves by wealth ; something repellant in him even, namely, a rude force of character, to be toned down hereafter into softness by success, but at present breaking its way and jostling foolish or pretentious men with a sort of proud discourtesy, — his challenge to the world that calls him poor and wisely refuses him rank in the great company of genius, until he win it beyond cavil in fair, sturdy fight for it. Not a brilliant man, one says, but still one of God's men, who, if chance favor him, will stand bolt upright for fair play to the weakest, where the baser sort would crawl in the dirt before Society or Power, and fight, what so few are men enough to fight, a man's battle. Indeed, I think so highly of Arthur Bassett as to believe that, upon occasion, he would show in this so commonplace life of ours the stuff of a Luther, or a Stauffacher, and brave the popes of our modern Protestantism, or keep almost any pass for liberty, as men like him have done through all the years of the necessities of our humanity; though as yet he is only an uncourtly, unknown, undeveloped student of twenty-two. Indeed, the main spiritual fact about Arthur is, a certain absence of any finish or harmony of nature. His intellectual attitude is chaotic. He neither knows himself, nor in any wise just how he stands in the universe, or his mission here. A nature blindly responsive to what is high in Art and History, lifted sometimes into silent ecstacies by the subtle inspiration of song and true human act of men, who raised thereby humanity still further above its shames and chains, — the undeveloped germ lying at the centre of his being, and able to bear beautiful fruits hereafter, — is to him the absolute unknown, and no voice or law as yet rules over it to lead him in through the gates of life to the inevitable arena. By the will of God, in every life as in every world, there is first chaos, until some mighty Eros creates out of it Cosmos. For Arthur, it is still chaos. Let us trust that in that severe path of life, wherein God makes His best beloved walk with suffering, — out of this blind, confused, chaotic, though loyal nature, — some Great Teacher of life may bring forth Cosmos.

CHAPTER IV.

ABOUT HOUSES.

" Thou gazest on the stars, my life!   Ah! gladly would I be
Yon starry skies with thousand eyes that I might gaze on thee."

PLATO.

THE history of the world is writ in houses. Human instincts, needs, cultures, origins, religions, civilizations, record themselves in window, doorway, roof-tree. Government, climate, soil, century, shape the commonest dwelling. The Alhambra and Cologne Cathedral, if more imperishable, are not more explicit monuments of Saracenic and Teutonic mediæval life, than are the peasant cottages by the Rhine and the Guadalquiver, wherein the religious races who listened for the Divinity in the falling waters or moan of night-wind in the Schwarzwald or Odenwald, or worshipped the One in the gleam of falling swords on a thousand battlefields, set up the penates of humble houses, and parcelled off for themselves from the immensity of the universe, with rafter and roof, a place that they called home. There is hardly anything so human as a house. It gains a certain sanctity, from the humanity that shelters itself from so many storms within. It is some man's plea for personality and recognition as a placeman in the great shifting world, who is set to meet life just there and so. An old, weather-stained, wooden house, such as one may see any day amongst the New England hills, is the most pathetic sight in the country landscape. Bowed down there under the elms, in the humility of its many years; stained into dark colors by storm and gust; embroidered with its clinging, sombre mosses, parasites that feed on its decay; wasting away without a moan under the rains that rot the eves and shingles, and dropping the straight lines and angles of its strong youth for the mellower lines of its age, where the crumbling beams sink down in faintness of long-continued task-work; and yet sheltering alike the little child that with careless step and shout plays through its spring-time within its aged walls, and the old man with the scars of life-long memories, that make all but the best in him withered; opening its doors to all comers with the same grave hospitality, and letting pass without a sob in peace many a weary man and woman, borne out to a more passionless home; in silent charity covering from rain and snow men and women, with their human and petty passions of love and hate; passionless and stainless itself from any sin, giving never rebuke but shelter alike to all, letting God judge all, so that it show its charity to all, — an old house has a certain strain of pathos and saintly charity written on its very front.

An old New England country-house is eminently historic. In cities, where wider wealth and intercourse give greater command of style and fabric, houses have a certain cosmopolitan air of kinship with elegant structures everywhere. But the country-houses are individual, provincial, unique. Their beams were hewn out of the neighboring swamp or forest by some rustic workman; their stones were dug out of the hill-side hard by; their ornaments are such as rude, rustic taste could fashion. Climate depressed the roof and lowered the rooms, to bear the snow-falls and save the heat against the rigorous New England winter. Necessity compelled men to wood for fabric; the white-pine trees of the woodlands have furnished a shelter to the best beauty, intellect, piety, patriotism, for nigh three centuries now. The earliest houses are largely English homes, and have been gradually receding towards a more national though nameless style. Puritan austerity banished all sweetness and all beauty, and wrote its creed over the doorway and the mantel. The sober, demure, primly-shaped, angular Puritan house, with roof broken midway into angles that depress it in humility towards the ground, seems to declare to every passer, "This earth is a vale of tears, and I am a worm of the dust." All true houses have a certain character about them, and physiognomy, like men, and the intense individualism of the early settlers, increased by the freedom of the wilderness, is recorded in the marked characteristics of the early dwellings.　Along almost any road where old things have not passed away, are scattered houses which reveal their builder's character: secretive houses, standing alone and self-contained, away from roadsides, with solitary reach of mysterious sheds and secluded granaries,—close, solitary, uncommunicative, with forbidding gates, and a certain air of inhospitality about them; and here another house close on the road, open-doored and windowed, and smiling as an old-time Squire ready to welcome his guests on the hall-steps; and here a third, bearing the impress of some ancient Englishman, hale, boisterous, and hearty, as old John Blackstone, of Norfolk, gravely astride his manageable steed with horns, riding to church, and compelled to emigrate, perhaps, not so much through spiritual zeal as by material wants,—a low, broad house, with numerous outbuildings that seem made to hold the worn-out family equipage, or store the corn harvest,—with a white-topped, irregular-sided stack of chimneys, and little windows set without order in its sides,—and standing in a little hollow that opened upon the road, along which grow luxuriantly the motherwort and raspberry and tansy, as from time immemorial they have grown by Puritan houses; and around it the ancient lilacs, with dead, scraggy arms thrust out from their deep green mouldy leaves, and curt, fat, warty cherry-trees, in all imaginable attitudes of sleepy barrenness, and the grass-grown, untravelled avenue that leads up to the unentered door of a decayed and tenantless home. So the dead have written their histories by all the traversed roadways of our New England rural life.

Bassett farm-house was a marked example of the older New England architecture. Its founder was one of that small class, who, divorced from Puritanism amongst the Puritans, had still found it necessary to transfer himself to one of the strictest of their communities. There had indeed been strange stories which implicated him in grave political intrigues abroad, and even darker rumors; but a straightforward, though somewhat solitary life, embellished with such amenities of generous living as he had been able to bring into the wilderness, had reconciled the early Sandowners to certain delinquencies of his in matters of church-going, and he died lamented by all who cherished good-fellowship and broadheartedness. The house had, therefore, from the start a certain elegance in detail and magnitude of structure, usually missed in such locality. It stood in the broad fields that stretched northward towards the sea, and its grounds sloped towards the marsh and beach. The primitive structure, a high, angular, wooden building, with the depressed, broken roof beforementioned, and large hall-door in the centre, adorned with some slight essays in Norman carving, had, in due course of years, received large secondary accretions in the shape of various suites of rooms and chambers tacked on without much regard to harmony, simply to satisfy the proprietor's convenience, and together formed one of those shapeless, uncouth piles, which, while they usually stand for thrift and family, are rarely found in later times, even in a New England landscape. It stood, moreover, under the arms of the old elms, and guarded by stalwart sycamores, in mingled garden and orchard, such as old mansions often display. In the late May-day, it looked sombre and grave, as the sunlight streamed through the gray elms and flecked it with alternate light and shade; and its gray mosses on the roof and weather-stained sides, and a general calm, deserted aspect, revealed at once its age and story. All this was to have been seen by Arthur, as in company with Sam Jones, " the help at the farm," he found himself emerging from the village into the quiet gray road which led between the rough stone-walls amongst thick shrubbery, set there as it seems to conceal such ugliness, to Bassett Farm. Whether Arthur was busy with such or far different matters, as he stood upon the broad stone-step of Bassett House to receive the courtesies and protestations of black Cloe, one of the freed bondwomen of that New England society which once dealt in Africans, as strict property, every student of the human heart can judge for himself. Here, then, was at last home; vacant, indeed, of some whose smile would have lighted up the old house into true transfiguration of love and tenderness, and whose voice should have repeated those dear old words, that, when they fall upon the heart, are always fresh and living, as if ten thousand crumbled lips had never spoken them to ten thousand crumbled hearts, — but still home. He looked around him in the garden. The old lilacs still guarded the entrance, as when he had crossed it as a little child ; the rows of the green box still led away in confused lines in under the old trees ; the early flowers were breaking their way up through the dry dead stalks of last year's foliage. Nature was busy here repairing her loss in winter, and ready to answer the strong sun again with beautiful offerings ; but the walks were overgrown and shadowed by rank dry grasses, and over all was a general aspect of the neglect and decay which come when ready hands grow feeble and masters change on the estate. He entered the house. The large hall, with its sombre paper and single mahogany table by the stairs, looks as it did to him fifteen years ago, only a little smaller and more sombre ; the parlor, with its huge painted oak beam overhead, and capacious fireplace, with the golden andirons, as the child once thought them, and quaint furniture, with the same lofty-backed, intricate oak-chairs, — some of them brought across seas they said ; and the same grim portraits of ladies and gentlemen in ruffs and feathers, whose eyes had followed him so with that merciless gaze of theirs, had hardly changed, though somehow they seemed older and more infirm ; the chambers, with their

3

sparse furnishings, and one where he remembered
as a little boy to have knelt down beside his mother
and prayed " Our Father ; " the rooms and ante-
rooms and passages leading up and down and away
into unknown and uninhabited nooks of the old
mansion, so silent and tenantless, inspired him with
that kind of awe one feels when entering a deserted
castle on the Rhine hills, or open tomb in the hill-
side amongst the Apennines.   He descended to the
study, where he remembered the last proprietor
had once received him with a sort of rough stateli-
ness that smacked of the Colonial times, — a single room built out upon the ground under the
shadow of the old elm that fed itself from the *débris*
of six generations of a now vanished life.   The old
books, dusty and silent, lay in disorder upon the
shelves ; the candelabras of his childish wonder
were on the mantel ; the study-table, with its ink-
stains and mouldy pens and littered papers, looked
as though its owner had taken long vacation and
left it to the care of dust and mould ; and everything wore a sort of dead aspect, as though the
human, with its concomitants of life, were wanting.
He seated himself in the huge arm-chair, and
thought of all that had been to him and others like
him, tenants in the old home.   How strange it all
was.   How much life and pride and passion and
humility and hope and fear had been here.   How
much tragedy and comedy had been played out
within these silent walls.   In these rooms little chil-

dren had been born, and old men had died, and mothers had wept, and brides hoped, and bride-grooms been eager for the wrestle and work of what was the great world to them, and ambitious men had been foiled, and humble men silent; and the sick had waited calmly for the destroyer, and there had been revel and wail and prayer and fair flowers and withered wreaths, and all those infinite and mysterious incidents of life, whereby its great drama goes slowly on from year to year, solemn, sacred, august, inevitable. And all this, and more than this, came to Arthur as he sat there, in some dim ways of consciousness, and he dreamed of his own future until he slept. So men sleep a thousand times in the arms of the great Past, until the inexorable Present calls them unto a still greater Future!

CHAPTER V.

GARRETS.

THE gray, cold week that followed Arthur's advent to Bassett Farm was in harmony with his mood. There is hardly any time so desolate as that interregnum between winter and spring, when the snow has gone and left the gray fields bare, to be cracked and seamed by nightly frosts, or inundated with the cold spring rain, and the dead grasses, without their pure white winter covering, rustle with that harsh, dead sound of theirs, in the dull, heavy air; when the barns are empty, and amongst the withered, red forest-leaves, the winter-birds search sedulously for scanty dead seeds and berries, and in the wood-hollows and on the north side of the wood-hills the failing snow-banks, half-ice under the rains, hide themselves from the fitful heat of the nearing sun, and man and beast and bird seem alike at halt, as if waiting for somewhat; when that immovable leaden sky, too passionless to show a gleam of red at sunset, and too merciless to disclose a field of blue at mid-day, reflects itself in the gray sea, and lends of its own hopelessness to the cold, watery, benumbed, and lifeless fields. It is Nature

resting awhile for the one great effort of her year,—
summer. Nature, alchemist, seems at rest sometimes in her laboratory, where, with that awful
secrecy of hers, she looks bent on some new discovery of the elixir of life for her worn-out children, when she is really busy preparing new crucibles, for her almost ghostly elements of air and fire
and water to refine into fresh and infinite life and
beauty. It was an impulse for society which drove
Arthur, in the gray days, into the fields; and they,
with their unsocial, barren manners, drove him back
upon himself. Sam Jones himself, man-of-all-work
and under-lord of Bassett Farm, had not as yet
dared to venture upon that sturdy wrestling with
them, upon which in great faith the New England
farmer must depend for harvests. Arthur found
him in the great barn-floor, mending rakes.

"No farming yet, Sam?" he said.

"Farming! you might as well plant potatoes in
the salt-marsh there, as anywhere about here. The
land's too cold. Things have to vegetate. Must n't
get afore the times, you know. The bluebirds have n't
come yet in the orchard, and I tells my wife them 's
my themomoters; and there 's snow-banks off yonder, and winter won't rot in the sky, and them
clouds there don't look much like planting-time,
anyhow. May frosts catch fools' corn, Squire."

And then they discussed farm matters, wherein
Sam's wisdom became very urgent, made up, as it
turned out, of what the old men had said, and how

the " Injuns " had done, and the way somebody's great-grandfather, who had the best farm in Sandowne, had managed, with certain wise saws and proverbs, brought across seas, and kept here for more than two centuries now in the conservative rustic consciousness of the Sandowners, though it never occurred to Sam to know how some of these last belonged to the sturdy Saxon churls, adorned with the silver collar of their Norman masters, who ploughed land in England nigh a thousand years ago.

" We plant corn," Sam said, " as the Injuns did, when the swamp-pinks come out; and them were wise fellers about fish and birds and flow'rs and sich things. Kinder natr'l to 'em, as for a pappoose to swim when the women throwed 'em into the river to toughen 'em; and old Saul Downer, though he does raise mighty great corn with his sea-weed and muck yonder, could n't find the best land in his pastures for a cornfield half so nice as them creeturs, the Injuns, did the warm, red land where the sun strikes first, and out o' the way of frosts. Kinder natr'l to them black skins, I s'pose," he said.

And thereupon Arthur fell to thinking how he had read in " The Birds of Aristophanes," that in Greece the coming of the crane marked the time of seed-sowing, and the kite the time of sheep-shearing, and the swallow the time to put on summer clothing; and how in lack of science, Nature provides for her needy children infallible horologues written upon the old hills, and even on the still older sky. The sublime democracy of Nature, wherein she provides for the lowest, the best, convicts even our wisest democracies of sham and partiality.

Arthur betook himself in-doors for occupation. The old homestead, so redolent of things past in this gray season, of the dead charities of the land, and in its cold calmness so unlike the warm instincts and harsh unrest of his afore-life, excited in him a sort of half-melancholy and half-restlessness, as everywhere the graves of a dead Past sadden a man and incite him to his life-long wrestle, that he may attain to their more than life-long rest. Cloe, housekeeper, was history, and he studied her. The old crone had known five generations of the Bassetts, and her world lay within the limits of Bassett Farm. Five generations she had waited on, with hardly a thought beyond her service; and she had so far forgot her youth that a wide blank in her consciousness, marked however here and there with certain figures and passages in the lives of the old proprietors, left only the narrow margin of her sleepy old age for solace; gleaning out of her narrow but long experience of life no theories, but only facts that to her mind were epochs, and whose faith (for Cloe was eminently religious in her own way) consisted of snatches of the old Puritan theology, interlaced with divers incidents of the Indians, who in her youth had still their wigwams up amongst the pine-hills, and came in the pinching winters into the farm-kitchen to beg corn; all toned, moreover, by a certain African superstitiousness that kept for more than half a century the blue bracelets on her withered wrists for amulets, and made her dance the moon-dance when the new moon came, and the harvest-dance, with those strange contortions and grimaces and barbaric jugglery of arms and feet which flourish along the Congo and the African slave coast, (so slowly does blood alter its methods even under new skies,) and sing psalm-tunes on Sunday mornings, mixed up with gibberish songs and broken strophes of what you might imagine aboriginal or African music, and introduce new names into her prayers, until the spectators thought her old head disordered. Cloe had a firm belief in the under-world, that did not square, indeed, with any recognized Christian creed, but had a wonderful control over her own little works and ways. If you found her under a clear sky taking in the wet clothes, with all the bustle of a man-of-war's man taking in sail with a squall ahead, she would give you as reason, "'T will rain afore night; I heard the natives quarrelling under ground." The "natives," whoever they might be, she held in profound awe. She would leave picking whortleberries in any place, if she heard "the natives" under-ground there; she prophesied weddings and burials, good luck or ill, and indeed everything that was of any matter to her from the goings-on of those mysterious, undescribed, invisible beings she called " na- tives." They were the black's goblins, elves, fairies, or whatsoever colony of spirits you please to name them. Cloe owned all Bassett Farm, and put on the family airs and honors as though such were a cook's perquisites. She was, withal, good-humored, though a little testy upon any slight interference with her vested rights as the oldest inhabitant of the freehold, and kept the same place on the oak- settle that stood on one side of the great, grim kitchen fireplace, when off work, smoking her black pipe, and dozing as a sable goddess of those sooty realms; or with a thimble on each thumb, singing piously all day long the edifying refrain, highly creditable to Cloe's study of the Catechism, " When I die I'm going home to Ginney;" one of the last of that patient race who carried our great- grandmothers in arms, built so much neglected stone-wall in pasture-lands, and who sleep now in nameless graves under the old elms of the village church-yard. Cloe, at Arthur's instigation, went through her long story with all its gaps and exag- gerations and colorings, with a confidence that ad- mitted no doubt from her auditor; a story about Massa John or James, and Mistresses Grace and Charity; of how such a Bassett was made Colonel, and how fine the regimentals looked; of babies the prettiest in the world, and of the loveliest brides that the same Massa John or James brought home; and how such and such grew to be such lovely boys and girls, and of how massa died, and what famous funeral dinners were cooked by her, Cloe; and how, when she was young, there were ghosts about the house, and what was done with the witch that Parson Churchill scented out from her hut on the beach yonder, and what she had seen by the church-yard wall when she came home after the famous dance they had in Squaw Crowfoot's wigwam, and such like matters that had lodged themselves in Cloe's consciousness, as one has seen dry leaves and branches lodge themselves on some dead tree reaching out from shore into the river channel; for to many another man and woman, like Cloe, the Time-stream in gentle charity brings its burden, though it be but dry leaves and twigs.

Arthur filled up the outline of Cloe's picture for himself, and read other chapters of History out of that Herodotean chronicler, the house itself. The house antiquities of New England are largely Puritan. No Sèvres vases, no statues, few paintings, — and these last, too, mostly ancestral portraits in the families of the better born; but here and there an oak-chair brought out of North England, from dear old fatherland, little china tea-sets and great china tea-sets, as the fashion of the age was, — the latter adorned with broad Dutch figures, reminiscences of the Puritan stay in Holland; a Puritan sword, a flint-lock from King Philip's war, or a " Queen's-arm " from the French and Indian war; continental equipments of '76, now passed into the dignity of history ; and above all, the worn family Bible, with its tattered, begrimmed leaves, out of which five generations of toiling yeomanry, between work and on Sundays, read the Word of Life, so that life under its rough garb became a true saintly struggle towards heaven ; a few theological works, like Baxter's " Call," and " Rest," and Mather's " Magnalia," — such are the gray and worn antiquities of the austere Puritan home. Arthur rummaged in the old closets with their dusty, dead scent of mouldy papers, and in the cupboards each side the chimneys, and under stairways ; and everywhere were tokens of some taste or habit of the old occupants, who had let slip these hints of their now silent lives for strangers to guess the rest. He betook himself finally to the garret, where the *débris* and sediment of the house-life had been silently bestowing themselves so long; to that mysterious upper realm under the rafters, where the bare oakbeams show their interlacings and all their seams and scars and knots so plainly, and the broad chimney-stack reveals the mystery of its ancient masonry as it springs through the roof; where the later rain sounds so soothingly on the roof in the still spring nights ; where the din of life below stairs reaches only in subdued tones, and little children fear its silence, and the black ways under the eaves, and the low passages leading they know not whither, — realm of dust, of spiders, the wrecks of work, pleasure, pain, of silence, of rest, — a New England garret.   Arthur surveyed the museum around him. Yonder, against the light that enters through the little square window, is the house spinning-wheel, whose hum sounded so cheerily in the autumn mornings, when the quick feet of the spinners were heard overhead, and out-doors the unhusked corn and yellow pumpkins and russet apples lay in heaps about the orchard, and man and maid wrought contentedly in the mild, hazy autumn-days. But now its broad brown circle, off which so much gray yarn had been spun, was dusty, and the spindle rusty, and the band crumbling away, as the fingers that so often stretched it upon the wheel had crumbled long ago ; and that diminutive windmill there is the measuring-reel, still, too, as off work now ; and the weavers' looms are piled yonder under the dust, whereon patriotic housewives wove the homespun to clothe the dear brave men that were away at Valley Forge fighting with worse enemies than Britons, when King George closed up every harbor with his ships.   And hung above, on the wooden pegs, are the cast-off garments of the old occupants.   That straw bonnet, a young girl's evidently, with its monstrous frontal elevation, looks sere enough, and the green ribbons on it are pale, but what of the face that smiled and chatted out of it ?   And that white dress, with elaborate flounce and plait, so yellow and rusty now ; — a bride wore that dress in the one great hour of woman which has centered in it all that has been or shall be to her.

But what of the bride herself? Did she win or lose in that old marriage? Did she gather little children about her knee in motherly pride, or were there no wheat-stalks intertwined with the wedding lilies? Or was it a young face or a worn face that lay open to the sun under the old elms when the townsmen came to another funeral at Bassett House? Shall we ask of the gray mossy stone over yonder by the town, or must we leave her with hopes for the best things for her, as one of an innumerable unknown company, kin of ours through the great Passion of our common life, who leaves us as the sole record of herself a faded wedding-dress? And these little shoes, and militia regimentals, and cocked hat with the rusty lace-band; the old rapier yonder, laid inside the family cradle,—what are these but sacred relics in that true Catholic Church of Life, wherefrom, with its mysterious Lents and Easters, and days of Ashes and days of Palm, all wise souls are born in faith, into the great hereafter? The " innumerable caravan " had halted here, and then moved on into the illimitable depths of what seem voiceless deserts. And these were as their footprints, and embers of their fires gone out upon the desert sands.

Something of this came to Arthur as he sat that evening by the crackling wood-fire in the huge parlor fireplace, and looked over by its light a lot of old papers he had chanced upon in the garret. They were of all sorts: justices' commissions, with the old colonial seal to them ; letters of business, and account-letters from the great war and from ship-board, and across seas, with the old marks on them ; letters about marriages and nativities, and betroth-ments and deaths; letters of absent husbands ; letters of absent lovers, men and women, each in its own peculiar handwriting, and telling its own story there after threescore years or more ; letters that meant so much to those who wrote and those who read ; letters out of passionate, warm hearts, with words that have not grown cold even now, so warm are they with an ever unalterable humanity, which kindles into sympathy hearts by hearts. Comedy and tragedy Arthur found in them, — a certain pathos and sweetness in these brown, stained letter-sheets, keeping each its message fresh, while so much else was voiceless and hidden. And Arthur tried to con-jure up before his mind the writers, and to learn their character from their handwriting; and won-dered whether the women were pretty and the men gentle, and much more about blue eyes and black, and fair-haired girls and brunettes, and such-like matters, as he sat watching the glowing red-oak coals building grotesque or fairy mansions for him in the heart of the fire that lighted up the room so cheerfully.   Just so, he thought, with the same demonstrative fashions of good-fellowship, the fire on the old hearth has lighted up this room for many of them as it does to-night for me, though it has no heart nor choice for any.   And he might have thought how the fashions of that fire were as old as the world itself; that just so it wrought when the Hebrews built their camp-fires around Mount Sinai forty centuries back; or the burning bush revealed the Jehovah to His kneeling servant. It was the immutability of Nature that troubled Arthur, as he thought how, without halt or wail, Nature on Bassett Farm went on in unalterable fashions, — whether children were born or died, or there was woe or wassail in-doors, — giving a grave alike to all without a pang for any, moving no summer flower in sympathy when the warm earth grasped them, nor deepening a single shadow in mourning when it gave a frosty grave in winter; and how buds were swelling now, and grasses were starting, and the flowers weeks hence would smile as serenely in happy May as though there had been no severe, stern drama of human souls in Bassett House. What seemed to Arthur the inhumanity of Nature, was but the settled purpose of the Infinite upon a subject world, — that without its let or hindrance, Humanity, as lord of it, might rise through it to Him.

CHAPTER VI.

SUNDRIES.

A FRESH warm day called Arthur out from the old house and its sombre memories into the fields. Arthur went; why he hardly knew, or whither; with no definite intent; partly, perhaps, through that natural restlessness of young men which, without curb or fixed course, misspends itself in a thousand fruitless or questionable tasks, and partly through a more subtle influence from that season, which, redolent with an upwelling life and aspiration for new beauty, leaves its aroma and struggle in all sensitive lives, and makes there a spring-time of new hopes and works. Life kindles itself into clearer flame with life, and the yearly spring lifts men out of leisure into labor with a strength beyond the measurement of our economies or bald utilities. However this might be, Arthur found a subtle and cheerful companionship in the fields. In-doors everything had a backward glance into the Past, and life, whether it were gay or sad, seemed to have end, and there was no future. But in the fields Nature, baptizing even death into life, out of her perennial fountains had a hopeful forward out-

look and prophecy of things to come.   Here again
was that mysterious Nativity, wherein, beneath the
same old stars, with choric melodies and ministering
magi, she was bringing her myrrh and treasures, to
lay them before her unalterable lord and master, —
man.   Arthur wandered away across the fields and·
in amongst the round, austere, mossy hills that
stretched away towards the south on the frontier
of the woods.   He marked the brown haze lying
seaward, and the placid waters without a sail on
them, and the quivering heat reflected in the air
from the warm earth, and the silent gray town below him, asleep, it seemed, in the mild sunshine;
and the patches of green in the hill-hollows where
the rain-waters had settled last winter-time ; and
the violets peering out from the mosses on the hill-
slopes, and the delicate green grass-blades shooting
up through the dead stalks of last year ; and the
white, downy oak and walnut buds still close shut as
against sudden surprise from frost or snow ; and the
fresh balmy scent of the pines on the hills above
him ; and the lazy gulls floating above the beach,
with its white sand-hills glistening in the sun ; and
the busy robins dashing across the open spaces between the wood, with chirrup and sharp quick cry,
in search of food and building-wood for the new
nest ; and in the rest and very sunshine that promised speedily a fresh, green earth, there was also a
certain inexplicable sadness and unrest for him.
Nature, which is in all lands the mirror of God,

even when most closely veiled, always reveals to us a double image, — His and our own ; and by contrast our fragmentary and discolored features shame us in presence of the ineffable Purity and Worth, and our aspiration towards the All-beautiful fills us with .struggle and inner pain.   The philosophy of all this escaped Arthur, as indeed it avoids all but our keenest intuitions, and even them it answers only in brief dim words, which teach the sensitive consciousness duty and faith.   Yet, as Arthur threw himself on the dry moss to watch the scene before him, he remembered how a gray-haired professor had told him once that of all places the old pastures amongst the hills recalled to him most vividly the Pilgrim Fathers who had made their homes here ; lands so austere and gray, with their scant herbage and desolate sand-patches breaking through the thin sward laid above the scanty loam and spare. sparse flowering weeds, with their almost negative tints, and curt blueberry bushes and clumps of barberry, and the stained mossy stones, and the scattered, low pines, — that they remind us of the Puritan, who, in poverty and struggle, fed with scant harvest and gleanings from the sea and forest, lived out with a severe humility that pure, true, simple life of faith which has become history. to the Church and ages. Ours is an austere realm, swept of east winds, and resting on granite ; and our landscapes carry in them the purity of the living rock, the severity of the frost and ice, and the colors of struggle and endurance beneath one of the severest climates. It is the Puritans' land.

In an old field amongst the pines, which by slow approaches were reclaiming it back to its ancient wildness, Arthur read a bit of Puritan history out of a sunken pile of mossy stones with a dwarf-cedar tree growing out of them, and a couple of white birches on the narrow ridge behind them. A Puritan house stood here, and these are its *débris;* and yonder beneath that narrow stone circle is the well, choked up now and waterless these many years; all but these wasted away to the dead mullein-stalks and long dry grasses on that stone-heap's edge, and vanished into the thin air. Here among the hills an old settler had set up his sanctuary of home, and gathered about him his household gods, and wrought, and set his heart here, with what prayers, and psalms, and hopes, and works, and fortunes, one cannot say, — and was laid asleep in the graveyard below, yonder. And Nature, pitiless, has hushed and covered all in silence, and has left, after a hundred years, only this pile of stones, and those scattered apple-trees, bowed down with their thick, dry, mossy arms, and a few slender shoots fed out of their rottenness and death; though the stars are as young, and the skies as blue, as when little children looked up in the winter's night, when the white snow covered all but the dark pines on the hill-side yonder, or the summer's sun went down from a cloudless day behind the western hills, when all was hope to the young hearts in this old home. A few years more, and the white-pines will cover with their sombre shade even these faint relics of humanity, and instead of children's voices, the sober requiem of the wind amongst their leaves. Arthur found the early violets here hid, and on the sunny edge of the pines the pure, sweet Mayflowers, creeping amongst the pine-leaves: those delicate first wood-flowers, some with their stainless white, and others blushing with the most exquisite tinge of red, which had also a striking purity about it, — children of the mild spring sun, and the pure, cold snow-waters of the early year. He found these scattered everywhere the cold winds could not reach, and gathered them along the woodpath which he followed, and also the modest, yellow buttercups. He clambered along the hill-sides, and found under the rocks the earliest wood-plants, and plucked the green brake out of the rock-seams, and the long velvety mosses from the stumps of dead trees; and, after a rather rapid descent and slide through the dead leaves and thick branches of the steep hill-side where he had discovered the rarest flowers, found himself, with slight propriety of attitude or motion, in the village wood-road, — and the presence of a lady. It was an adventure that Arthur had hardly counted on ; but he made the most of it by saluting the lady, who stood quietly watching him, with as much courtesy and ease of manner as his recent scramble amongst the rocks, and a somewhat flurried exodus from the last hill-side, had left him. " He was Arthur Bassett, from the farm yonder, on an idle ramble amongst the hills, to explore the country a little ; " and she was " Agnes Lawrence, and had heard of Mr. Bassett at the old homestead ; and the elders of the two families had been friends, and the meeting was pleasant, though without ceremony, and certainly a little quaint, in a wood-road, and they would waive an introduction," she said, courteously. And Arthur said polite things, and that he believed they had years ago met as children, and a certain inexcusable inaptitude for visiting had betrayed his purpose of paying his respects to his mother's friends, and, indeed, he half suspected the solitude of Bassett House had driven him out that very day to find society, and this was indeed a spring-day to him, as it brought him a new friend in Miss Lawrence,—a truly pleasant event in the very quiet Sandowne life he was living. And they walked on together down the road.

Agnes Lawrence, who is walking by the side of Arthur Bassett, is a young girl of twenty, maybe, and well worth a careful study for a moment. A *petite*, fragile woman, with soft brown hair carefully plaited to-day, and eyes almost blue, and features hardly Grecian or Roman even, and yet having a certain peculiar order and harmony of their own, and a varying expression of intellectual cleverness about the mouth and eyes, when lighted up, and a certain quiet dignity of manner, with an almost unobserved strain of sarcasm in it, which is the spirit and pride of the woman, (for she has both,) betraying themselves to careful eyes, — not a beautiful face, perhaps, but a pure face, and true and womanly withal; and if well noted, disclosing a strong, developed character beneath, — not an ideal heroine, but yet such a real woman as one finds oftenest in a New England village, away from the city, and the grand passage and march of what we call the world's life. One might call her a child of the soil, but that the same New England rears so many, so unlike her; for it requires some such culture of climate and of fellowship, as our northern Puritan realm affords, with its peculiar religious cultus, transmitted through such subtle and alterable forms as Puritanism for two centuries now has taken to itself, and such virtues and even narrownesses as our forefathers have left us, to make a country girl as pure, as strong, as self-reliant, and withal as noble, as Agnes Lawrence really is. She had never seen a city; and yet she had a certain polish and repose that comes from a large acquaintance with the world, and a certain delicate refinement and sensitiveness, which is never brought, but born in the most womanly natures. And behind all was a certain indefinite strength and certainty of nature, not gained from struggle with outward things, (for her nurture had been gentle,) but won from suffering, as is oftenest true, for Agnes had looked for years upon a great sorrow ; and there was about the young girl that which seemed gathered out of those dramatic incidents of life which discipline true souls into a gentle strength and sad tenderness of living. Agnes had not the learning of the schools, and yet she had made acquaintance with certain of those world-books that had strayed into the sleepy homes of the town's folks, and from close sympathy with such she had gained a certain fellowship and sensibility for the universal and sacred in the realm of letters. It is a secret, now revealed first to you, reader, that she had even written a girlish, twelve-act tragedy, founded on some Roman myth which she mistook for history, which, when she had grown wiser, she had thrown into the fire, together with certain girlish poems, — awkward and rough, perhaps, but not without a certain fire and blind struggle after the Perfect, — to keep them company ; a child's foolishness or conceit you say, but there is something touching and even beautiful to me in these improbable dramas and impossible, crude rhymings and child-verses ; for what are they but the inartful efforts of a fresh, pure spirit to express what lies behind expression in a mysterious being ; unmelodious songs and tragedies that a true melodious soul sings through a faltering lyre, inspired by what is tragedy to all those who cannot make level their Actual with God's Ideal, and sing their defeat and still unvanished hope as best they can ; and I for one would not burn one of these thousand failures that are hid away this very moment from the world's eyes, nor laugh at them : for a soul's aspiration after a divine Somewhat that you and I cannot even name, lies hid in them.　Agnes was no great favorite with young girls, to whom she was a perplexing puzzle, though always studiously kind; and the young men of the village had a certain vague fear of her, and feeling of inferiority when in her presence, and they naturally avoided her.　Even the mother failed to understand her, until they also came to live in two worlds, though under the same roof; and so Agnes had grown into a solitary, dreamy life, in an invisible realm that reached beyond the realm of Sandowne life about her, and was an indeterminate, inexplicable character to most, though without offence to any.　She was not even a member of the Sandowne church, and never employed the cant phrases of the times to express what lies hidden from most in the awful depths of that word, Religion ; and had even run the risk of suspected soundness in the Puritan faith, from expressing certain quaint and novel sentiments, not set down in the Catechism, in peaceable discussion with old Deacon Barlow, one day when he was warning her to flee from the wrath to come, in his harsh, stomachic tones, that in no wise reached Agnes's heart or head ; and had therefore daily prayers offered for her in six Sandowne families for a fortnight.　Yet a close observer might have

marked in the low tones used in speaking of divine things, and a sensitive shrinking from using the highest names, — a true, reverent, worshipful spirit lying at the very centre of her being. Indeed, one could not say how Agnes Lawrence had grown into womanhood any more than how the rarest flowers grow. Upon her heart Nature had laid her sweet, healthy influence of life, and fashioned it with her mysterious, sacred art, for such flowerage as renders life beautiful and fragrant.

"I often come here," Agnes said, "for the sake of the sea-view yonder, out of the reach of the roar and break of the surf that here seems but a white line on that restless blue field which from here looks full of peace ; and strange as you may think it, the scene affects me in two ways, — with a sense of ancientness, if I may so name it, and of the Infinite. I have felt in certain aspects of the sky — cold, gray-barred, motionless clouds, with a peculiar and delicately light green tint seen through their intervals, such a passionless, sombre sky as one sees in the late fall-time — a certain indescribable sense of time reaching back into eternity, and as if the ages, with their antique, dead lives and ways, (especially the ages that are the saintliest to me, as, indeed, the mediæval are,) were somehow falling in upon my own life and filling it with a certain indescribable sanctity and consciousness of long ago. And the same sense comes to me from certain aspects of the sea. That long, graceful line of the sea-horizon yonder, has always impressed me with a sense of the Infinite ; and if it be true, as I have read in books, that almost every traveller is filled with the same sense, when he watches from the spire of Milan Cathedral the long line which the Lombardy plain makes eastward with the horizon, and that the long, unbroken lines of ancient churches across seas fill the sensitive beholder with a sense of infinity and power, it must be true, beyond mere fancy, that long lines have a certain subtle foreshadowing and revelation of Deity.   It is always the " veiled face " in Nature, and though there be for us poor mortals now no burning bush in Horeb, there is always the voice beside us, and for the reverent heart, the draped and shadowy form of the All-Beautiful upon which it looks and lives.   And she repeated in a low tone, and as if half to herself, these lines from an unknown poet : —

I feel the presence of an unseen Power pervading
 The splendors of the spheres;
In all things high and low His course pursuing,
 Untired by length of years.

I see Him when the storm-tossed ship is drifting
 Beyond the distant hill;
And when the flowers kissed by the winds are bending
 Above the shadowy rill;

When the white snow-flake, child of frost, is lying
 Upon the winter earth;
When in the spring the powers of life are gathering
 To the mystic Nature-birth;

I feel Him as I watch the sea's stretch pointing
   To His infinity;
When in the voiceless autumn forest standing,
   Its sadness toucheth me.

I bow to Him where'er the sunshine falling
   Makes glad with crown of light,
And where the darkness on the human resting,
   Drives out its day with night.

And in such converse they went on until they
came to Agnes's home.

CHAPTER VII.

THE LAWRENCES.

"It is the property of crime to extend its mischief over innocence, as it is of virtue to extend its blessings over many who deserve them not." — GOETHE'S WILHELM MEISTER.

THE cheerful white house with green blinds that stood among the sycamores just across the meeting-house green, looking down from its modest plateau of flower-gardens and orcharding upon the main street of Sandowne, was the Lawrences'. "The Squire's widow, poor woman, lived there," the villagers said, as they pointed it out to strangers with a certain feeling of sympathy for the lady who dwelt there, and the sorrow that a heart was bearing there. "The Squire's widow never went out," they said, and the younger people hardly knew her by sight. The neat garden and grass-plots that gave a cheerful New England aspect to the dwelling were the work of her daughter Agnes. And intercourse with the outward world of Sandowne was kept up mainly through her.

A great sorrow had fallen on Mrs. Lawrence's life. It had lain there and deepened, until she had come to live under the night. The outward facts

of her sad history were well known to all the elders
of the village, and there were few so young as not
to have heard that the lady, who was sometimes
seen in deep mourning at the front windows of the
house on the hill, had known a withering wrong
which had wasted her life. The old folks remembered her as a light-hearted, sunny, singing girl
of twenty, gayest among the gay, and told how
sweetly she looked in the bride's dress, when the
handsomest couple in Sandowne stood up to be
married. It was in the unsettled times of our early
Revolution, when the young wife went in under the
old elms at Bassett House, (for the bridegroom was
of that family,) and there were happy, golden days
for the blithe heart that gave out its sunshine and
music in the old manse despite the political confusion of the times. Scarcely a year had gone, when,
on a dreary day, her husband had been brought
home to her dead, — shot through the heart, —
dead, too, without a word or sign for her. He had
been an active patriot in the arrest and manage-
ment of the neighboring Tories. He had gone out
that morning to look for some who were reported
lurking among the hills; and a hunter had found
him by accident in a lonely part of the forest, stark
and dead. That was the whole story. Strict, excited inquiry into the matter made nothing plain.
It was supposed that in attempting to arrest one of
the outlaws in arms against the new colonial independence, he had been shot. Besides the simple

conjecture, for many years now, nothing more had been discovered, and the affair remained a mystery. It was the one acknowledged tragedy in Sandowne history.

The blow fell upon a woman's heart and crushed it, — crushed out the sunlight, laughter, and song in it, and made only a grave of sad, hopeless memories in it. The young sufferer had spoken not a word, nor shed a tear, as she bent over her dead, — which her friends took for a bad sign, — not even a sob came through the white lips when the grave was filled, and she went back leaning in very weakness on an old man's arm to her desolated home. She shut herself away from her nearest friends for many months, and refused to see even the minister who proffered his ghostly consolations. She made, indeed, no complaint, and answered even the household with the briefest monosyllables, as if she were too busy with her own heart to talk, and she seemed to live in a bewildered dream. Her friends thought she would die. If praying would have brought death, two had been laid in the grave under the church-yard elms, instead of one. She lived because she could not help it.

It was a child that broke in upon her dream and brought her back to the world again, — a little girl that lay in her arms and was called Agnes, — and her consciousness of outward things seemed to return slowly, with the oversight of the little shoes and dresses, and the constant motherly care of her

only born.   Her she suffered no other hands to tend ; but with that sweet motherly sacrifice which makes motherhood so holy, she spent her days and nights with a gentle but firm assiduity for the new life that had been lent to hers.   She seemed to be always silently escaping out of herself and the dreary solitude in which her husband's death had plunged her, into the new world which her Agnes had opened for her; and yet never quite quit of that old world that had been glorified and solem- nized for her by the two twin angels of love and sorrow.   So, through the years, a little child had led her several stages in the path which conducted her away from her sorrow.   Better, had it led her unto the one Child who only can give us peace.   She grew calm and pale and passive under her cross, — silent, also, except on the one theme of her husband. It cannot be said that at any time she had reached the peace of true resignation.

"I must leave this house," she said, deliberately, in her sad, hopeless way, when Agnes was a few months old.   "I cannot live here without him, — here, where I have lived with him ;" and she had moved away to her present home, and had never entered Bassett House since.   Here she had brought all the mementos of her husband, — his books, his clothes, his fowling-gun, and even his fishing-rods, — and had them carefully bestowed about an inner room, which she arranged and kept herself, and which became a sort of shrine or sanctuary to her.

Here she was wont to pass hours every day in some kind of solemn intercourse or intercession with the dead ; and on memorial days, — such as the anniversary of their wedding, and a few other events of no importance except to herself, that marked the crises of their acquaintance, — she shut herself up even from Agnes, and spent the day alone.

It would be a curious as well as painful study, to attempt to analyze the elements of Mrs. Lawrence's life at the time when she is introduced to the reader. She had never been a queenly woman, bearing till her heart broke, and giving no sign of what lay at her heart ; or, better still, a Christian woman, taking to her heart what was sent her and moulding it into new forces of a positive womanly life, — only a loving, gentle woman, not over strong, perhaps, but capable of that great womanly passion, — absorbing and ruling everything else by itself, — that consumes and is not consumed, and which, when it loses its idol, fails often to find its God. The secret of Mrs. Lawrence's life for many years now had been endurance. She had taken her sorrow as something that had come to her, — perhaps that God had suffered to come to her, — though she could never see it, and it was only hers to bear it, and to be wasted by it, until death should free her from it and give her *him.* That was the substance of her Faith.

It is not meant to be concealed from the reader that in all this Mrs. Lawrence showed herself con-

quered and in vassalage of her sorrow. She had bowed and bent under the storm, and never stood erect again, like those queenly hearts which emerge from the wildest tempests of this life, with their treasures swept away, but who still look on, moving on with unfaltering step through this life, to find again their treasures in the hand of God. Mrs. Lawrence had buried her sunshine in a tomb around which her life revolved. She should have broken that tomb by faith, and lifted her life thereby above the strain of tears into that sunny realm where there is no death. It is easy indeed for men to counsel women to courage, when their hour has come, and to chide them for a persistent sorrow ; for men forget their grief in action, and throw down the cross at the footstool of some great success, while women wear it at their hearts, and find a subtile sort of happiness in holding it there in secret, and so walk through life with the old, unmoving pang. Do you think that this was a royal faith in sorrow which Mrs. Lawrence followed ? O women who grieve for your dead, and will not be comforted, hath not Christ broken every tomb, and did He not die in an agony that smote Mary's heart, and rent the temple's vail, that you might receive back yours through faith in Him, both here and after here ? So long, you think ? It is not very long, my sisters. Only long enough for patient faith.

Of Agnes Lawrence it suffices just here to say, that her mother had come to lean on her, and her daughter gave her a strong, steady support. The shadow had not failed to fall somewhat upon Agnes' life. Her mother's sorrow had lent its subtile influence to make her meditative, sober, and also strong. She was young; and her strong, fresh nature received the cloud upon it, and went on doing her work in the sunshine partly. In her care of her mother, she had·learned patience and self-reliance. But the life which she had led and seen touched her heart to other issues that oftenest come with her years.

Here, now, at least, were two lives that revolved in measure around a grave which murder had dug in the unquestioning earth. Had they sinned that they should suffer so? By whose justice is it that Mrs. Lawrence wears such a cross? Where is God that he does not pity? Perhaps it is fate that has achieved this. No! It is all God who pities. Every great sorrow that stands before a soul has two sides to it. On the one is written " Light; " on the other, " Night." Whichever we choose to read becomes henceforth the text for the story of our life. The legend we should always read is " Light."

CHAPTER VIII.

HOW TWO YOUNG PERSONS READ ÆSCHYLUS.

Arthur Bassett had become a diligent visitor at the Lawrences. So much we may affirm as history. He had gone to the house soon after his quaint rencontre with Agnes in the wood-road, and had been made a friend forthwith. Mrs. Lawrence had known his mother, and it was sufficient to insure her interest in him that he was a Bassett. The day when Arthur first came the sad lady seemed for a time to have forgot her silence, and talked a great deal of the old folks and the old life at Bassett House. It appeared that she had some knowledge of every one who had ever lived there, more especially as to how they died and when they died, and Arthur listened eagerly as she told him about his mother as a young girl, and her marriage, and the thousand and one little things that interest us in those who leave us, for Mrs. Lawrence had known her from a child. "As for me," she said, when she had gone through to him the story of her own sorrow, "I have never been to Bassett House for these many years, though it was once paradise to me. I should think you would find it very lonely in those large, uninhabited chambers, with only old Cloe for company." Arthur answered that he had been very busy of late, and that of course he hardly remembered when the house had been anything else than what he found it now.

Arthur's acquaintance with Agnes developed itself in very natural ways. They were both young and frank, — they were both lovers of books, — they had both common sympathies with Nature. That was enough. They had become friends.

It happened, therefore, quite as naturally, indeed, as it happens that the sun shines, that Arthur found himself very often in Agnes's society. When the oversight of the farm work, or his morning reading in the library, or his ramble on the beach or hills, were finished, the afternoon usually brought him to the Lawrences. It is remarkable, also, that he always half deceived himself into supposing that he had at such times a real errand there, — as to bring for Agnes's inspection some rare flower or stone he had found in his rambles, or a bouquet of spring flowers from Bassett garden for Mrs. Lawrence, to borrow a book or to lend a book, and a score of other things he felt called upon to do, — disinterested man, — and the errand was not so brief as pleasant. Why could he not tell himself that he made these pilgrimages simply because it somehow pleased him to be there? There is one shrine, at least, at which men find themselves constant applicants, where, at the start, they never ask Why? Latterly it had come to pass that he generally brought with him a book. One of the ancients at Bassett House had gathered from across seas a rare medley of old books, which Arthur was diligently turning to his own account in this way: rare books, often classic and mediæval, and among the rarest a folio Dante, with quaint devices; and Arthur, who had been at college a rambling reader, with an instinctive bias towards the shadowy and the religious which had made the two old Eddas of the Norsemen his favorite reading, was now every morning deep in the study of these authors. And Agnes, who had been for some-time now a student under the minister, Mr. Lever-ick, also found pleasure in like matters. Hence the books. At such times they would go out on the house-stoop under the lilacs, — Agnes with her work, while Arthur read the marked passages which had most pleased him, and with poetical sentences and quaint philosophies and criticisms that provoked dis-cussion, Agnes's work went on.

There was much that Arthur gained from this. She gave him a certain womanly sympathy in his admiration of these high things out of the great masters which was very grateful to him. He seemed to find new meanings in the author he read to her, and their subtler beauties revealed them-selves under a true woman's criticism. He felt his enthusiasm for what was eternally true kindling under her ready and emphatic commendations. It was not the first time, neither the last, that a young girl has taught us mortals of the grosser elements how to read aright. Above all, she excited him to intellectual activity. She was always finding out of the reading grave questions of Right and Duty that opened other questions, until the discussion very often ran back to those time-questions that underlie the universe, and which no age solves. There was, indeed, in what Agnes judged a certain clear, moral rectitude and loyalty to Right that touched Arthur sensibly. She seemed to have taken for her motto that noble sentiment of a heathen poet : " The truth is always right." Arthur somehow felt himself abashed, humiliated even, before what revealed itself to him as her single-hearted love of what was eternally the true. Hers was an absolute standard, above his, and he felt it to be a beautiful law which fashioned her life into a beauty and purity he was a stranger to. A certain sacrifice of self, a certain aspiration after a perfect life, joined withal to a certain strain of sadness, as he came to know her, seemed to separate her and lift her above him. Had it already come to this that Beatrice, beautiful lady in white, was standing again upon the Mount of God, and calling up to the " vita nuova," the new life, the reverent and kneeling worshipper. Nothing is yet confessed for Arthur. That does not yet appear. And yet how often in this world, for young hearts, it happens that the story of Dante's comedy comes true again, and a white-robed woman becomes the guiding angel out of the lower realms into the sunny lands that reach away unto the throne of the All-Beautiful.

Nor was it altogether in this aspect that Agnes was shown to Arthur. From the start, there were several things in their intercourse which pained him. His pride was piqued that a woman should be wiser and stronger than he, and he strove vainly against that thought until Agnes's simple moral steadiness caused him to yield the point. It did not please him that what seemed so beautiful in her was busying itself in no way about him, but rather in the study of that which was beyond him and independent of him. And there grew up in him a half-selfish jealousy of that over which he had no control. And her supremacy troubled him. Agnes was also a shade imperious, a little over-positive and certain, which Arthur most of all should have borne with, only that people are slow to tolerate themselves in others: she shocked him, too, sometimes, at least the traditional in him, by a certain plainness in talking about holy things, and by what was even real scepticism about matters he looked upon as fixed, though that pain vanished when he saw how implicitly she was yielding all her ways and wishes to what the invisible Sovereign, whom she was striving to obey, required. Indeed Agnes, as most young persons at some time of their lives usually are, was what nearly corresponded to a radical in social matters. She had her own complaints against what she thought wrongs to her sex, and wrongs that society engrafts on life. And she had some dim sense of somehow righting the world as a re-former, — a little only of which Arthur came slowly to understand.

In this friendship two strong, distinct natures, in certain mysterious attractions and repulsions, were striving to come closer together. It was a task by no means easy. Otherwise a task, if followed out, in which there must be much pain for both.

One of those afternoons at the Lawrences, which Arthur at least found so sunny, may stand for all its fellows. "To-morrow, Mr. Bassett," Agnes had said, as Arthur went away after he had been read-ing to her some of those strange legends out of the Heimskringla of Sturlæson, which they had dis-cussed and differed about as usual, "bring over, if you please, some one of the Greek tragedians, which you ought to have, as you have been a uni-versity man, and which have always a really strange fascination for me. Mr. Leverick read them with me two winters ago, in the evenings, and most of them, I think, ought to be read of stormy evenings, with the moan of the storm in the trees outside. I shall be indebted to your scholarship for the new pleasure of hearing them read again." When Ar-thur came next day, he said, "I have brought you, Miss Agnes, the Plays of Æschylus, as you asked; translated here for you, and in the original here for me, thanks to my ancient friend of Bassett House."

" Thanks, Sir Knight of the Books," was answered. And so they betook themselves to the reading.

" I found, this morning, looking over my papers," Agnes said, " some things I had written down out of these old masters when Mr. Leverick read them ; and also some things that he chose to say and afterwards wrote down for me ; and they shall be my contribution to our work to-day. They struck my fancy, and I never cease admiring the ever-fresh beauty of these heathen's phrases." And she read these excerpts out of Æschylus, making her comments as she went on :

" For pride, when it has bloomed, is wont to produce for fruit a crop of Atè, whence it reaps an all-mournful harvest."

" Wealth is no bulwark against destruction for him who, with a wanton heart, has spurned the great altar of justice."

" To be wise is the first part of happiness."

" The unwritten and unmovable laws of the gods are not of yesterday ; but eternally they live, and no one knows from what time they had their being."

" But the death of own brothers wrought by their own hands of this pollution, there is no decay."

" Doer must suffer." That is even briefer than our own " An eye for an eye, and a tooth for a tooth."

There is also an exquisitely poetical phraseology, especially, in Æschylus. He speaks of the

west as the place of " the wanings of the sovereign
sun ; " of night, as " the time when darkness tenants the temple of the firmament ; " of bees, as
" flower craftsmen ; " of fish, as " dumb children of
the unpolluted deep ; " of ships, as " the canvas-
winged chariots of the mariners ; " of mountain
peaks, as " neighbors to the stars ; " of lightning, as
" Jove's sleepless shaft."

" I am always reminded," Agnes said after she
had finished reading these excerpts, of what Mr.
Leverick once said of Æschylus, " that he was
Dante antedated about fifteen hundred years.   But
come," she said, smiling, " you are teacher, not I ;
what will you read to-day ? "

" I will read to you my favorite Greek tragedy, —
the Prometheus-bound of Æschylus," Arthur replied.

And so he read again out of the Greek to Agnes
Lawrence that weird, stormy, painful story of Prometheus riveted with adamant to Caucasus ; of the
god among the eldest born, pitiful to men ; suffering
at the hand of the Father of men for his good acts
towards them ; laid by merciless Force in the un-
trodden deserts of the outer world, beneath the
scorching suns and bitter, biting night-frosts, upon
his rocky bed of agony, alone through æons upon
æons of centuries to endure the pangs and thorns
thrust in upon him by the relentless Zeus ; silently
enduring Fate, confidently expecting his triumph
sometime over his persecutor on Olympus ; refus-

ing to yield or propitiate his enemy, stronger in bearing than Zeus in smiting; and enduring the unutterable agony in a kingly, mighty spirit that even Zeus could not break nor tame,—the most imperial struggle of all heathen time. It is a sombre, twilight story of the gods; and its passions and sorrows are all Titanic. Men have tried to measure and grasp its meanings. It is a Titanic thunder-cloud flung upon an ancient sky, and steadied there in all its awfulness two thousand years already, by that Titan, Genius. It has no measure nor interpreting.

The reading of the play ended in silence.

"Thanks, teacher," Agnes said at last. "One seems to live in the whirlwind hearing that, and breathes freer when it ends. It has always struck me that every true book or writing has, if we only saw it, a certain correspondence to some aspect or spot in the natural world. I always associate Ossian's Poems with a certain spot among the hills,—a bare, gray hill, sloping down by a shallow ravine to the fields below, with a few gnarled oaks thinly scattered over its crest, exposed to the wildest winds. And whenever I read Ossian, I think involuntarily of this place as it is when the northeast wind is sweeping in from sea on winter nights up above the moaning oaks, with their dead leaves rustling in it, and the black clouds flung across the sky. And Mr. Leverick told me once that he always thought of the Prometheus-bound as suffering his agony in

the Arctic night of Iceland ; bound somewhere on
one of those waste Icelandic plains that hardly a
footstep ever reaches : rocky, riven with immovable
frosts, eternally freezing under an absent sun ; without tree or grass, encompassed by the ice-mountains
frozen to their very heart, and swept of the wet
winds borne in from a sunless sea in a night where
the wail and moan of suffering elements echo over
the land, and there is no form nor substance visible.

"Indeed, I should like to read you here some remarks that Mr. Leverick made and wrote out for
me about this very tragedy of which I spoke to you
just now."

" Read them, Miss Agnes. I must know your
Mr. Leverick," he said, smiling, " and go to school
to him besides, as he seems to have such enthusias-
tic pupils and such quaint learning."

So Agnes read the criticism : —

" The Greek tragedies teach Christianity. They
teach by what they lack. Heathenism in its religion culminates in them. Their culmination is
eclipse. If cultured heathenism could do only that,
it is not blamable for that ; for it is human. If un-
cultured Christianity is infinitely more than that,
it is not human. What is not human is divine. In
the Greek tragedies there are sentiments, emotions,
but no principles. Without principles there is nothing fixed. When there is nothing morally certain,
there is certainty of ever-recurring sin. Many

things are very prettily said in Sophocles and Æschylus of filial duty. There is undeniable pathos in
the filial prayer of Antigone before strangers in
behalf of her blind father: ' O strangers, show pity
to miserable me, who in behalf of my father alone
implore, implore you, looking into your eyes, with
eyes not sightless. Grant the favor, I beseech thee,
by all that is dear to thee, — be it child, be it wife,
be it gold, or be it God.' Or when the blind Œdi-
pus is spoken of as ' touching with *unseeing* hands
his children.' So there are gleams of a tender phi-
lanthropy and self-sacrifice. Prometheus, in the
midst of his agony, is afraid lest his consolers should
suffer for their pity towards him, and warns them
of the risk they run with Zeus. That only proves
the aspiration after the Right was not altogether
dead beneath the chill skies of Paganism. It were
itself a miracle had Paganism not sometimes stumbled across the straight and narrow path of the only
true life. But it never saw that path leading away
before it, and never walked in it — only crossed it.
There is nothing immutable, eternal in Paganism,
except Fate, perhaps; and that was questioned.
Only that which is eternal is from God. In the
Greek tragedies there is always the sea, — there is
no land. The Greek mind, then, was never landed
in its faith. Where it is always the sea, it is always
cloud, unrest, toil. The thoughtful heathen mind
forever missed one word from its vocabulary. It
was the word peace. As to all the prime questions

of the universe, Heathendom answers only with
' It may be ; ' Christendom, with ' It is.'

"The early Church Fathers compared the Prometheus with the Christ.   The only comparison is
that of contrast.   That both suffered proves no
connection ; else every sufferer would be akin to
Christ, and the suffering of sin would lay claim to
righteousness.   The suffering of Christ was to restore a universe to harmony.   The suffering of
Prometheus was itself disorder, and ended anyhow
it produced no harmony anywhere.   There was
still Zeus to crush, and his inferiors to suffer.   But
Christ in his utmost agony was in perfect union
with his Father, without antagonism between them,
and he suffered of his own free will, submissively,
until he reconciled men with Heaven.   Prometheus
suffered because he could not help it, and Fate was
stronger ; and his sufferings could only widen the
breach between earth and heaven, so long as men
sympathized with their champion.   With him Fate
and Free Will were eternally in strife.   With
Christ, they harmonized themselves in that one
word ' Father.'   Prometheus had no victory, for he
never ceased to endure ; and his endurance was an
eternal strife that left no after-time for victory.
The dim prophecy that some time he should be free
does not change the statement.   And yet he could
not reconcile himself with his tormentor.   To sub-
mit, would have been confession that he had sinned
and Zeus was righteous in his punishment ; which

were a double falsehood. Release for him of any sort would have been to declare a moral chaos in the universe. It only remained for him to suffer. In Christ all is changed. Justice is satisfied, and love conquers ; and again, as before the fall, ‘ The morning stars sing together, and all the sons of God shout for joy.’ The new heavens and the new earth appeared by the power of the divine Prometheus, who died that man might live forever.

“ There are three historic invocations that prove Christianity : ‘ O dread majesty of my mother Earth ; O æther that diffusest thy common light, thou beholdest the wrongs I suffer.’ It is Prometheus chained to his rock.

“ ‘ Lord Jesus receive my spirit.’ It is the protomartyr Stephen dying beneath the stone-shower of his enemies.

“ ‘ Father, into Thy hands I commit my spirit.’ It is the Christ upon his cross.”

There were many things discussed by these young folks after the reading of the minister’s paper, not necessary to be repeated here. It was sundown as Arthur stood upon the house-steps going home. The little children were at their noisy games upon the common, the villagers, come home from the fields, were seated at rest in their doorways and talking to one another from their windows, and the gentle evening mist was gathering around the village.

“ How happy the scene below us is ! ” Agnes said.

" These honest folk give themselves no trouble about these old questions that have so pained and borne upon the wisest; and the Prometheus-bound, if they heard of it, would be only a very queer story, of no great interest; though the same imperishable ideas contain themselves even in this humble town-life of ours.   The visible world is sunny enough; but to me, within this is another invisible twilight world of spirits, — Titans, Divinities, Fate and the Furies; yes, even Prometheus still in agony upon the rock."

Yes, dear Agnes.   And if you could have looked through what now seems twilight to you, and entered that world a little, you would have heard a whisper and seen a legend written above a cross. The whisper is always, "*Venite ad me*"; the legend, "*Via crucis, via lucis.*"

CHAPTER IX.

THE MAY SEARCH.

THE next time that Arthur went to hunt up Sam Jones, to inquire about farm matters, he found that individual in the corn-barn, amongst meal-bags, old scythes, cider-barrels, and the thousand and one skeletons of farm-furniture which usually seek the shelter of that dusty mausoleum of old tools, with his coat off and sleeves rolled up, busy scrubbing an old Queen Anne's musket, that looked as though it had been through the wars, and now so long laid on the shelf that it had no more possible harm in it than any other old soldier on the retired list, addicted to rheumatism and red flannel, who had lost both arms and feet. Sam, however, seemed to think otherwise, for he scoured away at the rust on the barrel, and every now and then held out the gun at arm's-length for better inspection, with a certain affectionate, satisfied air towards it, as if he was sure something good would come of it. "Grandfather's gun, sir: was in the old French war, and spoke loud when there was anything a-going with them Redskins and frog-eaters up at the York lakes; and the old man said that Gin'ral Howe had 'spected that gun, when he and the rest of the boys stood in the ranks out at old Fort Ticonderoga; and the way he used to handle that gun, poor soul! to show us children how to use a baggernet when you come to close quarters with a tomyhawk in the underbrush, was a caution, I tell ye! Poor old soul! them days are gone now; and if 't was n't for me that gun 'd be gone too, long ago;" and he scoured away with fresh vigor as the last thought came over him.

Arthur ventured to inquire why he happened to be at that work to-day.

"Sarving my country," said Sam. "It 's May Sarch this afternoon, front of the meetin'-house and round there, and I 'm making this here " (holding up the gun) " pass muster; for it 's good, though pretty old," he said. " Govermint 's so good as to make us all train, to larn taktecs, and everlootons, and monovers; and you oughter see the grand County Muster, with the ginerals and officers, and the hollow squares, and all them things. You 'd think all the turkeys and osteriches and roosters in 'Merica had lost their tail-fethers, I guess, if you could only see that arternoon revoo, — some of them companies 's so fine and rigged up. Laws must be risspected, and times may come agin when them that 's able must shoulder a musket and fight Brit-ishers, or some other outlandishers, and we must stand by the country, wherever the enemy comes from, and we mus' n't forgit the blood that 's been shed to water the tree of liberty for us, as old Square Nye says, nor how our fathers did. When the red divils were eatin' up wimmin and children, and men had only a bushel or two of corn to live on, and some fish and clams to wash it down with, or when the King's Hesse'ns were about with Burg-wine and Cornwallis to ruin us all, them men took their old guns and blazed away right at 'em, and did n't run away only when they were 'bliged to ; and 'Mericans must fight for 'Merica when the time comes, and no questions asked, tho' the clargy tells us we must live peaceably with all men. But that 's what I say : if that old bull out in the field there comes at me with his horns, as the var-mint did last week, I hit him over the head with a fence-stake till he lies down on a sudden, as tho' he was dizzy, and does n't stir no more than a stone, and lets me alone ; and that 's what I call peace. Let him eat his grass, as his dooty is, and not run at me, as his dooty is n't, and all right. And there 's a great many bulls in the world that wun't eat grass, according to natur', but use their horns upon a feller, ag'in natur' ; and that 's why war comes, and I 'm scrubbin' up this gun, calca-latin' that I may want to use it some time against sumbody who won't eat his own fodder like a Christian, but wants to gore the country, — which 's me. And I say, so long 's bulls about, or roar-ing away off, t' other side the hills yonder, men must look to their fence-stakes, no matter what the

clargy says about peace; for what I say the Good
Book says in a gineral way, — and that 's a common-
sense book that has n't got no superfine nonsense
about dooties as is n't dooties, but shows a man up
just as he is, and tells us to treat him just as he is,
— though I ain't much of a scholar, seeing I 've only
ben to school o' winters; but that 's my idee. Sec-
ondly, as the parson says, govermint makes me
pay forty cents, if this old gun won't stand fire, and
ten cents for no ramrod, and so on for a wooden
flint in the lock, which lazy young chaps whittles
out and paints, sometimes, out of mischief, and so
forth; and I 'm calculatin' to save my cash this
a'ternoon," said Sam. With which elaborate expression of his sentiments, he proceeded with increased animation to scour the gun.

Arthur went that afternoon with Sam to the
May Search, — Sam in the uniform of a green
jacket, with huge pockets in its right and left flank,
to serve as a tobacco-magazine and store-house of
the remarkable red bandanna handkerchief he always sported, and a glazed tarpaulin hat, (for Sam
had smelt salt-water long ago,) and a pair of pro-
digious breeches, whose extremities were stuck in a
pair of capacious cowhide boots, and with such further
equipments as the aforesaid Queen's Arm, cartouche-
box, primers, ramrod, and so forth, as befitted so imposing a display as a New England militia training.
It was clear enough, as they came in town, that
something above the usual strain of Sandowne life

was going to transpire. Wagons, with huge loads of men and boys standing up in them to make room ; hay-carts, with a whole family of restless children munching gingerbread and dressed in their best, — the father at the reins, and the comfortable-looking mother with the youngest heir of the family, assisting her to be wet-nurse on the road, — were creeping along the ways that led to the village ; shaggy-maned, unkempt horses, dashing along in what folks are facetious enough to call pleasure-wagons, obeyed the whip of the more ostentatious country bloods, who left behind for the holiday the eternal farm of their thoughts and toils, except the aroma of the barn and hay ; less fortunate men and boys on foot, and a few on horseback, were wending their way towards the common centre. The centre, which no doubt seemed that day the centre of the universe to the scores of tangled-haired urchins who were running about under everybody's feet, in common with a great company of rural dogs of every pattern, size, age, and quality, who had followed their betters to the May Search, and who stood growling and twisting their tails at one another, with true military spirit, — had a picturesque and animated look, quite in contrast with its usual aspect of being profoundly engaged in sleeping, as Arthur remarked when he turned into the main street with Sam. The gingerbread and candy-stalls and cider-taps by the roadside had already drawn about them a gang hungering and thirsting after such vanities ; squads of the less enterprising citizens were perched here and there upon the rail-fences, whittling, or smoking their black clay-pipes in peace ; here a military man was putting the last touch to his arms, by a little private scouring of a bayonet in the green sward, or an inspection of his assets in cartridges ; groups of farmers· were laying their heads together before the village store, which to-day, in sounding metaphor, might be said to flow with cheese and rum, (so much dry biscuit and old cheese had to be washed down by old Jamaica,) in sober consultation about nothing more especial than the age of somebody's horse or the " heft " of somebody's steers, yet with a certain sort of deep inner satisfaction at being allowed to say nothing particular, though all together ; old men, with deep-red faces and a watery, vinous look about the eyes, were airing their knowledge of things in general before a select audience gathered round the town-pump, or a barn-door, or the street-corner, as if the thing they were saying no man had ever said before, and few men had been counted worthy to hear, and that they, — namely, the old men themselves, — out of the sheerest commiseration for all other men's ignorance, had condescended to reveal such matters, and that what they did n't know was hardly worth knowing ; the front windows and doors of Sandowne were thrown open to the family visitors who came in to take tea, Search Night ; there was a general circulation of men and dogs, and everywhere an aspect of jollity and good-humor.

Arthur made his way through the crowd to where a very fat man with a big drum, and another small boy with a very shrill fife were summoning the Sandowne military men to arms. The parade-ground in front of the meeting-house was already thronged, and in the centre were the Sandowne men of all arms, most of them in close consultation with an innumerable circle of friends, who insisted on frequent and affectionate interviews with the military, and everything in the most happy confusion. " Clear the field, Sergeant Ewer! " cried a little, short, fat man, in a huge cocked hat, with a mighty plume on it (the village postmaster, translated to a " responsible elevated military position," as his good wife, Mrs. Percival, used to say of her spouse). " Clear the field, Sergeant Ewer! " cried the little fat man with the great hat, and brandishing a vast sword that seemed to have an uncomfortable habit, somehow, of getting between his legs ; " Clear this field immediately! " Now Sergeant Ewer knew very well the rights of American citizens, and their impatience under restraint; and from his vast military experience had learned that, if you set a guard, there was great likelihood of its going clear off in the course of the next quarter of an hour, to get something " to wet one's whistle," or to gallant some female friend to the gingerbread and cider-stall, or to indulge in an independent scout after anything or body that might turn up, (such freedoms have citizen soldiery,) and therefore, in discharge of his very delicate duty, he displayed great nicety of judgment as to his methods. "Fall back, fellow-citizens!" he shouted; "do fall back, and obey the laws. Fall back, and help your brethren to preserve the well-earned glory of the Sandowne Guards!" "Squire Howe and Deacon Wiswell," said the Sergeant, as he observed these aforenamed dignitaries in the crowd, which, either in astonishment at the Sergeant's forcible address, or for some other sufficient reason, stood still, — "Do impress upon our friends the necessity of keeping the laws by falling back;" and whether out of regard to these two venerables, who, with great vigor, set about impressing this necessity upon the Sandowne mind, or for other cause, it is certain that the citizens did fall back for at least five minutes, and the order of the May Search began to be restored. "Form a line!" shouted the aforesaid military postmaster in the cocked-hat,—and who, truth to say, was not very like those taciturn Arab captains whom Mahomet's friend tells us of, too dignified to speak to soldiers, and looking for all the world as though God had tied a knot in their throats. "Fall in, fall in!" and the Sandowne yeomanry, in the course of time, did form a rather irregular, ragged line in the presence of their superior officer, the Captain with the hat. A longer line, indeed, than paraded before Miles Standish, when, with a mere handful of men, armed with steel helm and breastplate, and pike and halberd and matchlock, he set out with his sparse Puritan phalanx to hunt down a nation and subdue a continent, and having in it, no doubt, some of the Puritan fire that had flashed out with such fury against the cavaliers at Naseby and Marston Moor; but then, such a line! It seemed as if all the wrecked military glory and pomp of three generations had somehow floated down into it, and grounded against that fence-dyke: guns of what ineffable variety and efficiency, — rusty guns with bright bayonets, and bright guns with rusty bayonets, and guns with no bayonets, held in the hands of men seemingly unconscious that they had not deserved well of the government by the energy that had made a part bright; and cartouch-boxes that might have been a little cleaner; and uniforms, — pea-jackets with horn buttons, and bobtail coats with bright buttons, which seemed made from Spanish dollars, puffed out from the centre; and yellow continental waistcoats, reaching to the knees, and no waistcoats; and tarpaulins, — regular military hats, looking like inverted coffee-pots with a feather stuck through a hole in the bottom; and short men between tall men, and fat men somehow in close quarters with the leanest men in Sandowne; in short, it was a sight, as the spectators said, to be long remembered! There were some attempts made to better even that line by its ambitious Captain.

"Stand straight, John Place!" he said to a rather crooked-legged, round-shouldered private. John looked first right and left to his next neighbor, with a ferocious grin, as much as to say, " Thunder and lightning! *aint* I standing straight?" and moved his shoulders a little. "Fall back, Jim Black!" said the Captain to another, who had advanced ambitiously a foot or two before the rest. "Can't!" said Jim, with a look back; "the ladies is pressin' on." "The ladies must retire and obey the laws!" shouted Sergeant Ewer to a bevy of buxom country girls, who, as Jim was a favorite, were pressing in just at that point to get a better view of the Guards. And the ladies fell back and obeyed the laws. "Stand alone, you, sir!" cried the Captain to a jolly, round-faced Guard, who, a little unsteady about the eyes and feet, was steadying himself on his right-hand man. "Can't," said the Guard. "Got the rheumatis bad." All the "rheumatis" he had, he had caught in the grocery store, that never, on training days, was known to flow with milk and honey. "You 're drunk, Bill Sawyer, and you 're dismissed parade, and fined one dollar," said the Captain. And so, with much military genius, the Captain dressed the line of the Sandowne Guards.

The important business of inspection or search followed close upon this last military exploit of Captain Percival; and in due process it was brought to light what Sam had said about wooden flints, and a too common tendency on the part of the Guards to a deficiency of cartridges, and so forth, necessary, in the eyes of the law, to make efficient soldiers. However, all things considered, they might have been worse equipped, which was some consolation; and it was wonderful to mark how every man of the company, charged with any shortcoming, was absolutely certain that his were about the most thorough accoutrements to be found in the service. It was also remarkable that this miniature army had a new military quality under the sun, namely, a complete democracy pervading on all hands, to the exclusion of all rank and some little discipline; and how most privates seemed to know more than any officer, as if they had chosen for leaders men for their incapacity for high military skill; at least one would judge so from the general tone of the subalterns' remarks, and the tendency of the ranks to instruct their officers, just then and there upon that battle-field, of their, namely the officers', plain and bounden duty. However that might be, this truly democratic army were now called upon to perform the second part in this imposing military drama, and to march. It was no light duty, Captain Percival thought, — at least so the increasing solemnity of his mien might be interpreted, — either to set that army in motion, or, once aroused to that pitch of military enthusiasm, to stop its impetuosity in halt. He had privately another cause of anxiety, in the desire he felt to retrieve the fame of his corps from the rumors current about it, that last training, when it was boldly marching through a neighboring hay-field, its ranks had been scattered by an unfortunate charge of black wasps, whom the military clangor had somewhat irritated, and that the hatless Captain himself had been seen, the further side of a hay-rick, in a paroxysm of anger, examining, in the attitude of a Torso, the extent of his wounds, which luckily turned out to be located in no place which, according to medical science, is held to be vital. Inspired by such memories, or others equally cogent, the word was given by the illustrious leader—" March!" And " March!" said the drum and fife; and " March!" said the crowd that came pressing in upon that column; and " March!" emphatically said that array of shuffling warriors, as they stalked, each in his own time and attitude, along that route, which led them by the mill-pond, and round the school-house, and by the tavern, and back again to the parade. The subtle felicities of that peaceful march must forever elude the historian's pen.

It was during this celebrated military procession that Arthur observed a man, dressed in a faded officer's uniform and sword, sauntering along amongst the crowd which seemed hardly to know him; at least no one addressed him; and people made way for him, as Arthur noticed, with a half-side look, as though they had no wish to come closer to him.

He was a strongly built man of about sixty, may be, and a little bent, with features that had once been handsome, covered up under a long gray beard, and with deep lines, and a quick, darting, restless eye, which rather glanced than looked at anything, and a certain air about him as of a man in antagonism with the world in general, and this crowd in special.

"Who 's that man, yonder?" asked Arthur of a man next him.

"Oh, that is Old Treeman."

"Who 's he?"

"Nobody knows who he is, and I wouldn 't like to know; a witch, may be, or crazy, or the devil," said the man. "Who do you think he is?"

Arthur said he did not know, and asked how he happened to be at the Search in uniform.

"That I don't know neither, nor anybody in this town, I reckon. He 's always come to training and worn those regimentals these twenty years, Search-days. He lives up there on the hill, by the Injin graveyard, and out of doors among the woods and marshes, and everywhere and nowhere; and is no sort of a Christian, for he never goes to meeting; and nobody knows him and he knows nobody, — that 's to say he 's got no friends and won't have any; and he hurts nobody and nobody hurts him; and there 's a good many afeard of him, and he comes to training regular: and that 's all I know of him," said the man.

The man meanwhile had walked leisurely across the parade, where the soldiers had been left by their Captain to take breath after their late fatigue, previous to their dismissal. Apparently he was no stranger to the men, and some of the younger and more rollicking called out after him, " There's the Commodore, again ; " but he took no notice of them and walked on.

" Come, Commodore," shouted Bill Sawyer, who had not yet recovered from the rheumatis caught at the grocery, and who had not deigned to consider himself dismissed at the Captain's order, — " come, Commodore, and take a hand at soldiery. Them regimentals 'll spile afore long if you don't use them. We 'll 'lect you capt'n of the Guards, and you can ' put us through a course of sprouts,' afore all this company, and the parson and the square's widow up in the house, yonder ; and you shall stand treat all round when you 've finished."

The man turned sharply round and walked close up to the speaker.

" You call yourselves soldiers, do you ? I am an old man, but I 've seen soldiers, and you are not that, I tell you. You 'd run like a flock of sheep at gun-fire, and break your necks in the bargain over one another's shins running away. If you were my men a six-month I 'd make you sing a different song than the one you 've sung to your Captain this afternoon. You soldiers ? You 'd better go home and hide in your barns and stick hay-

seed in your hair, and swear you had never seen a
gun, if a dozen soldiers who knew their place, as
you don't know yours, came along to hunt you
up.   I am an old man who tell you this, whom you
should have let alone, and if it wer'n't plain murder,
I would n't mind taking a bout with any of you,
old as I am, with this here," laying his hand upon
his sword ; " but 't would be killing sheep like you.
Let me alone ; " and he walked away through the
crowd, which made way for him.

" That 's thundrin' curius," said Bill, " that the
old feller should flare up so, just for nothin'.
Who ever seed Old Treeman so uproarious before,
I 'd like to know ?   I 've heard the boys call after
him a hundred times, and he never took no notice
of them, and I don't know what he ever did take
any notice of that other people do ; but just as soon
as I axed him to take a hand at training us before
this crowd, and specified the parson and the square's
widow, he got mad mighty quick and talked onkind.
Pr'aps he 's got the rheumatis, as I have," said
Bill, in a milder humor, " and that accounts for
worse than that."   The bystanders did not vouch-
safe a different explanation, and the matter was
allowed to subside.

The formal parade of the Sandown Guards came
to an end in due course, like many another grave
transaction, and the law was satisfied.   " I don't
reckon that 's much of a turnout anyhow," said
Sam, as he came up to Arthur, after the company

had been dismissed; "tho' I 've been sarving my country a couple of hours for my country's good, and Old Treeman just hit the nail on the head when he said we wer'n't soldiers; but howsomever, we 'd make soldiers, if we once got where men wer'n't all officers, and we had something real to do. It 's in the blood, I reckon. It 's men's natur to fight. We 're Britishers, after all, with Yankee clothes on, and them chaps take naturally to ever-lootions, as ducks do to water; and ' what 's bred in the bone can't be beat out in the flesh,' and ' it 's hard to learn old dogs new tricks; ' and I say if the Captain don't know everlootons, and the men do take to wooden flints, trainin' times, it 's in us to fight, anyhow," said Sam, " tho' we ain't soldiers, as the old fellow said. That 's a queer chap, that Old Treeman. There is n't a man in this town can shoot half as straight with a rifle as him; nor can hunt a deer better, nor knock down a duck better, tho' nobody knows much about him, and my old woman, who knows everything, is mighty oneasy about him, as he puzzles her; and he keeps mostly out of everybody's way, and Bill Sawyer should have let him alone, for tho' he 's poor, he 's respectable, so far as I know," said Sam.

The May Search, as in duty bound, was to end with a grand supper at the tavern, and Sam, who had to go home to tend to " the old woman," and had " sown his wild oats," as he said, left the crowd, who were now dispersing to their wagons, and went home with Arthur; while the military men, and that large class in every community who find in that locality their Promised Land, set their faces towards the tavern, as thirsty as Philip de Commines's tired horse, who, thrusting his nose upon occasion into a pailful of wine, drank it at a bout, and was found of his master never better or fresher in his life. " The Indian Head " was very happy to-night, and with that excessive democracy evident in all our public houses, its doors stood open to everybody, and the bright tallow candles that sent a red, cheery light through the puttied and mended panes of its abundant windows, extended a pressing invitation to all to enter. It was an old house set out into the street, just as if somebody from behind had knocked it out there almost into the ruts; and it had a watering-trough in front for its customers' horses, while their owners were taking something stronger in-doors; and a sign hung on a high pole, with a huge pair of deer's horns nailed on the very top, which pretended to represent something like an Indian with monstrous feathers on his head, as he rested on a very long bow, with any quantity of arrows in his quiver and a tomahawk in his belt, quite in the Indian style, standing on the landlord's name, with the date of his stewardship over that mansion, — a sign which had swung there these fifty years, and in winter nights went creaking in the frost and wind like a skeleton swinging from its gibbet, and looking down from outside into the ruddy light of the bar-room, where so many acres of woodland and salt-marsh had been gulped down by the prodigals of Sandown; or, in day-light casting in its shadow upon the well-sanded floor, until once, late at night, old Bill Crane, who had the reddest nose and the greatest swallow of any Sandowner, and had been diligently fortifying that bad preëminence that very evening with deep drinking, came tumbling back out of the night air, holding on with both hands to his neck, to swear at the landlord for having set up a gallows by the tavern door; as if they had anything in common. It had, also, a large elm-tree in front, a great tee-totaller, as the same Bill Crane facetiously said, who never drank except out of the well where the tavern pump drank from; and its stable-yard was littered with the empty molasses barrels and sugar hogsheads, where the flies bred, which the adjoining grocery store had thrust out there; and a great backyard with a huge wood-pile in it; and a thick, fat chimney which somebody seemed to have knocked down into the broad mossy roof; and, altogether, despite the unfortunate sign-post, it had a fat, jolly, welcoming look, which had proved irresistible to many a Sandowner of the last three generations. To-night it was dressed in its best, and the house was filled with the din of voices and the rattle of glasses. The bar-room, with its oak fire blazing on the andirons, and its long, crooked-necked squashes and ears of Indian seed-corn festooned along the brown walls, welcomed, to-night, its most faithful children, and boasted some of the proudest specimens of its handiwork. These last were thin men, in rather dilapidated hats, with the felt worn off, and a woollen neckcloth about the throat tucked into waistcoats to conceal the lack of linen; and coats with very short tails and very broad collars that seemed to have imbibed an unreasonable amount of their wearer's fat from unreasonable usage, and very thick, rusty-looking shoes, outside of very thick, woollen stockings; men who blushed with the tips of their noses, and whose health sprinkled itself in the brightest vermilion spray over their cheeks, and who kept up a perpetual moisture or weeping in their inanimate eyes, and had a habit of keeping their skinny hands, with the dull blue veins starting out of them, in their pockets, as if searching after sixpences for grog, or to keep sixpences away from the grogman's hands; and walked slowly, as if they were going after nothing, and stooped as if they had deep thoughts about something; and stared at you a moment when you spoke, with a vacant, hopeless look, as if they felt they knew, and the world knew, there was something gone wrong with them which they did n't know exactly how to right. These were the completed specimens of the bar's handiwork; and there were many others in different states of finish, who had begun to revolve about the same ghastly flame, to be burned in

the same dreadful fire. But to-night there was
only jollity and rough, hearty fellowship amongst
the crowd who came to drink and eat and talk
over the Search, and terrestrial things in general ;
and a hum of satisfied men crept out through the
doors and even across the broad street beyond.

It is one of the privileges of high military rank
amongst New England soldiers to always provide
a befitting supper after the Search for such of the
honorable and independent yeomanry. in uniform as
choose to partake ; and one might have found this
evening in the dining-hall of mine host of the " Indian Head," a rather talkative company engaged in
the peaceful pastimes of roast-pig and rum. There
was Captain Percival and Sergeant Ewer, and a
half score of Captains and Majors on the retired
list, with a plentiful sprinkling of village Squires, as
the brighter lights of this military banquet, from
whose benign presence the poorest private in the
Sandowne Guards was not excluded. And strange
to say, amongst that company, though hardly of it,
sat the quaint man who had attracted Arthur's notice, — whom Bill Sawyer had saluted as Commodore Treeman. Sergeant Ewer had run across him
after the training, and with his customary delicate
diplomacy, though for some reason he had not seen
fit to mention, either a sentiment of military companionship with the man in the worn uniform, or a
desire to raise his estimate of the Guards by a well-
directed hospitality, had pressingly invited him to

supper, without the least idea of his acceptance, and he had accepted, against all his ideas, and was there, to the disgust of several and the surprise of all. But the feast was furious, and the cups deep; and with rough jokes and proverbs and liberty-songs, and a deluge of cries and outcries, such as mark such festivals of the sons of Mars; and compliments to the distinguished officers, return of compliments to the disciplined privates, healths and toasts of exquisite and subtle flavor, such as only spring from black bottles inscribed " Jamaica," the night wore on. It was a pastime to which the company quite as naturally, if not as righteously, betook themselves as to psalm-singing and the Catechism. These Sandowners were sinking down tonight through a thousand years to the level of their Norse forefathers, who revelled with mead and boar's flesh, on board the galleys of the Sea Kings, or after the carnage of Danish battle-fields, and were carousing just as they, in spite of the Pilgrims and Plymouth Rock. It was well that Squire Howe had refused to say grace before that company, with the gentle excuse: " It is hardly worth while, is it, Captain, — them young fellows are so noisy." Grace was not a weakness of the Sandowne Guards.

" A toast!" shouted the Captain. " Many returns of this happy day!" Drunk with profound emotion. " A toast!" cried Sergeant Ewer, with a voice a little thick from roast-pig and Jamaica. " Alexander Hamilton and the tariff forever!"

" That 's politics ! " shouted a dozen voices. " Turn him out ; that 's nothin' to do with training "; and the Sergeant sunk back in disgrace to his pork and platter. A dozen sentiments, one top of another, caused the black bottles to suffer terribly, and some additional confusion. " I give you a toast, gentlemen ! " cried Squire Howe, from the head of the table, " which must appeal to every patriotic American : ' Our Revolutionary Fathers and Bunker Hill ! ' " " And damnation to the Tories ! " shouted Bill Sawyer ; " them 's my sentiments." Bill's amendment was not rejected. " Now all together, gentlemen, standin'." And they all stood up as well as they could, considering the roast-pig and the fatigues of the Search, and made ready. " Stand up, Commodore ! " shouted Bill to old Treeman, who had silently sat through all the revel, and had taken little part in the feasting ; " stand up, and no shirkin' them sentiments." And all eyes were turned down the table where he sat without moving. " Stand up and drink the toast." " I won't drink that toast," said the man. A volley of ejaculations, which savored more of strength than of righteousness, followed the refusal, and half a dozen glasses were levelled at him. " I beseech you stop, gentlemen," said the Squire ; " he does n't appreciate the sentiment, and I know he won't refuse to give glory to our Pooritan ancestry who fought for American rights." " I do understand it all," said the man, gruffly, " and I won't drink to that. Who are you, to talk of Puritan ancestry, when you are all as drunk as a fiddler's dog, and slobber and swill like anything but Puritans? What rights did the Puritans give you or anybody else in this town, but to go to the meeting-house and sing psalms through your nose, and then go and get drunk privately in a tavern? What religion have you got, with all your catechisms and hymn-books? They took all the life out of men with their eternal mumbling about Divine Providence and their 'Five Points;' and made men curs, afraid to wag their tails on Sundays, or against the parson's sermon and the Church of the Elect. I hate the Puritans for an unmerciful set of Lord Bishops, that lorded it without stole or mitre over better men than themselves. They stole the Indians' land from them, and cut their throats when they refused to give up their own. They called King Philip, in every pulpit, a red-devil and son of Satan, when he was one of the truest martyrs that ever fell in defence of justice for the weak against the strong; and they quartered his dead body as though he were a dog, as it lay in the swamp by Mount Hope, where he had fled in famine, and because his friends were cowards, to die, where he had always lived, a king; and they sold his little son, nine years old, in slavery, though the brave Church, who was a poor Puritan, and all true men, begged against it, and wept for it; — and I say they stole and murdered, and then whined and prayed over the spoils as though they were the hosts of the Lord, and not children of the devil, against the poor, ignorant red men. And I hate them, and I won't drink to them, if you cut my throat for it. And you say ' damnation to the Tories ! ' The men that might answer that are mostly in their graves, where you flung them, or in foreign lands, where you drove them ; and you have it your own way here, as though there were none to answer. But I tell you they were men who hated hypocrites ; and the eternal snivelling they were sick of ; and they stood by their king, and liked him better than the knaves who put on a liberty-cap to preach treason in against the best government under the sun, and stabbed liberty to death, except such liberty as they chose to give you, — men who lost their all for loyalty to principle ; and if they had won would have had a crown, instead of the contempt your historians heap on them ; and they are in their graves, and I knew many of them, and loved them ; and you shan't trample on them, if only an old man is to stand between you and them ; and I drink to King George and his liegemen, who lived and died true to him " ; and he emptied with a steady hand his glass, and set it down.

It was peace before in comparison with what followed. The old man's audacity, and the fire with which he spoke, had checked for a moment the impulse to interfere with him ; but the bitterness of his words exasperated men already excited by the night's carousal, and they sprung at him as if they would trample him under foot just then and there. But the devil in him seemed roused, and springing back with a sudden bound, he stood on his guard, without a word, and with the air of a man, who, with a stout sword, was not to be trifled with. "Kill the rebel!" shouted Sergeant Ewer, as he made a drunken pass at him, which the man replied to by dashing the sergeant's sword out of his hand, and by a blow upon his head with the flat of his own that sent the sergeant reeling back amongst his friends. Evidently there was one good swordsman in that room who had served out his apprenticeship somewhere, and the men let him alone. "No murder, gentlemen!" cried Squire Howe, in a deprecatory tone. "Let the law be respected! Call upon the selectmen for help! Don't shed blood, I beseech, on this festive occasion! 'Wrath is mine, saith the Lord!'" And the old man, sheathing his sword, without a word walked unmolested out of the room.

CHAPTER X.

MYSTERIES.

As Sam Jones did not make his appearance the next morning at the usual hour to report about farm-matters, after breakfast Arthur sought the mansion of that individual for information. Sam's domicile stood a little way off, down the old lane that led to the marshes, and had been from time immemorial devoted to the uses of "the help" on Bassett Farm, — a little squat, dumpy house, with a rather huge, squat chimney, looking as if both were making an unsuccessful attempt to get their heads underground out of the way of the rough north-easters that came sweeping in winter across the flats; with a great display of economy in windows, and its sides painted a glaring red, and a yellow door in front, and Sam's name printed with emphatic black letters on the floor of the front entry; and a prim yard, embellished by a few straggling hollyhocks and marigolds in season, enclosed by what was once a picket fence; and a back yard, where all in the domestic *ménage* that was not intended for the public gaze found a resting-place: putting, as it were, — and as plenty of people do, —

the best foot forward, though it be not a very good foot, and things are sadly dilapidated in the rear, — a house, thanks to Mrs. Sam, kept always on its good behavior, and home of humble though clean penates, where Sam by permission hung up his hat and lived. "Come in," said a voice, as Arthur knocked, which the latter recognized as belonging to the aforesaid occupant. "Come in, without standin' on ceremony, and don't make a slave of yourself knocking." A low, indescribable bustle, as of a sudden confusion amongst wooden ware, as if the chairs in the house were knocking their legs together in a hurried minuet, and a suppressed, expostulating voice, "How *could* you, Mr. Jones?" made it clear that there was somebody else in-doors, who, at any rate, was not so much averse to the aforesaid ceremony; and Arthur went in, with becoming deliberation, to meet for the first time Mrs. Sam, who, having hastily thrown the broom in her hand into the back bedroom, and Sam's hat after it, as the said hat happened to be in its usual place, to the disfigurement of her especial vanity — her white kitchen floor; and taken a turn at the chairs, which Sam had managed during the morning to get a degree or two out of their appropriate latitude or longitude, according to his wife's kitchen geography; and made a dash at her hair with both hands, to smooth that female consolation; and shaken the wrinkles out of her calico dress, and otherwise made ready, received her visitor with some little

confusion of manner, consequent upon her late la-
bors, but with remarkable volubility and warmth.
" Wife," said Sam.   " 'Bliged to you for calling,
Mr. Bassett.   Take a cheer if you can find one,
Mr. Bassett.   Long time since I 've seen you, Mr.
Bassett ; " and she seized a chair as she might a dis-
obedient child, by the nape of the neck, and giving
it a slight dusting with her apron, out of sheer
habit, for there was no dust on it, set it down before
Arthur with emphasis, who thereupon sat down.

Mrs. Abigail Jones, or as the townsfolks curtly
called her, " Aunt Nabby," had it in her very bones
to be a Yankee, and she did n't deny it.   She had
lived in the woods and been brought down to the
marshes, when Sam had looked round for " a help-
meet," and her inner consciousness was a mixture
of wood and marsh.   Not by any means that her
temperament was either wooden or muddy, though
it, perhaps, had a smack of both ; for it had, also, a
little vinegar, and her speech and acts, within their
peculiar limits, were as bright and sharp as steel,
and on occasion she had a tongue of the rasp order
in her personal machinery ; but somehow she had
managed to live for nigh forty years now in Sandown, without having any more philosophical idea
about them than that the woods were to furnish
cord wood for the fire-place, and the marshes salt
hay for the barnyard, and on that theory of the
universe she had been content to live along without
asking questions in that quarter, at least.   And

Nature, that at the start always comes to a fresh soul with beautiful gifts, and when they are not taken with thanks, avenges herself by sealing up the empty chambers, so that after a time no truly beautiful thing can ever find its way into it, but all her music, pathos, poetry, are as though that soul were deaf and blind, had, on sufficient grounds, long since parted company with Mrs. Sam, and in her own peculiar way had avenged herself by leaving her with a sublime indifference to everything in the universe, except what could be put into her house or stomach. So Mrs. Sam did not think much of anything she could n't either eat or wear. And as so good a feeder could n't live on sunsets, and so real an entity as Mrs. Sam could n't exactly replenish her wardrobe out of the clouds, (though in the latter case she would have been out on a hunt for them before sunrise, so thrifty and always looking after the main chance was she,) she never condescended to give a thought to either, except to prophesy about the hay weather, or the state of the tides for Sam's expeditions after clams. In plain English, Aunt Nabby was a matter-of-fact person, who knew that two and two make four, and if you put a tea-kettle on the fire it is sure to boil; — one of our intense New England Realists, found everywhere, without any poetry or sentiment to speak of, who never saw in a corn-field anything but so many bags of Indian meal, potentially, or in a meadow anything but so much fodder for the

cows. Is Mrs. Abigail Jones to blame for that?
Do you, who are without sin, then, cast the first
stone at her. Remember, the world is divided
between the crickets and the ants. Have n't all
such people a stock of necessary virtues, by which
society subsists? and what should we careless crickets come to, who lie in the warm sunshine and sing
out of glad hearts our thanks for the Beautiful
about us, if it were n't for these careful ants that go
grubbing in the fields for grain, and lay it up in
safe cellars, and spend their lives watching and
moiling for what may keep us full and warm?
By immutable law, there will be always ants and
crickets, and why should we prodigals quarrel with
such useful laborers.

Yet Mrs. Sam had shining virtues of a certain
sort, and her house spoke volumes in her praise.
The true antichrist in her theology was dirt, and
she hunted down that demon in all quarters with
a persistent, though quiet rage, and neither gave
nor took quarter with that enemy and bane of her
existence. If her Christian stewardship here had
consisted in scrubbing the kitchen floor, her seat
would have certainly been in the seventh heaven
hereafter. You could afford to eat quite as well
off that floor as from the family table. She prided
herself on that floor; she gave her mind to that
floor, and loved to hear her visitors admire its
whiteness; and woe to man or beast who dared to
set unseemly feet on it. After every fresh scrub-

bing, Sam had learned by experience to avoid any rash trespass upon it, and even the thick-set, yellow dog, at such times walked demurely across it to his nap in the chimney-corner, with a side glance at his mistress, as if to say, " By your leave, Madam." In fine, the old Saxon proverb, " Cleanliness is kin to godliness," covered very much of her practical theology in house matters. Next to dirt, the bane of Mrs. Sam's life was laziness. In this respect Sam's conduct was not above suspicion, and while she was often heard to declare " she had n't a lazy bone in her body," she had been known to insinuate that, " If it were n't for her, they would n't have a roof above their heads very long." She had a bitter contempt for all eye-servants, who all day thought of nothing but " salt pork and sunset," as she said. She mentioned, in terms of reprobation, the lazy saying of Old Bill Swain, to somebody who ventured to suggest that he should preserve his valuable life by a little work occasionally, — " Let them that has n't got souls work, I 'm thinking," said Bill; " as for me, I 'm a Christian, I reckon." Thus on scrubbing-days she made the house a little too hot for comfort, and Sam was glad to escape to the barn for refuge while his spouse was putting things to rights; and there was a certain despotism in her industry that was always interfering with Sam's hat, which loved the aforesaid floor, and with his boots that did n't love cleaning, and gave him a sort of permissive right in his own domicil; but he was a wise man, and yielded to the inevitable destiny of his wife's broom and mop without a murmur. Indeed, it was sometimes said in the neighborhood that " the off-ox was the best team," — which meant that Sam was a little too much under petticoat government; and Sam, himself, in the early part of his married life, had instituted some inquiries into that matter, and had been forced to the conclusion that it was best " to let well enough alone " in-doors; and Mrs. Sam ruled her house, henceforth, with an unchallenged sceptre. True, she had her faults, for she had her trials. The soap would n't settle, or the butter would n't come in the churn, or the chickens would parade across her white floor, or some such calamity would disturb her temper; at which time she always betook herself to one solace, — she punched the dog. Whereupon that individual would get up with a surly but very dignified air of conscious injury, and walk out of doors, while Mrs. Sam, with anger modified by the explosion, would betake herself to repairing damages. Yet she was a busy, efficient housekeeper, and good-hearted withal, and according to her kind, was bent on discharging all her duties with justice towards all. Only Mrs. Sam was a little human, and had both too much and too little of the woods and marshes in her to make her a paragon. So much the worse for Mrs. Sam.

On ordinary occasions, Arthur would have found himself overwhelmed by Mrs. Sam with all sorts of questions as to his future plans, mercenary or marital, and been compelled to give that lady a diary of his own existence for the last ten years. For Mrs. Sam had a strong thirst for that sort of knowledge, and a peculiar way of worming out the truth, as to what were often only her very shrewd conjectures, by a well-directed course of cross-questioning, as, " Is it really true, Mr. Bassett, as folks say, that you are going to tear down Bassett House ? " and so on, until, before you knew it, she had guessed or jumped at the truth, in spite of you. She had, indeed, a wonderful gift of minding other folks' business, without neglecting her own. She ruminated upon the town gossip while she scrubbed. She rolled any bit of fresh scandal, like a sweet morsel, under her tongue, as she made a daily warfare upon the dirt. Not that she was a malicious person, or had an ill-will against any ; nor so much as La Rochefoucauld has said, and just missed the truth in saying, " Because in the misfortunes of our best friends we often find something which does not displease us," but as a punishment that Nature inflicted on her, because, as I have said, she shut up her heart from her beautiful charities and meanings ; and now, when from year to year that troublesome tenant, hungry and thirsty, was restless and complaining, though less loudly as time wore on, she brought and laid at its prison door such dry husks as petty rumors, scandals, gossipings of Sandowne life, in self-defence. So intimately does life depend on duty, throughout the universe, that I suppose, if the clearest diamond could and did refuse to take to its heart and flash back therefrom the sunlight, it would soon crumble away like the dingiest slate-stone of the hills. And when any life set amidst Nature refuses to receive the beautiful light thereof, to transfigure its inner sanctuary with gleam and sunshine, in due course that life becomes dark and crumbles into dust ; and what we call foibles, faults, vanities, are the *débris* at the base of the crumbling and sunless hill. If the Switzer refuses to take up into his own life the great Alps, the Alps bury him, with the awful rigor of offended majesty, in the sunless grave of a narrowed and menial life, as one may learn among the beggars of the Oberland. We meet plenty of men and women in every country village that startle and pain us by a certain deformed and dreary life, out of which all sentiment and poetry seem to have dropped, and left behind them only the desert sands of menial and servile tastes and tasks. And for them Nature, in her royal robes and gentle persuasive voice, has been speaking these thirty years, and now, at last, to blind eyes and deaf ears, in vain. Electra, amongst our northern hills, wears no Hellenic robes of grace, may be, but her mien is as awful, and her wrath as iron as when she stood in the halls of Atreus, and marked that Thyestian banquet, at which, in very horror, the coursers of the sun stood still in the pathway of the heavens. Punishment comes with leaden feet, but strikes with iron hands, and its coming is seldom sadder than when it brings avenging content to a human soul, sinking half consciously beneath its petty cares and cravings into utter night, where there are no stars, and into a sunless life, where the flowers of pure and subtle yearnings after the Infinite Good and Beautiful are dead. In a higher economy than ours, life misused turns to death transfused ; and on many a life, guiltless before human law of any crime, and diligently satisfying the demands our worldly economies and societies make on it, and yet lacking the divinest things, the pitiless, avenging Furies, in strictest justice, enter that solemn verdict, DOOMED.

But to return from this digression, inspired by Mrs. Sam. Arthur found her this morning quite too excited to talk of anything but the events of the May Search yesterday, and certain mysterious transactions, that, together with Treeman's strange conduct, had thrown the Sandowners into a state of great excitement. "Heerd the news?" was her first inquiry. "Orful, is n't it? ' This is a world of wickedness, (Mrs. Sam always broke out with some such Scripture when she ran foul of any fresh scandal,) and a vale of tears.' I don't see what the world 's comin' to! To think of that blasphemer, abusin' the sacred ordinances of religion and the Caatekism and the ministers! I wonder the airth did n't open to swallow him up. I should n't be surprised if he were carried off sudden, by him he 's been sarvin', afore long. He 's got a spray foot, I guess, if they 'd only pull off his boots. I would n't be in his skin for all the world when the Great Day comes. I 've always been afeerd of that man; he 's always prowlin' round and runnin' up and down the airth, and folks are always meetin' him everywhere they go, — gunnin', or choppin', or berryin', — and he 's always out in stormy weather, as if he liked it, and 't was natr'l to him, and he 's ramblin' on the beech down there when it blows like great guns, though if he 'd been an honest man, I can't see what he 's there for; and men has met him, when they were black-duckin', roamin' on the sand-hills almost down to ' the light'; and always kept away from 'em, and won't speak to 'em; and what 's he there for unless he 's a pirate and hunt-in' for money, or leastaways is diggin' for money where the Black One tells him? and he 'll come to some bad end afore long, that 's sartin, and to think how he sarved the company at ' The Head' last evenin'."

Arthur ventured to inquire, as soon as Mrs. Sam found time to stop to take breath, after this out-burst, to what she alluded. "*Haint* you heerd," said Mrs. Sam, in great astonishment, " how old Billy Treeman has been goin' on? Why, he 's nearupon killed Sergeant Ewer, who reproved him for swearin' so bad agin the meetin', and callin' folks such bad names, and holdin' up the Tories; and he 's an infidel of the worst sort, and they say it smelt brimstony about there arter he went off; and Deacon Wiswell sez there was a sort of blue light about his hed as he went along the road last night, and I 'm afeerd he 's a witch, or a divil, or somethin', and desarves hangin'."

Mrs. Sam was much nearer the truth about what went on at the supper than some of her neighbors; for, upon the first report, brought to her by one of the farm hands who happened to be present, she had dispatched Sam in hot haste to the seat of war, and he had managed to pick up at the tavern such information as his wife had just imparted to her visitor. The affair had indeed caused an universal uproar in the village. As the day wore on, Madam Rumor, who never has shown any signs of decrepitude in a New England village, and as far as I know, for the next ten thousand years, will merit Virgil's description of that dame, —

> " The great ill from small beginnings grows,
>   And every moment brings
>   New vigor to her flights, new pinions to her wings.
>   Soon grows the pigmy to gigantic size;
>   Her feet on earth, her forehead in the skies.
>   Swift is her walk, more swift her wingèd haste,
>   A monstrous phantom, horrible and vast;
>   As many plumes as raise her lofty flight,
>   So many piercing eyes enlarge her sight;
>   Millions of opening mouths to her belong,
>   And every mouth is furnished with a tongue,
>   And round with listening ears the flying plague is hung.
>   She fills the peaceful universe with cries,
>   No slumbers ever close her wakeful eyes.

By day from lofty towers her head she shews,
And spreads thro' trembling crowds disastrous news;
With court, informers haunts, and royal spies;
Things done relates; not done she feigns; and mingles truth with
      lies," —

had with swift feet carried into the outskirts of the
town a terrible story of at least a dozen men being
killed, and how the Devil had appeared bodily at the
supper, standing behind old Treeman's chair, and
going out with him at the end; and the countrymen came bustling into the town to have a hand in
the matter, or at least to bring back the news to
their anxious families.   Several things had been
proposed by the company at " The Head ; " as, for
instance, that the selectmen with the sheriff and
Deacon Wiswell should proceed to old Treeman's
house by the woods and arrest him for assault and
battery and blasphemy against religion, and Toryism, — in fine, on a dozen charges that plausibly
presented themselves ; but in the multitude of coun-
sellors there was disagreement, and consequently
safety for the offender, who was still at large.

" Times has changed since my time, or that fellow would be put in the town-stocks, and have had
' forty lashes save one,' " said Squire Howe, with a
sigh.   " Stocks 's jist the thing for curin' such people, or the duckin'-stool ; vagabonds like him are
afeerd of rotten eggs and cold water, and some of
'em 'd be a great sight better for a little more of
both." — " Give him swamp law ! " said an old farmer, with a very red face ; " ride him on a fence-rail

and drum him outer town 's the best!" —"Respect the law, gentlemen," said Squire Howe. —"String him up on the guide-post!" said a third; "and he 'd soon say, as the Tory did in the Reverlootion, when they let him down the third time, black in the face, 'It 's a very queer way, gentlemen, to make a Whig; but, by heavens, it 's a very sure way!' Give him a hist, the Tory, and he 'll soon cool off about King George and all them Hessians!" But as it was a very delicate matter for an exasperated though order-loving community to settle, and as the offence was largely against the spiritual powers, it was finally determined to refer the matter to the parson, Mr. Leverick, and a deputation was appointed to call upon him for advice. And so the matter stood at Arthur's visit to Mrs. Sam.

"Things are comin' to some bad end, I 'm afeerd," continued that lady, with a long breath that was meant for a sigh. "The powers of darkness are in the air. I don't know but Sandowne 'll be destroyed for the sins of the people. The Church is so dead, and there aint ben an outporin' for a long time, now, because we don't wrestle for the blessin', as poor Deacon Barlow says, and people are gettin' so stuck up nowadays, and wearin' sich finery, and stayin' home from meetin'. And there 's a new wreath of flowers on the cross, and the garden has been fixed again in the graveyard, and I 'm afeerd the Evil One is a rulin' in this town, and agin the Lord's chosen."

"Why, you see," says Sam, in answer to an inquiring look from Arthur, "there was a man murdered a good many years ago, up among the hills yonder, by nobody knows who, — a relation of yours, too, and belongin' to the House to which you belong, — Widow Lawrence's husband, who 's a connection of your 'n, somehow ; and people never knew how it came about, — somebody cross with him for marrying his wife, I think I 've heard father say ; and somebody 's set up a cross on the spot where the body was found, down amongst the trees in the swamp, where nobody likes to travel after sundown ; and every year just about this time somebody puts a wreath of May-flowers on that cross, and though it 's been watched, he 's never been found out ; and some people thinks it 's spirits or angels done that, because the poor man did n't have his rights at the hands of his feller-men, and they 're makin' compensation for it."

"It 's just this day of the year, too," said Mrs. Sam, " when it happened. Old Cloe, who 's got all them things in her head, said so, yesterday ; and that she knowed Master Alfred when a boy, and brought him up at the House, and one of the handsomest young men in all Sandowne, and she seed him when he was brought home shot right through the heart, and his poor wife never shed a tear, but looked as white as a sheet as she kissed him just as he lay in the entry in his huntin' clothes, as they brought him in, and she has n't been herself ever since, — so folks say who knew her afore."

" It 's all very singular," said Sam, " but what will happen will, I s'pose."

" But what about the grave ? " said Arthur, eagerly, — for that such things could be a part of the sleepy Sandowne life he saw about him seemed incomprehensible, — " what of the grave in the burying-ground ? "

" Nobody knows nothing about that," said Sam. " Somebody 's buried there who died twenty years ago or more, I think, — not a Sandowner, nor from these parts ; killed in the great storm, when the sea broke over the beach and did such damage to the salt-marshes here. You may have heerd of that storm," said Sam. " Men out all of ten days on the beach trying to save somebody, and vessels coming on shore, and not a soul saved, — only one dog, — and the graves there by the meetin'-house, — mostly men, and some women and children, buried all together, and nobody to know their names, though at the Great Day that 'll be easy enough, I s'pose ; and when people came down to inquire, nobody to tell them much, only they were buried."

" But the grave ? " said Arthur.

" That 's one of them, I reckon," said Sam ; " a woman's ; she was so beautiful, and looked so as if asleep when they found her in the surf, that they buried her and marked the grave with two great stones, and called it ' the girl's grave,'— kinder lov-

ing like. And somebody has made a flower-garden
on it, and set out rose-bushes and them things, and it
looks so cheery in amongst the gravestones, and
every spring somebody works in there; and last
week, when old Mason's funeral was, there 'peared
a gravestone amongst the rose-bushes with a strange
inscription, which I 've heard, but which, as I 'm
no scholar, I don't quite understand. And people
don't know what to make of all of it. They 're
afeerd something 's wrong. I 'm not superstitious,
and don't believe in ghosts and witches and all that,
but I feel rather queer with all this going on, and
nobody knows who 's at the bottom of it."

" *I* 've seen a ghost," said Mrs. Sam, " and my
grandmother knowed a witch, and I believe in evil
spirits, and I know who 's to the bottom of it,
though I don't see how *he* dares to go to a graveyard, amongst the dust of Christians, and where old
Parson Snow, who hated him so, is buried, and so
many texts out of the Good Book on the gravestones. *I* think it 's the Evil One."

As Arthur left Mrs. Sam's house, he forthwith
forgot that lady and her amenities to meditate upon
the grave matters which he had heard ; and a certain sadness, through sympathy for what must have
been a true passion or suffering of souls long ago,
took possession of him, which was in marked contrast with the gay, happy, quiet day about him.
Here, then, amongst these sleepy hills there must
be also that strange drama of life — half comedy

half tragedy — which is never absent where man is, advancing to its own strange and pathetic conclusions. The life of two thousand years ago, which in its stormier moods finds fit portraiture in the Antigone of Sophocles and the Prometheus, is one in essence with the rustic life of our country villages, and has the same grave meanings and sorrows always; and is the sacred fire from heaven that sanctifies the rudest altars and the most prosaic rituals.

Arthur seemed to hear unseen footsteps that crossed with him the threshold as he came slowly back to Bassett House, and entered the hall where years ago a young man had crossed one day and been carried back dead to a crushed wife; but there was no wail to-day, and only a young man entered. Cloe showed him the portrait, and went through her story. " 'Deed, Massa, the handsomest young gentleman in all Sandowne. Cloe babied him in these arms; " and the old crone rubbed at her eyes, which were dry. The portrait was that of a very young man in a semi-Puritanic dress, a trifle stiff, — a round, ruddy, New England face, without a wrinkle, with blue eyes, and with that hopeful expression, borrowing so largely from the future, which many young faces have. Yet it was only the face of a man who had died, with a story to it. And what was that to Arthur? Had not many men died with stories, and were not many men dying that very moment and leaving legends of many sorts? Only this, — that Arthur had heard this story, and this man was his kinsman. For the rest, it was only needed that the one great Friend of strangers should hear all stories and be as He always is, the immutable Kinsman of the forgotten.

A young man at Bassett House watched the embers go out that night upon the hearth, and then fell asleep to dream a confused dream of murderers and their victims; and he saw sleepless demons driving the red-handed ones up and down the earth with whips of fire, until in flight they fell into a surging sea of fire, which closed in over them and still kept heaving its molten waves without rest or halt. And the fire seemed to be sweeping round him, and he felt it at his heart, and it awoke him. What was this? A red light in that dark room was poured out over him. Was it light from that sea he dreamed of? He looked up and round him. Wonder of wonders! It was light from the portrait of the murdered man upon the wall. That picture seemed on fire; and yet it did not burn. But the face upon the canvas was lighted up, and light shone through the eyes, and a red glare was on its silent features, and an indescribable distinctness seemed given to every line and color of the painter's work. Arthur started up. Did the dead come back to reanimate their busts and pictures? He had read some such fable in the old books. Was this some sign of an unquiet spirit, who, on this anniversary of its grievous wrong at human hands, came back again with such lurid protest and reminder of its ancient passion? Who could answer Arthur as he stood spell-bound, gazing at that flaming countenance? The same red glare on all the furniture in the old room, and on the other faces that lined the walls. He turned to go to call help. He stumbled against a chair. It was utter darkness. He groped his way to the hall-door and opened it. There was no one to call but Cloe. Cloe came stumbling along from the kitchen, mumbling something at the disturbance.

" Well, Massa Arthur? "

" That picture — the dead man's — has been on fire, Cloe! " he said.

" Fire? " she muttered: " Fire? " rubbing her sleepy eyes as if trying to remember something. " Yes; I remember. I 've seed that twice. That is the natives under ground. They comes up here on sich days. I knowed they would. The natives have been oneasy all day long. They 've got him afore this, down there in their fire, — him that killed Massa John. I knowed it." And the old crone went mumbling back to the kitchen.

CHAPTER XI.

MEMORIES.

THIS chapter is history. It has no place nor time to it, however. It is written of a man without a name. Perhaps it is also the history of many men whom history does not name. After all, the splendor and the sorrow that weaves the garland of life out of immortelles for mortals is not always writ in history.

Let the curtain rise a moment from before a heart. It is a man sitting at eventide in spring-time looking out upon the sea. He has looked out on the sea in spring-time under other skies, when he was younger. The sea is placid and asleep this time. Yonder on the headlands the setting sun casts fading sunlight upon the black woods, and transfigures the white sand-hills beyond them into more dazzling whiteness. What legend is there to this man watching the sea? A legend very, very old. It is of a heart that suffered and grew strong.

The sun goes down, and the man sits in the evening twilight beside the sea. What thoughts are in the heart, under the night? In a pure human sympathy we will command them to grow audible to us across the years. They are old memories. The heart under the night, says, " It was such a night as this when I left her with a kiss in hope. Has either failed ? Neither. Though a grave came between us. Should one complain? No! The hand that takes our dearest from us is never iron. Dear Father! why should one waste beneath it? By it is a new life, though it seem heavy with pain, and denotes sometimes a grave. Men think of me as solitary. They are the solitary; not I. They go out of their homes to their voyage or travel, and lament the absent. But her home is where I am ; close to me always as the shadow that follows a man in sunshine. Other wives die, but she cannot die; other wives fail or disappoint, and love is frayed out under the cark and care of life ; but she has grown transfigured to me ; and our love is above the strain of temporal things. True, sometimes the heart sinks down into a sense of solitude, and the shadow comes back again. It is only the shadow of the eternal sunshine, — ' dark with excess of light.'

" I see other brides stand before the altar wreathed with flowers. Shall I feel agony with the uttered words ' What God hath joined together let no man put asunder,' when I know that my bride is crowned with flowers that do not fade, in a marriage solemnized of that high priest of Immortality, — Death ? I love all for her. I feel a new tenderness towards the little children in other men's homes, since mine is childless. In one I have come to love the All.

Henceforth there is no grave, nor loss, nor death, since she has conquered them all for me, by leading me above them all to her. To her? Well, then, to God. Is she not very near to Him? I have conquered them for her. My heart went up to God with her. And I am strong through both. It is not pain, but peace."

How is it with the heart under the darkness by the sea? Is it not well with it? Drop, then, again the curtain, and leave it to the two who dwell in it, —a wife and God!

CHAPTER XII.

THE PARSONAGE.

"A pastor is the deputy of Christ for the reducing of man to the obedience of God. Therefore neither disdaineth he to enter into the poorest cottage, tho' he even creep into it. For both God is there also, and those for whom God died." — GEORGE HERBERT.

THE REV. HENRY LEVERICK was tenant in Sandowne Parsonage. The Parsonage itself was the gift of men and women who died long ago, and testified their zeal for the Puritan faith by this disposition of a tithe of those worldly goods which they could not carry with them even to the graveyard that lay just beyond their doors. It included not only the comfortable house that looked out on the mill-pond from amidst the lilacs, but also sundry pieces of salt-marsh and woodland and neckland scattered over the township, all and several of which the townspeople dignified with that one name, — The Parsonage. The older tenants of the demesne, — who had eked out their salaries with so much cord-wood, or monopoly of pitch-making in the town, granted them in open town-meeting, — had been farmers as well as parsons; but the present incumbent had given up his temporal rights in rent, and the Parsonage-lands were tilled by lay-brethren of the worshipful fraternity of farmers. The Parsonage proper was a by no means remarkable edifice, — except in the eyes of the urchins who watched on Sundays for the parson as he came through its front-door, dressed in his stately black robes of office, on his way to the meeting-house, or of the few who knew a tithe of what had gone on inside through the century and a half of its house-life. Here those clear, hard intellects had thought out, with weariness and solemn zeal, as though life and death waited upon their meditations, their personal answers to those subtle and sometimes terrible problems which the Puritan theology thrust upon them. In its library those sermons had been penned (written in a firm, decisive hand, and closely-lined, in economy of paper), which on Sundays had been followed to the end (though the parson turned the hour-glass on the pulpit twice), by his sober, toil-worn audience, to whom the sermon served as strong meat on week-days, and who never tired of discussing among themselves the abstrusest matters, relishing a tough point in ethics as spiritual food and feasting for the sinewy Puritan mind. Here refugees from across seas, for conscience-sake, had been harbored with simple but unfaltering generosity, until, as ministers, they had attained to a new parish in the wilderness, or, as laymen, been provided with work and became townsmen. From here had flashed out the fire of liberty into a patriotic address, read, maybe, at a county gathering of King George's malcontents in the years that made ready our Revolution. From here, and from houses like this, had gone out indeed those subtle, spiritual influences, backed by no mean culture brought from the Universities, which had given tone to the public and social life of the Puritan States. And under its humble roof had been thought thoughts that travelled into that domain of thought which has no bars nor years on it, and had been lived lives which made their owners citizens of a quite other municipality than that of Sandowne.

Henry Leverick, the present incumbent upon the parish properties, had been settled for nigh a score of years. A blue-eyed man, past forty as one would judge, and a bachelor, to the silent chagrin of several in Sandowne. He had come here on recommendation of the President of the College at K——, and had discharged with conscientious industry his duties towards his charge. He had somehow settled down amongst his people without challenging their curiosity; and as he entertained no visitors from abroad, and had no near of kin in the neighborhood, his parishioners knew and asked little more about him than what immediately concerned themselves. He happened both to be the pride and the enigma of his parish. Not uncommunicative, and always ready to explain or advise in holy things, he still left, even with those of obtuse sensibilities, an impression that

there was something behind which he did not say,
— somewhat in him at which they could not get ;
and many left him piqued at a certain reticence
which they mistook for scant fellowship, or some
such defect, as minister. Yet all admitted the
single-heartedness of the man. The more staid
church-members thought him odd. His sermons
on Sundays were hardly explicit enough upon car-
dinal points of doctrine, some said. He was more
apt to impress on his hearers practical duties than
speculations about .election. Others thought him
unintelligible when he set about showing how some
sublime law of the universe showed through some
simple act or thing, and he would have lost the ear
of his audience if every now and then he had not
struck their hearts with some plain truth, quaintly
put, with a power few could withstand ; and even
the more stolid, when they could not understand,
came to feel that somehow he was a solemn, earnest
man, who had great truths on his mind which he
wished to make theirs also ; and his influence in
the parish, though subtle, had been for a long time
now surely lifting the Sandowne mind to a broader
and more religious life, though men hardly saw it,
as they do not see when life lifts the flowers, or the
soft air paints a child's cheek with health.

Mr. Leverick's oddities entered into week-days
as well as Sundays. He had a habit of strolling
through the country, and it was said of him that he
knew every swamp and marsh and outlandish nook

for miles around. He was like the other apostles, a fisherman, and had at first shocked the more godly of his flock by being seen across-fields with something that looked very much like a trout-pole; but this had come to be overlooked, and the townsmen often met him in the early spring tramping through those low sunny ravines where the first tortoises and swamp-cabbage show themselves, or resting on the green sward under the May apple-trees, apparently busy about nothing in particular, and passed him without surprise. It leaked out, through his old housekeeper, that there was a room in his house filled with the queerest things : birds' nests, with eggs in them, of rare species, who halt occasionally in their passage to other latitudes, — strange, silent visitors, that only the trained naturalist finds out : stuffed squirrel-skins ; spiders and insects of all colors, that lie under men's feet, working out their strange destiny, without any to see them once in a century ; and rare plants and rarer vegetables, *ludi naturæ,* which he had found in the woods, and pebbles which he had picked up out of the beds of trout-streams or on the beach, and sea-weeds from the creeks. All this had seemed nonsense to many, until one spring he had taught his neighbors how to save their apple-trees from a strange insect that was destroying them. The reaction had then been so great that his reputation for skill in occult things cost him a new annoyance, that culminated when an old crone out of the woods had applied to him, after Sunday services, to cure her and her house that were both bewitched. He could not work miracles, and in that case the cure was not performed.

There was one thing in the minister's favor, — the parish children were not afraid of him. They loved him. No matter how awful he might appear to the younger as he stood in the pulpit in his black gown on Sundays, — so awful, that, in their confused consciousness about holy things, they sometimes were afraid as if the Holiest was speaking, — there was not a child in the parish who would not wait an hour by the roadside to be patted on the head by their week-day friend. Children intuitively took to him, and never failed to come to him the first time as confidently as they would have gone to their mothers. There was something in his low, gentle voice, or eyes, that brought them, why they did not know. Perhaps because he was a child somehow, and in this world it is always like to like. By consequence, Mr Leverick's walks through the village were garnished with children. Children were to be seen almost any fair day playing around his door-stone, until every absentee of tender years was regularly hunted up at the Parsonage, and most knew their way to the library-door. He had indeed the unclerical habit of romping with his little visitors, and he might often be seen on summer afternoons with a group around him on the Parsonage lawn, putting flowers in the girls' hair, and enveloped in a crowd of happy naturalists, who, with an exquisite air of childish wonder, were learning about the specked stone, or the fragile blade of grass which he held in his hand as text; until many a household were perplexed with the new learning brought in-doors; and many a little one in Sandowne, as it said its prayers at evening, thought or said, "I have seen God to-day." It was only a child's comment upon the wise shepherd of young souls who that day had been tending the lambs of his flock, and the still waters and green pastures in which he led them made the sleep of many little slumberers sweet.

Sandowne Parsonage also could boast one child as permanent occupant. It was the boy Frederick Maud, commonly known in that household as Fritz. A slight child of five years, with that golden hair which Guido gives to his Madonnas, and deep hazel eyes, gentler than most women's, that looked out upon you from under the long eye-lashes out of liquid deeps, in which, to a close observer, a sensitive, thoughtful child-soul played and lived its dreamy child's life, so soon forgotten by most of us, and as we age, so inadequately computed by all of us. Frederick Maud was an orphan at birth, and had been consigned to the Lawrences, as kinsfolk of his, in infancy. He had grown into a strange attachment to the minister that had begun from the very hour when they two had met, — attachment as strange and as strong in the older as

in the younger party to the friendship. Every day
he had been carried in arms to the Parsonage, and,
after his daily frolic with the august master of the
same, had been as regularly laid to sleep upon the
latter's library sofa. For some time now he had
become regularly domiciled here, to the satisfaction
of both. They seemed to understand each other
from the start, and took each to his several avoca-
tion. Fritz's business was to be at home and
happy ; the minister's, to make him so. Fritz had
the range of the house, and did not abuse his privileges. The stuffed squirrels and birds he knew he
must not meddle with ; but he knew also what was
in every drawer of the minister's study-table, or on
it, climbing thereto to wonder at the pens or peer
into the huge glass inkstand, and where the sermons kept themselves, which he had fits of reading
childwise, and pursued grave studies amongst a pile
of books, until he became an adept in frontispieces
and black-letter, — all in his quiet way, as if busy
with most pressing pursuits, and careful not to disturb his silent friend, bent over his papers in mysterious handicraft of some sort, unknown to him, —
the aforesaid Fritz. Sometimes a little head stood
beside the table, waiting to be patted by a great,
gentle hand, when it forthwith silently disappeared
again among the books. Sometimes a pair of eyes
looked over the great man's shoulder at the desk,
and a low breathing was in the great man's ear,
and somebody had climbed his chair to wonder at

what work was being done there ; and none spoke, and there were two happy lives. Sometimes, when the minister had done writing, a little scholar came to be taught: about everything and nothing generally. And his thoughtful hazel eyes saw everything, and a little soul drank in wisdom of many sorts, and yet it seemed playing, not schooling, which the child got. Sometimes he came with a tangled thread he wanted untwisted ; sometimes with a fly's wing he had found on the window-sill; sometimes with a new flower he had found on the lawn ; or a pretty stone from somewhere. And always there was a question and a gentle answer that sent him away satisfied upon new discoveries. And Fritz was all faith, and some little wisdom, and much perplexity in these school-hours, when love played teacher. And the confidence which grew up between these two one could not describe nor explain, certainly not the silent man who sat at his desk and wrote. The housekeeper was impressed to say that Mr. Leverick made the child an idol. I know the wise man in this life has never but one idol, and that Mr. Leverick had lost his long ago. Henceforth he had only gifts from God that he stood ready to restore when asked. He spoke truth when he said, " I am better for this child. When Fritz is asleep by me in his corner on the sofa, and I am troubled in my writing and alone at night, I look at the child's face and doubts resolve themselves, and I find friends

again. In him the peace that passeth understanding. It is a child asleep." So Fritz possessed the
Parsonage and its master, and slept in his corner on
the sofa.

These two Arthur found as he came to the Parsonage for society, with an indistinct expectation
that somehow Mr. Leverick might help him in the
strange matters that troubled him, — the minister at
his writing and Fritz asleep. The former received
him cordially, as of a family he had known, and of
the college where he had been entered. " I am glad
to see a Bassett," he said; " and you like books."
Arthur said " Yes;" and forthwith they fell into
such conversation as befits friends. There was
something in Mr. Leverick that seemed to Arthur
very much older than himself, and yet something
that made him comrade. The minister, at Arthur's asking, told him many of the traditions of the
Parsonage.

" My predecessors were often quaint, but always
good men," he said : " emphatic men, often of ac-
curate university culture, set in the wilderness
among wrestlers for bread, who turned in upon
themselves for society, and lived two lives as most
men do : the one inner, with those great lords of
learning with whom they had spent their youth,
and which was buried with them in the graveyard
yonder, or rather rose with them when they left the
Parsonage ; the other outer, which went into Sunday sermons and their parish intercourse, and, soli-

tary as they were, they not seldom grew quaint or odd, as men said, with eccentricities which furnish the stock for many legends in these parts; men of broad humor often, garnishing the *res angustæ domi* with a certain genial grace of scholarly bearing that gave them a patent of nobility in all the neighborhood, though they had only this for castle. Some were called thundering preachers in their time, and others said quaint sayings out of their pulpit, which are still remembered hereabouts; and one, reported to have been the strongest man in all the country round, and who had upon occasions drilled his parishioners in arms before the Parsonage here, had fought with Puritan stubbornness at the most famous siege in Ireland, and been followed to his grave by his sorrowing comrades in arms who had emigrated with him; and others had left names behind them as martyrs for truth that are still spoken in the Puritan homes of England. They are asleep now in the graveyard yonder, and I fancy that when this land is covered with cities, men will forget the debt they owe to the country parsons of long ago, whose lives lie at the roots of the most vital virtues of the land. They have always seemed to me like travellers in a wood-path when the storm covers forthwith their tracks in the soft snow; but they who come after, through the level snow, feel though they cannot see the tracks beneath that bear them firmly up in a march made easier by these forerunners.

" As you are just from the learned bustle of the university," he said, " you may think that life here is too level and tame. Perhaps you think, with the old proverb," he said, smiling, " that ' One man is no man.' I try to carry the university into life, and make living, scholarship. That one word, Life, covers all art, learning, music, mystery, pathos, beauty in this world, and I find it never commonplace. I have books here, you see : they are my old friends, and they never change their courtesy or charity towards me. I have men outside me, and out of them I study the same passions, the same aspirations, the same wants and wills that over this world have built all, destroyed all, and have made or unmade nations from Pharaoh until now, and they reproduce for me history without my asking. I have the country, and in it a history older than any man, — a university with a charter older than any race, and in it a greater than any Chancellor teaches me ; and I go to school in my old age," he said, " as Michael Angelo went to the fish-market, not simply to study nature, but to read in every leaf of it the letters which everywhere the intellect finds to spell the Infinite, and the heart to spell ' our Father.' And then I go to school to this little boy here asleep. I study Nature in him. I find in him the Infinite. I learn what God is like in him. I say Heaven shines through a child's life, though the flesh sometimes colors the ray. I test philosophies with him. He is true, — a true work of the Highest, — and whatsoever contradicts childhood is not true. And these are my masters in this town," he said.

Arthur understood something of this. How should he understand all? We understand mainly with our lives, and Arthur was only twenty-two. The minister was older. Arthur finally told him his errand, — what Mrs. Sam had said, and what he had seen last night at Bassett House.

"I do not know. It is very strange," the minister said. "I have known things equally strange in this life, sometimes, hereabouts though. I advise you to patiently wait and see. The murdered man," ——

What the minister was about to say was interrupted by a loud hum of voices coming towards the Parsonage, and a very decisive knocking at the door, which was now surrounded by a crowd of men.

And Fritz awoke.

CHAPTER XIII.

AFTER THE SEARCH.

It was a motley crowd which entered the parson's library or waited outside. They had come to arraign the culprit of the Search Supper before the minister, as a proper person in their eyes to determine a cause half civil and half ecclesiastical. Treeman had spoken against the Catechism and against the clergy, and Mr. Leverick would no doubt vindicate his office and themselves by a suitable verdict. The culprit had strolled into town that morning past the respectable group before The Indian Head, who were discussing his arrest by the selectmen, and when Squire Howe stepped out to tell him of the proposed inquest at the Parsonage, he had answered bluntly, " Well ! " and had come with them. To-day he had doffed his regimentals and wore a grotesque dress tied up with ribbons of all colors, and carried in his hand a stout oak cane stuck at the bottom into a sheep's marrow-bone, and stood silently apart as if waiting for the case to go on.

Squire Howe, who had been a seafarer in his early days, and on his retirement from business had been made Justice of Peace in that ilk, — a little spare, quick-motioned man, with short, gray hair, in a suit of black, forever taking snuff out of a black snuff-box he always held in his hand, — was spokesman of the party. He related with tolerable accuracy the events of the Search Supper, and was especially emphatic about what he supposed to be Treeman's blasphemy against the Church. "We have brought this man," he said, in conclusion, "to ask you what shall be done with him for thus breaking the peace."

"They did not bring me," said the man, addressing the minister; "I came with them because I chose to come, and was not afraid to come. I should not have come unless I chose, and I chose because you are a minister and can judge better than these blockheads whether I am to blame. All I wish is, to be allowed to live and be let alone; and I live as though I were a wolf, with a pack always baying at my heels. I harm no one, and I ask none for bread, and they teach their children to be afraid of me, as if I were going to eat them; and when I walk the road they run in-doors from me — an old man — as if I were the Devil. They make me an outlaw here and call it godliness, and I am tired of it. If I am let alone, I shall go to my grave soon, and save these gentlemen all their trouble about me; but while I live I wish to be let alone. I did speak harshly, maybe, the other night at their supper. I suppose they asked me there to laugh at me; and they insulted me, and those who are dead and dear to me ; and I stood by my friends as they had stood by me in life, and had made life something else than a wild beast's hunt, as these here have made it for me. And I said what I will say here and everywhere, if needful, and men force me to it by their hard words about the dead. I am not a brute, but a man. I am no saint, nor are the rest here. I am only a man who wishes to be let alone to die and be buried away in a grave which has more mercy than these who cry out against an old man."

" You are a Tory," said Sergeant Ewer, "and deserve hanging on the furst tree. You spoke against the meeting-house and the Reverlootion. Maybe you 're a spy and wish to bring back the Hessians here ; and you 're no good," said the Sergeant.

" That 's so," said several in the crowd.

" Who are you ? " said the man, turning sharply upon the speakers. " You are saints, you are patriots, — are you ? and you come here with clean hands to strike me down, — do you ? Now listen. I knew you, and I knew your fathers, and I knew your Revolution, as you call it ; and I am not the man to believe any of you were saints. Hear now."

And they did hear a story that surprised them all. Somehow the man seemed acquainted with the secret history of every family in Sandowne for the past hundred years, and had gleaned together what was most sinister and desirable to have forgotten. That story was never repeated out of the Parsonage. The men who heard it felt that it had better be put out of sight as soon as it was spoken. It was a story that compromised the good name of many, and it was said by the less reticent afterwards that it seemed as if the bones of some in the graveyard ought to fairly shake with rage or fear if the story told to-day was true. The man seemed to feel a sort of increasing pleasure as he went on with his sinister narrative. Every now and then he would single out some one in the crowd, and, addressing him by name, recall some transaction of long ago, which seemed a by no. means pleasant memory to the. man addressed. It was hinted that Squire Howe himself was not one who escaped. It somehow oozed out long after, that Treeman's story was one which dated back from the Indian times, — about men who had robbed the natives, grown godly in old age, and slept honorably in the graveyard ; about men who had spent their lives altering bounds in the woods, defrauding thereby the orphans and the friendless ; about men who had changed the records of the county courts, or cut out leaves therefrom that destroyed titles ; about men who had shot down their Tory neighbors to gratify some long-standing feud, and then had possessed themselves of some coveted field or lot ; about men, and even women, who, underneath the rigid garb of Puritanism, had sinned sins older than any Puritanism, and proved that they were only men and women' needing pardon at the hands of the one great Pardoner of sinful lives, whose mercy, always tasked, is always ready for the repentant.

Things had come to wear a dramatic aspect in the Parsonage library. The half-restrained anger of the townsmen, and the resolute, dogged air of the old man, who stood apart from the rest, ready to repel assault in any shape, furnished that which was stormy in the scene. Fritz, who at the first seemed disposed to resent the untimely intrusion which had disturbed his nap, during Squire Howe's harangue had managed to slip off his sofa and quietly ensconced himself in the minister's lap, where he had watched with wondering eyes the speakers, and these two seemed the only persons who retained any sort of tranquillity when Treeman ended.

" You might as well have left these things unsaid," he said, mildly, to the old man. " None of us are better for them. You are not. You have asked me, my friends," he said, in answer to the townsmen, " to decide this matter. I can only advise. I advise you to leave this old man to himself. He says truly. He belongs to the grave rather than to us. The old are God's subjects, with whom not even kings may lightly meddle. You say he has spoken against religion. That which is true cannot be spoken against ; and if he has assailed the Church with blame, the Church that is blameless can receive no hurt from him. The fact that the Church *is*, after all blame, proves it. You say he is a Tory. Many good men, though mistaken men, as you and I think, have been that. They have failed in that. We should forget that. This man is one of the last, and he is harmless. We should fill that breach between countrymen with charity. Charity cures all. I advise you, let this man go free at your hands and in your hearts. As to you," he said, turning to the accused, " what you have said or thought remains with you. Let God judge, not man."

Whether this advice pleased the company is more than doubtful; but it was the minister who had spoken, and one by one they went out. The old man did not go.

" You have spoken kindly to me, and that is a new thing to me. I came here because I needed justice, — not the justice of the laws, but the justice of charity. We all have need of that. I am not a bad man, as I may seem. Life makes many men seem what they are not. I seem to be a pauper and outlaw. I have been something else. There are few men who have not been children and had mothers, and I am like the rest. I do not come to the meeting-house. I do not despise what you call religion for all that. You said let God judge. So say I; for God knows me, and His knowledge is mercy."

The man turned to go. Something made him stop and look down. It was the child playing with the bone on the end of his staff. He bent down to the child as if he would have kissed him, and moved his hand as if to lay it on his head. He did neither, but gently removing his staff, left the room.

"What is sin?" said the child, when he had gone, with an anxious, puzzled look towards his great friend by the study-table.

"I cannot tell you," said the minister.

And the child came back to him, and climbing up into his arms, lay there silently as if asleep.

CHAPTER XIV.

SUNDAY IN SANDOWNE.

SUNDAY came to Sandowne as it comes to many another hamlet and realm of this world, bringing its own holy rest. It came asking no questions as to what had gone on the week past in any of its homes, but bringing alike to sinner and saint its benison of peace. It bore a lesson in its daylight that some read not, and others had found to mean hope of another Sabbath to be spent with Him who, in the great week of Immortality, wherein is no death nor sin, provideth for His still greater peace. It was Sunday in all the Sandowne homes, and upon all the Sandowne lives that had fretted and worried themselves with the drudgeries of their narrow tasks ; Sunday over all the fields, where the plough stood still in the unfinished furrow, — over all the meadows where the grasses and flowers bathed themselves in the gentle yellow sunlight, — more yellow and gentle to-day than ever ; Sunday up among the hills and in the woods, where even the leaves seemed at rest in the still air ; Sunday over all the marshes, and upon the silent tide moving in along the creeks where the fishermen's craft, anchored upon the bank, seemed deserted of their noisy crew ; Sunday among the white sand-hills of the beach beyond the marshes ; Sunday upon the blue, waveless sea that to-day seemed to have forgot its customary unrest and babble ; Sunday up among the white, fleecy clouds that lay as if asleep overhead ; Sunday in the passionless blue-dome that rested upon the hills, and seemed as a tabernacle not made with hands, built for a day of prayer like this, over all worshippers, by Him, the Invisible within it, who heareth prayer.

And when the meeting-house bell sent its gentle summons over the hills to the peaceful Sandowne homes, it was as if a saint's voice were calling to those within to come out from their cares and dwell this one day in a home where there was no care. And many had heard the saintly music of its voice for some time now, and it brought to them pleasant memories of long ago, when they as little children had obeyed the call, as they walked with other little children, who had grown into greater wisdom as they slept in the graveyard yonder ; and many had heard that voice, who this Sunday listened to quite other voices in a more gentle Sabbath than that which came to Sandowne.   And that bell said several things to many, and especially to the old who heard its voice and rose up again obeying it.   All the morning groups of people might have been seen wending their way along the roads towards the meeting-house, — some on foot, a man with his wife on the pillion behind him, riding double on a farm-horse, along ways over which their fathers had rode in winter, — as the sons of royal Clovis are said to have rode forth from their palace, in carts or sleds drawn by oxen, — all with that grave decorum which befitted their errand there. Every now and then a village house emptied itself of a crowd of children, dressed out in their best, and walking hand-in-hand with a demureness befitting elders, while the white-haired grandfather, with his spouse, slowly brought up the rear. So in good time Sandowne found itself at the meeting-house.

The Puritan meeting-house had been from the start the centre of the Puritan activity and life. It was a visible sign of that great cause of free hearts and worship for which they had perilled seas and savage men and wildernesses. They had brought it with them from that fatherland, which, though it might have cast them out, had once been home, and it carried them back to the gray ivied churches in the old fields across seas, where they had prayed until a cross or surplice had drove them out; with their church-yard under the shadow of their Saxon spire, where their kindred were crumbling into dust. They had built these houses as a solemn duty for the most solemn services of which man is capable. They had given them an austere furnishing, as befitted men who felt that the Invisible was to be approached without form or symbol. They had been just to themselves in doing that; and in their meeting-houses the Puritans had wrestled and aspired, with what results only the Highest judges, for that great blessing at which all worship aims.

Other than religious affairs had been transacted within and without their walls. Around them, in the Indian times, they had built palisades and breast-works against the onset of the savages. Around them stood those oak-trees under which there had been the first gospel preaching, and the old folk sat between services to smoke their pipes and gossip. At their doors armed sentinels had stood on guard while the rest worshipped within. Before their porches oxen had been roasted with Puritan festivi-ties when Quebec fell and Montcalm died. On their sides wolves' heads had been nailed when some young hunter had gained the bounty, and thus pub-lished his success. On the open lawn in front the train-bands had assembled to march off upon an In-dian trail, or to strive with the French by the Can-ada lakes, or to join our great Fabius in his en-trenchments southward. Within their walls what prayers and sermons had been offered, and what a grim, earnest company gathered to listen, until life became more grim and earnest in the Puritan war-fare against the very elements themselves. In Taunton meeting-house had been that strange con-course, when Philip with his Indians — coarse, long-haired savages, with belts of colored wampum and little tinkling bells for amulets, bow and arrow in hand — had stood gloomily on one side ; and on

the other the fair-haired Saxon, with his steel and
, matchlock, grimly set on trampling down his ene-
. mies. And these two had gone out, after sharp,
brief words ; and many Puritan homes were ashes,
clotted with Puritan blood, and Philip and Philip's
race perished before the white man.

Sandowne meeting-house had its own history.
On this spot, indeed, the Pilgrims had met out-of-
doors under the trees for worship, before they had
hardly built themselves a cabin to live in on week-
days. A century and a half ago it had taken the
place of a rude board-shed, thatched over in winter,
where the Puritan heard the sermon and brushed
off the snow that came drifting through the seams
of the wall. It had given up the flag that was
hung out at first as a sign of meeting-time, as also
the trumpet and drum, which, in their lack of something better, had been beaten, — as the old traveller,
Sandys, tells us, in the East a plank used to be
beaten with two wooden mallets to call Christians
to church, — and now rejoiced in a bell-tower and
bell. It was a huge, shingled, unpainted, many-
windowed house outside, with doors under the bell-
tower and at the side, and its broad steeple, sur-
mounted by a weathercock, rose up in front from
the very ground, till the sailors saw it far off at sea
and turned the helm homewards. In its ample
porches the old sat between services, and the young
people displayed their finery. Inside, it was filled
with square, unpainted pews, with carved balus-

trades on top, (in English style,) and long galleries
occupied three sides of it; and over all were the
huge oak-beams and braces where the men piled up
their hats during service. A pulpit, bare of orna-
ment, and the singing-gallery opposite, finished the
whole into a meeting-house. It had also its own
religious symbolism, written on its very front. For,
as the square Norman towers across seas typified
resistance against worldly aggression, and the soaring Gothic spires the aspirations of the soul towards
heaven, so the Puritan meeting-house symbolized
the austerity of a faith that required no outward
sign, and the severity of that Puritan life that had
been purified as it were by fire. Democracy and
aristocracy were strangely blended in-doors. Puritanism was equality for the saints; but time had
stole this quality away, and the world had long
since asserted its own privilege of rank and wealth
against the elect. In the old times, and even now
somewhat, the citizens were seated with some regard to rank, — the more notable nearest the pulpit. The " seating " of the meeting had cost no
little jealousy and heart-burning amongst the Sandowners; but long before this, matters had settled
to their natural level, and there was peace within.
The bent old sexton still tugged at the bell-rope in
the porch, nodding gravely, in the intervals of labor,
to his acquaintances as they passed him. The warden, with his long, white pole of office, still kept
in check unruly urchins, or gently tapped a man's

head, asleep ; and the choir, composed of the most blooming Sandowne youth of both sexes, led by Sergeant Ewer, with a huge pitch-pipe in hand, dispersed sacred harmonies among the multitude. It is, unfortunately, a part of every town history, to be verified in any year, that village choristers are as sensitive and unmanageable as Charlemagne's twelve singers, whom the great Emperor begged from Rome that the chanting of the service might be uniform throughout his empire, and who, dispersed among his bishops, despite the Emperor and Pope, sung each in his own tune and method, until the despairing monarch sent these unruly spirits back to Rome and prison, — and the Sandowne choir was flesh and blood like other mortals.

The galleries were black with worshippers as the minister, leading the child Fritz with him, walked slowly up the pulpit steps. A hymn was read and sung ; a prayer offered, when the congregation all stood up ; Scripture was read ; another hymn sung, and then the sermon. It was a simple service, as befitted the place and people. It was a Puritan service, which it had cost fifteen hundred years to render possible, and they who offered it were children of exiles in the wilderness, and sons of men who had fought against kings for it.

The sermon to-day was about the sea, from the text that speaks of " those who go down to the sea in ships ; " and the chapter which the minister read was the one hundred and seventh Psalm, wherein occurs that sublime description of the sea in storm which no painter or poet has ever equalled in his art. And, as it was the time now when the young men were leaving the neighborhood for the eastern fisheries, there were many of these seafarers who listened earnestly to Mr. Leverick's words. He told them that God was in the sea, — in its wave, its surge, its current, its spray, its blueness, its blackness; in its depths, where no eye reaches, and where the unseen sands bear up its vastness in eternal silence; in its winds, that come how no man can say ; so that everywhere it was His mirror; —reflecting His awfulness and strength,— His infinity in its waves, — His eternity in their eternal motion. And they who lived on it, should live by it in two ways, — not only from what they caught out of it in food for the mere body, but much more, from the glimpses of God which they caught in it, as food for the soul. And he reminded them of how it was said of those who went down to the sea in ships, " These see the works of the Lord and His wonders in the deep " ; and that they who do not see Him never truly behold the sea, but are as blind men. " You think the sea cruel," he said. " I have heard some of you who have been in shipwreck call it a wild beast without mercy. Nothing is cruel in which God works, — it only seems so. The sea is only legal, not cruel. In this world there are mainly two aspects of God, — that of the sea and that of the land. The one is His aspect on

Mount Sinai, when He gave commandments; the other as He showed himself in a little child at Bethlehem. And as the earth is so beautiful only through the sea and land together, so in all lives, and in His life who died for us, the sea and earth still unite themselves, and create a divine beauty. The sea is God's law expressed in matter; the land is God's love also inscribed therein. No flower grows *in* the sea: *by* the sea, all flowers. The earth gives you fruits and flowers, growing green with spring and ripe with harvest; but the sea has no spring, nor season, nor grain-field, but through all years solemn, immutable, unsparing as infinite Law were without an infinite Love.

" Life, in many of its aspects, is like the sea ; and a man's first duty is to learn that he sails upon this sea, and to wisely regulate his voyage. You know," he said, " how great the mystery of the sea is. You grow acquainted with your fields and roads; but several old men, living all their lives by the sea, have told me that it was always a stranger to them. In the creeks and bays and channels thereof, which are the streets of the sea, who knows the processions of the travellers over its roadways. The dry-land men explore and delve in, and leave their mark on it; but sailors sail only upon the surface, and their trail is erased the moment the keel has divided its uppermost waves. And life is the great sea of mystery, rounded by a horizon of clouds that no man penetrates, with depths that no man sounds;

ever altering, ever unknown, — some gleam upon
its surface, but the abyss beneath black, shadowy,
solemn, nightlike, fathomless.   And when a young
soul goes out upon this sea, from start to port, mystery is everywhere, until it enters that greatest mystery of the Hereafter, where all is known and seen.
You have found, also, how changeable the sea is, —
how it is never two hours or two moments the
same; how never once in all the ages has it been
ever twice alike, — not even in a single wave or
spray of its white foam dashed against any cliff or
keel, though it be always the sea of old.   Sameness
in infinite change, like Him who, beneath the infinite shadows and shapes of this world, is always One.
And our lives are like the sea in that.   For though
man is always, mark how men change or vanish.
Childhood into manhood, and the grave for all, while
a train of little children follow close on those who
mourn and those who sleep.   How many have sat
in these pews, think you, that have given place to
you?   You yourselves are of that innumerable caravan that never halt twice by the same waters or
sleep twice by the same fires.

"The sea is the realm of labor.   It is always
doing something.   It is always forcing us to do
something.   Its waves, as they silently lift themselves against the horizon, far off at sea, seem like
the chained captives of the under-world that by
the poet's fables are made forever to move heavy
rocks up a severe hill, whose summit is never

reached. It puts men to their metal. It tests their watchfulness. It sends often a storm on swift wings to answer the careless crew with shipwreck, and it sweeps with black tempests round the well-manned bark, and tries the quality both of ship and crew. So Life is labor. Man's destiny is not to enjoy as one who has won, but to labor on as one who has to acquire. He that endures is not overcome. The sea is Spartan, and it breeds Spartans. It is an ordeal by fire for most men; the ordeal of the sea for all. For if we would reach port we must watch, meeting storms with carefulness and courage. I know how severe the voyage sometimes is, and how it wears men. But when in life the sea seems to overwhelm us, and we are as men struggling on a frail plank amidst the waves, and we would cry out like the Hebrew prophet, 'For thou, Lord, hadst cast me into the deep, in the midst of the seas. The waters compassed me about, even to the soul; the depths closed me round about; the weeds were wrapped about my head. I went down to the bottoms of the mountains; the earth with her bars was about me forever,'—remember also that other Scripture of hope, 'And God shall wipe away all tears from their eyes; and there shall be no more death, neither sorrow, nor crying, neither shall there be any more pain; for the former things have passed away.' 'And there was no more sea.'

. "The sea separates you who sail out together. No two ships from the same port ever follow in the same track. Hull down before sunset often, as you go out to the same grounds. Wind, tide, current set you apart, and each must make his voyage alone. So life separates friendly hearts. So the great waves of interest, passion, and impulse separate us with unknown distances. There are in the things of this world only two perfect solitudes, — the solitude of the sea and the solitude of the desert; but God so sends a man sometimes out upon the sea of life that the solitude of his soul is vaster than any.

"The sea also shipwrecks men. It takes life from men. How thick the wrecks lie upon the floor of the sea, — wreck of gold, wreck of precious stones, wreck of iron, wreck of war-galleys that sunk in red battle; wreck of merchantmen, gone down before hidden rock or black storm; wreck of crumbled bones of victor and vanquished, — all alike in their silent mausoleum of the under waters. Life shipwrecks its mariners, — prodigals in disgrace, saints in weakness or in martyrdoms; lost of appetite, mischance, or men's wrong, — all bent or broken before the storm, and hid away in the silent grave of the Past. And all these must be rendered back the day when the sea gives up its dead.

" The sea," he added, " is not only destroyer, — at its heart it is creator. It has its own way with men, and it is a way that leads through ruin often, but the end is life, but life in its own way. Plant your roses upon the sea-beach, and its salt spray withers them ; but when that same spray is lifted upon the soft wings of winds and borne in the great tides of the upper air over the land, it makes· a summer among the hills ; and where roses are fairest and lillies purest, there the sea is gentlest giver of life. The sea, then, is God's, as life is God's; and we should be God's mariners, sailing for Him and to Him ; voyaging not in our own right or wit, but under Him as the great Master of mariners, remembering how .a wise man has said that ' Reason is like the stars, which can guide only when the sky is clear, while Faith is like the magnetic needle, that guides the ship when it is wrapped in darkness.'

" Beyond the sea is heaven. Let us give thanks, as we all go forth upon the sea, for the land beyond the sea. For heaven, whose spring-time brings not its flowers to eyes dim with the tears shed for those asleep beneath spring violets, nor pours its autumn fulness upon those bent with bowing over their coffined dead ; — heaven that gives back wife to husband, and has no missing sister, nor sin-shipwrecked brother, nor Rachel weeping for her children ;— where no storm falleth, nor wave breaketh, nor current hindereth, nor sad sea sobbeth ; for St. John, beloved most of Christ, beloved now by us for his divine assurance, tells us in his rapt vision of the New Jerusalem : ' I saw a new heaven and a new earth, for the first heaven and the first earth were passed away ; and there was no more sea.' "

CHAPTER XV.

AFTER MEETING.

> "The loud deep calls me home even now to feed it
> With azure calm out of the emerald urns
> Which stand forever full before my throne."
>
> SHELLEY.

IT would have been a curious learning that one would gain were he able to see the thoughts about the Sabbath worship which the Sandowne people carried with them to their homes. On the minds of the younger, the chief impressions made were those of an ill-defined awe respecting the rites just celebrated, and a sense of being very hungry on Sundays. Of the older, each man carried away with him just that which he had chanced to hear; but many had been put to thinking, and the sermon furnished staple for discussion. Some had heard what was not in the sermon, and more did not hear what was. Upon the whole, the answer to this uncertain state of mind, in which Sandowne is by no means the only parish that finds itself, lies in the old question, " If thine eye be not sunny, how canst thou behold the sun ? "

One did not know what the parson was driving at. One thought the parson would preach a better sermon on that particular text if he would only go a three months' voyage in a fishing-smack to the Banks. Another thought him a great scholar, but a little misty. And a few went away silent; and sometimes at sea, when the day's work was done and they stood leaning over the tafferel, remembered the parson's words. The drift of the Sandowne thought about Mr. Leverick's discourse made its appearance as distinctly as any way in a quite private conversation which Sam Jones held with Mrs. Sam on their way to the cottage of the immaculate kitchen-floor.

"Capital sermon to-day," said Sam, " as far as I know."

"Yes, Mr. Jones, for them that likes it, and can onderstand it. I 'm afraid the parson is hardly Gospel enough. I don't see why he talks 'bout the sea that 's under everybody's nose in this town, and says sich fine things 'bout it. It 's good enough in its place, but it 's a bad neighbor when it drives all the salt-hay ashore off the staddles in the September gales, and there 's no end to quarrellin' 'bout who 's owner. As for me, I 'm glad them hills 's between it and me; and though I 've nothin' to say agin it, I 've somethin' else to do than meddlin' with it, and I don't care 'bout hearin' of it Sundays in the meetin'-house. How does the parson expect to save souls, talkin' 'bout the sea? *I* love doctrines. You would n't catch old parson Wareham, who christened me, talkin' sich things in the meetin'-house; and he preached the good old doctrines, and had a revival reg'lar every year."

"That may be," said Sam. "I like doctrines myself, and my father jined the meeting, and I like the parson's doctrines. I 'm not much of a sailor, though I 've ben afore the mast, and have stayed ashore ever since you jined me; but the parson and I agrees when he says that the great Being is everywhere. What 's the use of having a sea if it 's only to seine macker'l in? And what 's the use of having land if it 's only to go scrubbin' and grubbin' in. I should feel somethin' like a yeller dog tied in a tread-mill, as the parson says, if I 'd nothin' else to do than go hoein' and mowin'. There 's something in a feller that speaks rite out to him afore he knows it, and preaches him a sarmon in his every-day clothes; and a feller feels better after it. I aint no scholar, and can't talk like the parson; but I know it 's all very strange what 's made; and I don't think it made itself, or looks out for itself. I 'm no Christian as the meetin' is; but when I see how things goes on at the farm, I believe in the meetin'-house, and more than the meetin'-house. Scriptur' and the farm agree jist as if they were made for one another. When I see a corn-hill better looking than the rest I hoe that, kinder natrally; and Scriptur' says, ' To him that hath shall be given, and he shall have abundance;' and there 's one sermon afore breakfast for you.

There 's no cheatin' in the farm. If I sow rye I gets rye, and if I sow bad seed I gets nothin'. ' For whatsoever a man soweth that shall he also reap.' And I know that if a man goes plantin' in the tavern, he 'll go reapin' at the poor-house or the graveyard before fall. The farm tells no lies; men does. If I treat it well, it treats me well; if not, not. I can't cheat it by rising ever so airly. I go to do about right with it, and no foolin', if I expect to get along with it. And, I conclood, tenthly, as the parson says, that if a man wants to get along well with the great Being, here and after here, he must go about right with him, and no foolin'. Them 's my sentiments."

Agnes Lawrence waited in the porch for the minister, as he came down from the pulpit, leading the child; and Arthur joined the party as they walked down the road to the Lawrences', — Mr. Leverick to visit the invalid, and Arthur in his sympathy for society, and especially the society he found there. Mrs. Lawrence received them with her placid, gentle welcome; and the boy Fritz went to his customary chair at her feet, looking up into her face for his smile, which from time immemorial had not been denied to him.

"I have been at the meeting with you to-day," she said, " here in my prison-house, in these chains you see. I sometimes think I should be young again if I could get there. But I miss so many. I should hear in the singing other voices I cannot well bear. It is only the young that have merry Christmas or merry meeting. Agnes told me the other day out of her reading that the German women used to fasten up their robes with a thorn. I could not help asking whether in those old times the thorn never reached through the flesh to the heart."

" Maybe they laid aside the thorn with the robe, as something which should not be worn at the heart," said the minister, mildly.

The conversation naturally turned to the day's sermon, which had excited two hearers at least to mental activity.

" I have observed in Homer, and the old writers," Arthur said, " a certain terror of the sea as an unlovable thing. The father of poets generally speaks of it as the ' hoary ' or the ' barren ' sea; his tenderest word in his Odyssey that I have found is the ' divine ' sea, which has also a shade of fear about it."

" You might trace the advance of the human mind towards Christianity and in it," said Mr. Leverick, " in just this gradual change of men's minds towards the sea, strange as it may seem. I have taken pains to study this very matter in the old writers, and have gathered several curious facts which I could hardly use in to-day's services, and which I should be glad to give you in a lay sermon. The old legend that the earliest voyagers saw at the farthest islands a menacing figure which said,

' Go no farther,' expresses well enough the relations of antiquity to the sea. They called the Atlantic 'the sea of darkness.' Even in later times, they built their houses away from it, and the mediæval ages hated it. It is only in later times, thanks to science and Christian faith, that men at sea have dared to look the tempest fairly in the face and conquer it. It is only in later times that men have come to see the Providence in harbors scattered so skilfully along its coasts, whereby is the life of great cities, like London, and have flashed out the benevolence of Christianity in a thousand watch-fires where danger is. The ancients had their Pharos, and the Etruscans kept the night-fire burning upon their sacred stones among the hills, but it was rather natural instinct than a fixed faith that did this. And men have gradually conquered the sea by a science built on faith in love. I remember our old professor surprised us by a dissertation that went to prove how the blue of the Virgin's robes in mediæval art was a subtle symbolism taken from the sea; that mediæval churches, like those of Freiburg, in the Black Forest, which had so many things from the land carved on them, and so few from the sea, were planned by men who had the mediæval hate of the sea; and how the curving lines of Greek temples were copies of the lines exposed everywhere in their sea-coast and in their islands; and how civilization shaped itself by the sea.

"I made an extract in the pages of my sermon

from an ancient prayer used in the consecration of
the communion in the early Church, both for its own
unrivalled sublimity and poetry, and because it expresses the substance of what was said to-day.   It
is this: ' For Thou art He who hast established the
heavens as an arch, and extended them like a curtain ; that hast founded the earth upon nothing by
Thy sole will ; that hast brought light out of Thy
treasures, and superadded darkness for a covering
to give rest to the creatures that move in the
world ; that hast set the sun in the heavens to govern the day, and the moon to govern the night, and
ordered the course of the stars to the praise of Thy
magnificent power ; that hast made the water for
drink, and the vital air both for breath and speech ;
that hast made the fire to be a comfort in darkness,
to supply our wants, and that we should be both
warmed and enlightened thereby ; that hast divided
the great sea from the earth, and made the one nav-
igable and the other passable on foot ; that hast
crowned the earth with plants and herbs of all
sorts, and adorned it with flowers, and enriched it
with seeds ; that hast established the deep, and set
a great barrier about it, walling the great heaps of
salt waters, and bounding them with gates of the
smallest sand ; that sometimes raisest the same to
the magnitude of mountains by Thy winds, and
sometimes layest it plain like a field, — now making
it rage with a storm, and then again quieting it
with a calm, that they which sail therein may find

a safe and gentle passage; that hast begirt the world that Thou didst make by Christ with rivers, and watered it with brooks, and filled it with springs of living water always flowing, and bound up the earth with mountains to give it a firm and unmovable situation.' "

" I have taken at least a woman's interest in the sea," said Agnes, " since you told me it often puts• a soft roselike color on the cheeks of those who live near it ; and that in the sea-coral, as in woman's lips, it is iron that gives the coloring. The sea makes me sad. I associate the dead with it. And yet I have rather studied its happier moods than those you speak of. Here is something I found the other day on the shore." And she brought from her portfolio a paper which she read. It was entitled, " WATER IN REST." " Down amongst seamed and fractured rocks, just on the edge of the channel, where the restless tides sweep in over the summits of sunken rocks in ceaseless eddy and whirl and clamor, is a modest pool of water in rest, — strife and peace beside each other. Around it is the passionate impatience and foray of the sea. Twice a day through the year great tides lift themselves up beside it in solemn procession, but its waters are not lifted by any advent of the sea. Here in this sheltered pool there is no tide, eddy, surge, break, current, or clamor. Only a bit of salt-spray sometimes flung into it across the sheltering rock. And for the rest, peace. And in this sea-side pool

sea-mosses of delicate emerald hues have set themselves, clinging to its rocky sides as if half in fear
and half in faith, and throwing out their tender
branches upon the friendly element around them, to
shadow with gentle drapery the passionless rock
beneath ; sea-mosses more delicate than any land
leaf or flower, asleep in life it seems upon the soft
waters that with a gentler than any mother's care
embraces these sea-children in gentle rest.   And in
this silent sea-forest, many inhabitants of this fairy
realm disport themselves and live out their stormless life, with what loves or dreams one cannot say,
— creatures of sunny lives, who escape the passions
and pangs of men, — silent citizens of a stormless
realm among the rocks.   For though this be not
the grandest, it is still a sea-palace, and its peace
and purity and beauty surpass all human habita-
tions."

Before they separated, the minister had prayers
with Mrs. Lawrence, and they sung this Vesper
Hymn : —

> Thy night, O Lord, o'er weary worlds goes trailing
> 　　Its curtained rest.
> At hearth and altar where are worn hearts praying,
> 　　Be Thou the guest:
> Sleep we, as child in mother's arms is sleeping,
> 　　Upon Thy breast.
>
> Thy stars, O Lord, o'er men serenely shining,
> 　　Pure vigils keep.
> So be Thy love, with glance serene, down looking
> 　　On us who sleep;
> Pour tearless slumbers from Thy hand o'erflowing
> 　　On eyes that weep.

Thy darkness, Lord, toil's wasting chain unloosing,
    Bids labor cease;
So from the yoke and burden of our sinning
    Our lives release.
In Night's great temple star-crowned mercy crowning,
    Grant us Thy peace.

Thy worlds, O Lord, refreshed of rest are sweeping
    Out of the night.
No night of sin or pain our lives beclouding,
    But in Thy sight.
Lead us from out this dim world's shame and sorrowing
    Into Thy light!

CHAPTER XVI.

FRENCHMAN'S HEAD.

It had been arranged that the minister should take Arthur and Agnes with him on an excursion to Frenchman's Head. The Head lay about an hour's walk from the village, and was only a hard, round sand-hill, pushed out a little further than its neighbors into the sea, where the latter had long ago formed itself into a sort of cove or harbor sheltered in measure from the rougher winds by the enclosing hill-ranges that lifted on their broad backs the more primitive of the Sandowne woods, — a quiet, secluded nook, where unfortunates had settled. It had its name from a colony of Acadians, who, weary and heart-broken in their banishment, halted here and for many years had given a name and a sad interest to the spot. They had brought with them, out of the shipwreck of their touching sorrow, their rural habits, their religion, and even their little tastes and ways : had with industry built up among the hills by the sea a thriving, peaceable community, governed by the most exemplary virtues : had won even the good-will of their Puritan neighbors by the singleness of their inoffensive conversation, though practising rites which the latter held idolatrous; had even intermarried with several town families, and, far away from the scenes of their childhood, had lived out their gentle lives on the shore of that sea which separated them from home, until, forgetting their hardships, they had fallen asleep in those peaceful slumbers where no king molests and no priest insults. After several generations their village had become deserted, and Frenchman's Head had only its simple graves and ruins for garniture.

Mr. Leverick had proposed a visit hither, and the two young people looked forward to what one might call a pleasant field-day, and such other pleasures as such young people find together. Mr. Leverick had from the start, and with the tacit assent of both, assumed the attitude of elder and teacher. The three had many things in common. The inner life in each was an aspiration towards the good, the beautiful, the true, or howsoever else you name those immutable elements of life that have God for their fountain; and yet the attitude of each towards life was different. With the two younger it was spring, — spring with its fire, its unrest, its struggle, — often so blind, so trusting, and yet not without a sense of aspirations unsatisfied; with Mr. Leverick it was verging towards autumn, in its calmness, and laden with fruits from that tree of the Past which has such choice fruitage for the wise wrestler beneath its branches; and the supremacy which he exercised over them was due to their unspoken appreciation of the fact that he was richer than they, and master. The great difference, after all, between people, is always this same attitude towards life, which, while men make it so different in the understanding or the misunderstanding of it, is the same essentially to all. To Arthur, the most wonderful pages of its Book were sealed, and his honesty made him an humble student ; and although Agnes had that wisdom of womanly intuition, given that woman's spiritual insight may make her in holy things mistress of strength, and which makes a woman's " because " often sign of a learning beyond all books, — she, too, still stood upon the threshold of that inner life which opens mainly towards the unseen, and is itself unseen of all but One. But Mr. Leverick had somehow seen, had known, had wrestled, and above all had suffered in plucking the fruit from that tree of knowledge, which to the highest' natures is forever the tree of Life. That the deep, gentle tones of his voice said, and his grave, placid smile, and above all, a certain influence, like a power, which unconsciously exercised itself on his young friends. Somehow he had found certainty and its peace, — which these last, as all young persons, wanted. It was a true life, lived through and out, become a lamp to guide the unworn feet in the great temple into which we all are led unto its one altar, from which the wisely devout pluck peace. So much is to be said of the deeper relations between our tourists to the Frenchman's Head.

The party halted, as they came out of the village, under a broad oak-tree that was throwing out its tender green leaves in the warm sunshine, as if it were still young, and as if it were not from heart to branch an oak. There were many dry branches, however, among the leaves, and its arms were twisted and knotty as if it had been a wrestler with the winds for a long time now. " This tree is a Sandowne antiquity," said the minister, "a boundary-tree in the old township bought from the Indian tribe here, who had their village nearer down to the beach. It has been spared as a relic of the old times, and is one of the points in the town survey. Look here a moment," he said. And he showed them, branded down deep into the tree, an arrow. " That is the king's mark. The king's surveyors marked every tree they wanted for the king's ships with this arrow, and the tree became sacred only to such uses ; so that the best trees often rotted with that mark on them, or were lost to the settlers. Loud complaints were made about this matter by the men who became restive under the king's rule, and this arrow is one of the few remaining relics of the age. At ' the Head,' and about here, we shall find vestiges of the old men who once lived there ; but after all, our grayest antiquities are these fields themselves. Land is older than pyramid, and more royal than any Pharaoh's tomb, and has more solemn legends to it. When I look at these spring fields, they seem to me like that Egyptian sphinx with a smiling girl's face to it, keeping in its profound silence its riddles and its wonders, older than anything but God. Mysteries everywhere are in the land. That Indian-corn yonder, which the farmers have just planted, where it came from, what its honors were at the hands of Peruvian Incas, and a thousand other questions about it, no one can answer. Across seas one meets everywhere with the monuments of dead men. But the country here seems like a tablet out of which time has eaten the inscription men made on it and left it blank. Here our antiquities seem but of yesterday. An Indian grave, or corn-mortar and pestle, or arrow-head, or heap of shells. Are these all? The land says nothing. Whatever was once upon it, whether city or temple, equal in time with Pharaoh, has fallen into it. The land hereabouts is dumb, but if it could speak, I have sometimes thought that on this silent continent, almost without a temple for us to point to, it might tell of wonders enacted here by nations who fell asleep and were crumbling into dust before the pyramids were built. And there is truly something awful in this silent land, without a sign or history. However, I will show you one of the few monuments we have," he said, " on that hill yonder. The habits of the country-folk themselves, brought from across seas, are, indeed, amongst the most ancient things, and they have everywhere a slow conservatism about them which preserves the old. The sharp-pointed tin lanterns, which most farmers use,

are of the Saxon times at least, and have a certain
air about them of the age when England was a
land of peasants, and all but lords laid their heads
at night on oak-logs for pillows."

They climbed together one of the round, bare
hills that lay open to the sun and sea. "Under
the red loam here," he said, "are Indian graves.
This was their church-yard, — an airy, open place,
where, maybe, they thought the Great Spirit would
find them readily. They chose open, sunny spots
among the hills. I have dug into some of these
graves, and found a few arrow-heads and a little
black dust occasionally, but their only monument is
the hill itself. This is a favorite spot with me to
sit in the spring days and look out on the sea yonder. Everything is so full of peace here; but the
peace beneath, of the dust, is greater. The writers
say that the most lasting monuments of a people
are their graves; and the merciful Mother keeps
indeed the sleepers graciously in peace, letting
none interfere with what is hers, as if to hint at
that greater care with which One keeps the imperishable lives of those who sleep, and as if the peace
which fills the lighted temple lingered even at its
portals.

"The old professor, of whom I spoke to you, was
an enthusiast about grave-lore as well as about the
sea. And he had some strange facts to tell every
class about graves and their occupants: how they
found Charlemagne, five hundred years after burial,

12

sitting bolt upright with the sceptre in his hand, as though he were still a king, instead of the spiced and perfumed dust and ashes that he was; how, when they bore Charles V. from the parish church at Yuste, where he had slept for eighty years, to repose at last in the Escurial, they found the face unaltered, with the same features he wore alive, and the thyme in his grave-shroud as fragrant as when laid there; how, in Siberia, they hollow out frozen graves with fire; and how, in Southern Italy, the earth has been planted with the dead three times at least, — Roman above Grecian, and beneath the last, under lava from a mountain whose fires went out before Moses's mother laid him upon the Nile, still the dead of a forgotten race; how, indeed, were it not for graves, Antiquity would have had but slight history for the moderns; always closing his dissertation by the story out of Plutarch, of how Solon proved the Athenian claim to Salamis against Megara, by opening the tombs and showing the men of Salamis turned the faces of their dead to the same side as the Athenians, but the Megarians to the other."

The path they followed took them in among the hills where had once been the land-locked hamlet and harbor of the Acadians. There was to-day utter silence in the hill-hollow where the village had been. The storm had long since choked up the harbor with sand, and the sea, breaking over the narrow beach, had now taken possession of the exiles' choicest fields, and the tide ebbed where their corn grew. All the pain and strife of that village had ended years ago, and the place was, as I have said, deserted.

" Opposite, on the hill yonder," said the minister, " where the grass seems the greenest, under the turf, are the foundation-walls of the Acadian church. I have been told it was — like the houses of those times — but a thatched board-house, whereon, to the horror of the neighborhood, they set a cross. The neighborhood in consequence named the spot Babylon Hill, in open allusion to her whom here was always called mother of idolatries; but the inoffensive lives of the Acadians saved them from any further molestation. On this cross they used to hang at night a lantern as signal to the villagers out on the fishing-grounds ; and here they came on their holydays to listen to those ancient litanies of their Church, so full of aspiration and tenderness, which have followed all exiles and all unfortunates with the benedictions of hope and promise. Even now the seamen about here think they sometimes see in dark nights the light on Frenchman's Head, and hear in the tempest the tolling of a bell borne over the waters sometimes as a solemn chant, until it has become a common saying among sailors, ' There was mass at the Frenchman's Head last night.' "

The party found in the hollow as they came to it hardly a trace of the Acadians. A solitary pear-

or apple-tree here and there kept guard with its mossy and shrivelled arms over a gray heap of stones where an Acadian's house had been ; but out of the clear brook that ran its brief course over the clean, many-colored pebbles, from a hill-spring to the creek where had once been the harbor, no child drew water, and among these hills no house-wife sang or wrought or waited. They followed the path by the stream, and Mr. Leverick led the way to the marsh. They came at last to what seemed sand-flats, which the tide had now left bare, except in the shallow pools, where the salt-water still stood, through which a sluggish stream crept seaward. " Here is the Acadian graveyard under the sea," said Mr. Leverick. " Why they did not bury their dead by their church is not clear, — perhaps because the hill summit was too scant for all ; but they buried them in what was a long meadow, until in the great storm some twenty years ago the sea broke through the beach and took possession hereabouts as you observe, and sends its waters over the graveyard of these wanderers as though even in death their fate was to be stormy and restless. I have been told that at that time the remains of a wharf which they had built, and also of a tide-mill wheel used for grinding their corn, were disclosed to view, where the sand had washed away. And you see the tide still ebbs and the sand drifts over these Acadians and their works. When I strolled over here the other day," said Mr. Leverick, " I chanced upon a relic which I will show you," and he led them across the flats to where the beach still held its place against the tides. " There it is." He pointed out a gray stone cut out into a cross. " That must have been a gravestone," he said. " There were once some initials on it, but they have been worn out, and the cross on some wanderer's grave has wandered away even from him."

" It is sad," said Agnes, " that even in death these poor people have such a disturbed resting-place as this under the sea ; as though the sea followed them even in their graves to rob them of that gentle sleep the red men on the hill yonder enjoy. A grave should have peaceful externals always, and that is what men always aim at, and to me the last sleep of these Acadians is truly pathetic."

What Agnes's thoughts were, are best set forth in some verses which were read by her at the next meeting of the friends. They are these : —

THE GRAVEYARD UNDER THE SEA.

Under the sea the sleepers now are dreaming,
In their shroud of the wasting sand;
Under that sea is never loss nor sorrowing,
Though they sleep on a foreign strand.
    Overhead the sea-weeds creep,
    Overhead the billows sweep,
    Winds in wrath mad revels keep.
Wanderers under the wandering waves,
Storm round their hearth-stones and storm round their graves,
    Deep down in the restless sea.

Across the trembling sands the wailing waves out-thunder
Weird battle-hymn and funeral dirge,

White-plumed battalions of the black waves wildly **wander**
With their foam and whirl and surge.
    Madly now the breakers roar,
    Knocking at the sleepers' door,
    Pale with rage the heralds hoar.
O'er grave-guarded exiles, as sheep on the lea,
Pours the unslumbering stream of the sea, —
    Asleep in the passionate sea.

Under the sea no flowers are fragrance flinging,
Through its shadowy halls of gloom,
Where waves with salt the barren sands are strowing,
Nor roses nor violets bloom.
    Wasting rock by wasting tide,
    Wasting sands where the horsemen ride,
    With angry foam of their stormy pride.
O'er the dead that waste on the wasting shore,
Breaks in dreary clamor and sullen roar,
    The pitiless strain of the sea.

Under that sea are never tired feet hurrying,
Life's wrestle and wage to win:
Under that sea are never sad hearts sorrowing,
The strain and the cross of their sin.
    Thick the air with hurtling snow,
    Wild and chill the night-winds blow,
    Swift the eager currents flow.
Passionless, careless, the exiles now sleep,
Hearts stilled to ashes, and eyes that ne'er weep,
    In the rest of the shroud of the sea.

Out of Life's sea God lifts in love His sorrowing
To a realm without sea or night;
In fragrant fields the asphodel is flowering,
In the soft sun's wooing light.
    There now no wild winds rave,
    There is never salt-sea wave,
    There no more the barren grave.
Henceforth the tired ones rest from the strife,
Henceforth no wasting nor passion of life,
    In the passionate foam of the sea!

" There is another relic of these Acadians which I will show you at the head of the brook yonder." As the tourists turned back again along the brook, they entered a short ravine between two hills, until they came to the little pool or spring of clear water, under the white-pines, that all day long cast their shadows into it, or sang to it with that sad *susurrus* or plaint which these trees always have. "There," said the teacher, pointing to a pile of rough, unhewn stones, tumbled upon one another, " are the vestiges of the Acadian water-wheel with which they managed to lift the water from here into their homes above on the hill-side. And this water-wheel always has seemed to me like a true saint, as it lifted up from among these hills, under the shadow of these pines, in its secret, unnoticed labors, the clear waters to the thirsty lips above."

They seated themselves on the floor of pine-leaves the place afforded, and Agnes furnished lunch. " A right royal dining-hall," she said, " under these trees, with the world shut out, and the blue of the sea yonder between the branches, and the rhythm of these pines and the brook below us, for orchestra." Arthur, who had brought the cross with him from the sands, laid it on the pine-leaves. ·

" Do not lay it there," she said, " on those dead things ; lay it rather on these fresh leaves of the arbutus, among the flowers. The cross should be trimmed with flowers — with nothing dead."

. " A very poor Puritan are you, Agnes," said

Mr. Leverick. " The deacons, good souls, if they heard you, would put you down as a full-fledged papist, ready for a nunnery, or a gunpowder-plot, or any other pleasant pastime in which they fancy any child of Rome is ready to indulge."

" Are you the best of Puritans ? " Agnes retorted, smiling. " If so, please your lordship, give us the old war-cry against images. ' No popery,' is a very winning cry hereabouts ; and we Protestants in the woods have been always famous for our charity. What would you say, now, if I, your daughter, were to wear a cross, as indeed I would if I were not afraid of a town uproar ? Would you think me a heathen, or worse than that, as folks judge, a Romanist ? "

" No," said Mr. Leverick, gravely. " I do not think that. I am of the order of the Puritan clergy, but I gave up long ago judging in that way. I do not join in the Puritan horror of one of the oldest of churches. It is time the old bitterness were laid aside, especially by us, who have suffered nothing from Rome. Our forefathers wrestled with a strong man in triple armor, — namely, the Church of Rome, — and conquered, after many wounds, the right of being let alone. Among the Saxon race that man has been shorn of power, and yet many are eager to strike against a skeleton which is but dust and ashes. As to the cross, as a sign, the men who speak of it should not object to seeing it, or even wearing it. Across seas

I have met it in many places: up among the
Alps; by the road-sides, on the Rhine plain; and
always with a sense of somehow being made better
by that simple sign. To-day is not time here; but
a to-morrow comes when the Church will receive
the cross, as Constantine did, as the sign under
which it conquers. For prejudice is temporal, but
the cross eternal. There is a certain mystery of the
cross, and I should not wonder if the Universe, as
many old churches are, were built upon it, and into
the shape of it. A very common, a very natural,
a very facile shape for men to pattern after or in-
vent in their architecture or mechanics, and long
ago men painted it or graved it in Egypt, and before Egypt, until its origin is lost in antiquity, as
many of the most wonderful religious ideas of the
heathen are. I have been interested in the story
which the early Church Fathers give of that Egyptian apple, in which, whatever way you cut it, appears always a cross. And I think that if we saw
clearly enough, we should find beneath all substance
a cross, as a sign of how the world lives and thrives.
Men, apt in signs, have found the cross in many natural attitudes of men and things. The world, they
say, is in its fashion, — east, west, north and south
being the arms thereof. No bird, they say, flies
through the air but the cross is there; no man lifts
his hands in prayer, as one may see in the cata-
combs, but makes it; no ship sails the sea but
writes it upon the waves; no husbandman ploughs

the land but inscribes it in the furrow; and men
have set it on temple, on mosque, on church, on
the king's throne of state, on the chairs of bishops
that ruled a priesthood more splendid than the Jew-
ish or the heathen; stamped it on letters that bore
tidings from friends at sea or ashore; on title-deeds
that transferred the wealth of kingdoms; bore it on
banners that conquered on a thousand battle-fields;
wrote it in baptismal water upon the foreheads of
little children; signed dying men with it; and introduced it in the affairs of a world as a symbol of
Him above and within the world, by whom the
world lives and moves."

CHAPTER XVII.

A KITCHEN.

The conversation which our company carried on had so interested them that they had not noticed how the shadows under the trees had been for some time deepening, until Agnes broke in upon the discussion abruptly, —

" The clouds are moving in from sea, I think ; and the storm-spray before the rain-clouds have been for some time passing overhead landward. It would be ill-faring to be caught just here in a tempest, though I do not happen to be of that order of women reported to us by the Saxon bards as made by magic out of flowers ; but nevertheless I trust to you, gentlemen, on your honor, to save me from a storm, after an invitation to a sunny ramble at ' the Head.' "

" It is time to be going, then," said both. And they moved homeward under a threatening sky, Arthur carrying the cross.

" Many sunny days end like this, my friends, before night often, let wayfarers make ever so much haste, and in ever so pleasant company," said Mr. Leverick. " And that is not the worst that could happen either. The worst would be to have always sunny days without storm. However, I am glad we have put so much between us and the storm on the sea yonder," he said, as they halted a moment on the last range of hills that lay between home and 'the Head.' "Look yonder a moment!"

And over the Acadian hamlet that once had been, and reaching along the headland, thrust into the sea, lay the thunder-cloud, seething and moving on, and throwing cloud, height above height, in an angry cloud-range, as if ready to hurl them swiftly upon the land beneath. The quick, forked gleam of the lightning pierced its lower blackness, and the cloud was shutting out "the Head" as they turned homeward again.

"The storm will reach Sandowne before us this time," said Mr. Leverick, "and we must find an inn somewhere. Under the oak with the arrow on it is dangerous; under Farmer Barlow's roof, in the farm-house yonder, is better. So now, Agnes, let us see whether you are made of flowers, or have a little of the nature of that lady fair, writ in the old books, who followed on foot her lover from France to Holy Land, to find him at last before the Holy Sepulchre, praying for her."

"For this time I am her kin," said Agnes, laughing, — "at least in running away from a cloud."

They passed under the antique oak of the morning, — which seemed to have grown older and darker, — now hurrying towards the farm-house.

" The oak has changed its mood since morning," said the minister, " or at least the weird, ghostly storm-shadow is at its heart, so that it greets us with a frown, though it greeted us as we passed it with a stately courtesy, befitting its years and honors as a royal oak, predestined to the king's navy long ago. The storm changes the most familiar places often, until we hardly know them. Moonlight does the same, and lends a sort of mystery and magic to the landscape. And in a heavy snowstorm, when the feathery snow lies upon the elms by the town-road yonder, as I have passed along, somehow the storm seems to have lifted the landscape into a dim, solemn cathedral, with arches of the tree-tops, and aisles reaching away right and left, — shadowy, mystic, ghostly ; while the snowflakes and the sullen sweep of the winds through the trees on the hill-sides, sound like a litany of muffled music, repeated by unseen choristers before an unseen altar, under the bending oaks in the woods where the storm is king. And the landscape changes every hour, being never twice alike, as all changes but God."

" There is Thor, breathing through his beard again," said Arthur, as the sharp blast that precedes the rain fell down upon the trees beside them ; " and yonder at ' the Head ' he is hurling his hammer at the giants, as though there were wage of fierce war to-day between them."

" Thor, as you say," added the minister, " is

busy and angry withal just now, and his breath has the tone of his rage in it. And as we must get the rain, I will also get one thing more out of it. The storm has a stormy sound of strife and passion in it, and all things in Nature give out a voice that mark their condition. The crack of a withered branch under your feet has a sharp, dry sound that denotes decay: the break of a green branch has a softer sound. The strongest wind amongst spring-leaves has something soft and gentle in it; the rustle of autumn-leaves has a weird and withered voice; and in mid-winter, the dash of the snow in storm, on the dead leaves, has something cruelly heartless and grave-like about it. And so everywhere Nature speaks her condition and her attempt. And in a moment the rain will be upon us."

And they had hardly found their inn in Farmer Barlow's kitchen before the fleet rain came, — first slanting, as innumerable spear-shafts hurled by an unseen warrior, and then drifting over the fields before the blast, falling and drifting in the wild confusion of the storm, and shutting out sky and land with its gray darkness, and over all the solemn burst of the thunder-roll and the break of the flash through the mist, — trumpet, cohort, gleam of fire in the angry battle.

Farmer Barlow's kitchen was the summer-quarters of the family, which, like many another in this realm, moved every spring from the front-door to the back, from some ill-defined impulse of emigration, like that which has sent the Saxon to sit by so many door-ways under every sky. It was an apartment well ventilated through the seams of its broad sides, with a huge fireplace at one end, and at the other a windlass-well, with its black-oak bucket, out of which the household drank, and between, the table set out now for supper; and on the sides the usual litter of household and farm equipments, managed into a certain decent primness which all good housewives strive for. The white-haired grandfather, and his wife, who sat in the chimney-corner opposite him, knitting, and the grandchildren, and the house-dog, with the hard-handed farm-help, and the farmer and his bustling helpmate, three generations at least together, composed a patriarchal picture such as one might often meet in a farmhouse of the old times.

The fugitives from " the Head " were greeted, as they came in, with a blunt though hearty welcome, and the family stood up in honor of the parson.

" Where did you come from," said the farmer, " in this rain ? "

" From ' the Head,' where we have been to see the village."

" It used to be haunted once, I 've heard, and we boys never went over there; but it 's a peaceable place enough now, I reckon; at least everything seems dead enough when I go there for sea-weed or with the cows. Make yourselves at home, neighbors; the rain is not long when it comes from ' the

Head,' and we shall maybe have clear sunset after this rain; that 's just the thing for the new corn."

" How does it look at ' the Head ' now ? " said the grandfather to the minister. " Everything but ' the Head ' has gone," was the reply. " I remember as a boy," the old man said, " going over to Wife Francis's, the last of the Frenchmen there, who would n't leave there when her daughter, who married in the town, wanted her; and she was always scrubbin' around there, looking after every pear-tree when there was nothing left but the roots; and I 've heerd used to say her prayers mornin' and evenin' on Babylon Hill, where the cross was; and when she died wanted to be buried with the rest where the sea is now, and to read something that nobody could understand out of a foreignish book that had a cross in it. And she worshipped the Pope, I understood, poor creetur."

" You are very old, then ? " said Agnes.

" Yes, Miss, past ninety, as I remember, though it don't seem so long, neither, only when I think how many has gone before me to the graveyard by the pond. My father was more than a hundred, too, when he went, tho' maybe I sha'n't last as long, and there 's many as has been older than me in this township."

" You remember the Revolution, then ? "

" Yes, Miss; I was a sojer then, and I remember it very well; only it seems strange, like a dream now. And Betsy over there remembers it, —old woman, don't you ? "

"What?" said the knitter, slowly looking up.

"Why, the Reverlution, to be sure; and when the man on horseback rode through Sandowne and said there 'd ben fiting at Bunker Hill; and when everybody turned out with their guns, and the parson, afore the meetin'-house, prayed over them as was going to jine our folk; and all the young gals was there; and you never looked at me, tho' I knowed you 'd ben crying, when you was n't Betsy Barlow, old woman."

"I remember it," said the knitter, beginning a new needle.

"But you don't remember as I do what we went through when we jined the army. 'T was bad enough gitting no money but continental bills, when it took a hat-full of 'em to buy a doughnut and a bit of beef; but then we was froze so at 'the Valley,' with no boots to keep our toes out of the snow, and no hats to our backs, until we made regimentals out of bed-quilts, and whatever we could rummage up in the camp; all the time expecting the Britishers, and not knowin' a word of how the folks were to home. And Sam Green, and a lot of other boys from this town, was carried out feet foremost, with a drum and fife playin' ' Good-by Boys,' and covered up like dogs in a field without a coffin. You don't remember that, old gal; and you did n't think none of me, — out of sight out of mind with all you women, — tho' I kept the mittens you knit for me, kinder sly, and did n't wear them only on guard, and when the General came round; and you 've forgot all that, p'raps. Nor you don't remember when Cornwallis was marched out, and all the Frenchmen looked so fine; and how we burnt up all our old clothes when peace was made, and lit bonfires, and hurrahed for 'Merica. Them was tough times; but they 're gone now, and the men that was in 'em, too, all except such old hulks as I, going round on a crutch, and good for not much but keepin' bread from mouldin'. Them were white-oak men in them days, and had white-oak heads; and there was only here and there a pewter-head, like Arnold, the rascal, and he was n't a pewter-head, only he 'd got the devil in his head. And the General, — God bless him! — he was a white-oaker all through, without a knot or a rotten speck about him; and how fine he looked on his horse ridin' down the lines, and how kind he spoke to us, as though we was his children, tellin' us to keep up courage, and all would come out right. It 's a long time since I seed him, and people 'll forget him, p'raps, folks have so much to think on; but his old boys 'll remember him as long as wood grows and water runs. God bless him! And it seems like a dream, how that I 've ben where men were falling, and all you could see was baggernuts through the smoke, and the Kurnel hollooing like mad, ' Give it to 'em, boys! ' and we walked rite over the dead and wounded, crawlin' about, as though they were only eels. You don't remember all that, old gal, do you ? "

" I remember," said the knitter, looking over her spectacles gravely, " when peace came, and you came home, and a great many other things I sha'n't tell you ; and after all you say, I think it was about as hard for the folks at home as for them who went off."

" Who was sick abed ater word came how I was shot at Long Island ? " said the grandfather.

" Your mother, likely," said the knitter.

" And who did I see singing in the choir, who turned as white as a sheet the Sunday we came home, and marched rite into the meetin'-house, afore folks expected us, and the parson stopped his sermon, and said, ' Let us pray,' and the parson prayed thankful like that we 'd so many come back ? "

" I don't recollect," said the knitter, soberly shifting her needles.

" P'raps I dreamed it," said the grandfather.

The rain was now over, and the visitors straightway took their leave. A clear, fresh evening on a clear, fresh earth, baptized out of the heavens, in a solemn perennial rite, through which is all Beauty ; and the low, soft sun, aslant the glittering fields, greeted the three as they came out-doors.

" Well, friends," said the minister, " in the kitchen we have found antiquity ; and yonder," pointing with his hand to the west, " is that which is forever old and forever new."

CHAPTER XVIII.

TROUT-FISHING.

> "Knowest thou what wove yon wood-bird's nest,
>   Of leaves, and feathers from her breast, —
>   Or how the fish outbuilt her shell,
>   Painting with morn each annual cell, — ·
>   Or how the sacred pine-tree adds
>   To her old leaves new myriads?"
>
> THE DIAL.

> "Who taught the raven in a drought to throw pebbles into a hollow tree, where she espied water, that the water might rise so as she might come to it? Who taught the bee to sail through such a vast sea of air, and to find the way from a field in flower, a great way off, to her hive? Who taught the ant to bite every grain of corn that she burieth in her hill, lest it should take root and grow?" — LORD BACON.

MR. LEVERICK had a passion for trout-fishing. In this he was not altogether singular, inasmuch as the first apostles had been fishermen. Without indorsing the opinion of the old writer that Judas, had he been a good fisherman, could not have been so bad an apostle, Mr. Leverick still held there was something canonical and edifying in trout-fishing. It was said that he had once preached a sermon on trout-fishing, very instructive to those who heard it, for the especial benefit of a very prim female parishioner, of that especial class among females, of no especial age, who elect themselves overseers of the clergy, who had taken him to task for what she was pleased to term " the worldliness of catching trout, poor things ; " the drift of the discourse being that trout-fishing was spiritual discipline and culture. All of which the aforesaid lady neither understood nor believed.

The Monday after the visit to Frenchman's Head, Mr. Leverick had set apart for a day's trout-fishing with Arthur Bassett. The sun only an hour old that day found them among the hills that led to the head of the trout-brook, where the minister, as he said, looked for rare sport about this season. " For trout," he added, " seem fickle creatures, often, and appear and disappear according to no laws known to fishermen. Where they go in winter, or in the summer droughts, is still a mooted question ; and the trout is a mystery to all, I dare say, but himself. Lucky if his whereabouts prove no mystery to us, to-day."

" Stop here a while," he said, as they both came, after a dash across fields, to the bare top of the hill that looked down upon the ravine where they were to fish. " The king of fishermen in these parts, Johnny Trout, who has caught fish and talked fish all his days, has a proverb, that luck and leisure catch most fish. And, as I have told you, I go about this county angling after several sorts of game. It is my picture-gallery, where I study paintings ; my museum, where I study history and art."

And they sat down to look over the marshes and the beach below them, to the blue sea beyond, and upon the spring fields bathed with the yellow sunlight, with the purple mist among the distant forest, and such universal peace and harmony in the landscape as enter into a sunny New-England day in spring.

"I do not wonder," the minister said, after they had watched for some time in silence the scene before them, "at the Greek mythology, or even the rougher and more Titanic creed of our Norse forefathers. I only marvel how men can live in the country and not have a religion of some sort. In great cities it is not so strange, perhaps. But this is the eternal temple, built about all other temples, and the spirit in it seems always to speak something to us. I am always filled with a sense of the nearness of some one in a landscape like this; and Nature was meant to be a voice, a presence to every open heart. I think that for a true soul, on every landscape is written the legend inscribed over the portal of the temple at Delphi, contained in the Greek word E'I, which some supplicants for oracles interpreted to mean ' Thou art,' and others to mean ' If.' And first here and everywhere when I look, I find ' Thou art,' and then straightway fall to questioning if things are so and so, as a Christian supplicant at a shrine older than Delphi. And it strikes me, as I read so-called mythologies, how the men who thought them out had been on the same errand with myself. They studied Nature as they found her, and she toned and colored their confessions. Their sunshine or their storm, shines through and lowers through the creed of every race; and rests on their hills of granite or of marble, as they were Norse or Greek. They were children, indeed, seeing things in the twilight, and they saw a little of that other world which lies about us, and which too much sunlight so often darkens. And they left off searching, with a belief that within the visible work dwelt the workman, who wore a crown and was the highest. And so men came to hold natural things to be altogether sacred, and the veil of some divinity. Thus the Etruscans divined from the motions of birds the will of the gods, and the legend of the Cranes of Ibycus has the same origin. The German women foretold from the murmur or the eddies of the river. With the same sentiment, the Swiss, in mediæval times, were urgent to bathe their war-banners in streams of running water; and the women of Cologne, on St. John's day, strove to wash away their sins in the Rhine."

"But come," he said, starting up, "to work!" and they went off down the hill to the ravine and the woods. "We bait hooks here," he said, kneeling down on the white honeysuckle, and searching for a worm in his basket. "Trout-fishing is a discipline, as you may find before you are through, and especially with me, as you have just found from my sermon on the hill. You put your wit against the trout's instincts, and as it is a matter of life and death with him, he must be wary who conquers. The trout is a right royal fish to do battle with, — cautious, alert, and sensitive to sight or sound, and whosoever gets him wins him by sheer forethought. No noise, then, — a steady hand and a patient mind, and I will show you a Sandowne trout-brook in the trees yonder. I have been here before, but this is my first time this year, and I have always some curiosity to see how the winter has left my old friend the trout-brook, after I have been a six months' absentee from it."

So they made their way through the dry weeds and brushwood in under the pines. Under the pines, among the hills, was a quaint place; such a place, indeed, as men who travel leisurely along well-conducted roads never see. Men who go over the hill would find it much to their profit to halt and see what lies under the hill. Nature delights in "under the hill." If you would see Nature in her happiest mood, go not to the well-hedged and planted fields, for there she is subject to the strong arm of Labor; but go, gun or rod in hand, down under the hills where the brooks hide themselves, and where Nature is out of sight, and there you shall find pleasant things. There she is, away from man; there she has the youngest, freest look, and revels in her liberty until she creates a wood-garden in the ravine hardly equalled by any civilized gardening known to me. Under the pines was a dome built of gray branches hung with the spear-headed pine-leaves, lifted by the stout mossy trunks that gained a livelihood under the dark ferns down below the swamp-hummocks in amongst the hidden springs flowing up out of the clear, clean pebbles under ground. Under them, for mirrors, scattered here and there, were the clear pools of spring-water, hemmed in with their dark-brown banks of curt moss and heather, wherein the trout hide themselves ; with no sound but the sighing of the pines, and no visitors except birds and sportsmen. Under the pines had a very ancient and very peaceful look.

As they made their way there through the swamp underbrush, Mr. Leverick motioned Arthur with his hand to one of these pools, while he crept silently to another, and they were at once at work. Trout-fishing is a calling full of meditations. You suffer your line to find its way down under the brook-banks waiting for its finny visitors, and think meanwhile of ten thousand things, maybe, in the great world, and all your judgments and thoughts come to have a little of the peace around you. You bring the world with you, and the world is made sweeter for you by the pure air that lies around the still waters of the pool. A sharp, quick dash of Arthur's line under the bank. He pulled nervously. That was a good bite. The first trout, perhaps, to-day. No ; a miss. The trout is off ; and Arthur's hook is tangled in a dead branch under water, and holds fast. Patience! Let no man who has not patience go out for trout. Haste spoils all. A perturbed mind makes the hand unsteady ; over-eagerness defeats itself, and you catch only provoking branches with strong affinities for trout-lines, and no fish. Arthur had been too hot-headed, and had only to clear his line. Did you ever undertake, reader, to clear your line in the face of a fine trout, which you knew was quietly fanning the water with his fins just under the bank, and waiting to see what next might come down to him from over the edge? It is a grim necessity that loses you the game.

Arthur laid himself down and looked over the bank after his line, and a fine trout that moment shot in under the opposite bank and left behind him only a little puff of black mud at the bottom. Arthur looked where he had gone, and then around. What fairy palaces there are under the clear spring-waters. Water tones down all, softens all, and lends a certain enchantment to all, and besides a certain mystery, with just a tinge of awe to it for those who look. A dry brook is commonplace enough. — but common-looking sands and pebbles, and the banks common earth, — and you can walk in it, and search it through and through ; but when the water flows through it, at once a certain soft, mystic character is imparted to everything, and it is yours no longer. It belongs to the nymphs and dryads of the fountain.

Arthur found a softly marvellous realm below the waters. On its soft floor were scattered leaves and dead branches, covered now with sombre-colored mosses, and its sides were clothed in gray, and it reached in far away under the pine-roots, and back underground to its neighbors in avenues where the trout hide, and the green pines reflected their branches, and the sky through the trees its blue or cloud in its gentle realm ; and it took starlight or sunlight, or shade or cloud, through a twelvemonth, without choice, lending to all its own liquid softness and peace.

Arthur's reverie, as he lay looking into the pool, was interrupted by a slight sound in the direction of the minister. It was only that person's trout-pole striking against the branches in an attempt he was making to draw in a fine trout he had just hooked. He drew him in at last safely, and having stowed him away in his trout-basket, proceeded with that absorbed air of a man wholly given up to his work, — which marks the true fisherman, — to angle again in his pool. Arthur watched him until he had caught several, and had been waiting for some time now, without any further sign of trout, when he drew in his line and came over to him.

" No fish ? " he said, as he looked into Arthur's basket. " Patience, my friend. If you are determined to catch trout, trout you will catch. I have sometimes thought that when, after bad luck for

hours, I have determined upon catching fish, somehow I have begun very soon to succeed. And I
have observed that those who persevere against
hope almost, come out well at last. Perseverance
is the first law of trout-fishing. And so trout-fishing, as I have said, is discipline. However, if you
catch none, you can learn resignation, which is another virtue ; for it is the most useless undertaking
to fret where you have failed, and no true fisherman
ever does that. And if one comes with great expectations to a trout-brook, and there are no fish for
him, he learns the vanity of earthly hopes sometimes. And so one is taught several things in trout-
fishing, whether he gains or fails."

" Very well," was the answer, " I shall catch
trout."

" The next fishing-grounds lie some distance below here," the minister added, " and, as you know,
trout have their favorite resorts, and dislike apparently some parts of every stream, for one finds none
in such spots. From here to there the stream takes
a stroll underground in several directions, and breaks
out among the hummocks in small pools that have
the gray gleam of steel on them as I pass by them.
I fancy that here in the old time the beaver resorted
and burrowed and sported, and these may have been
their breathing-holes. Lower down I have seen in
the meadows holes fifteen feet deep, which these
creatures made, filled now with the purest water.
They have gone now, as completely as the elephants

have gone from Siberia, and left only this memorial, in one of which I came near losing my life once when I was out fishing. So now for a dash through the swamp."

Whoever has had a tramp through a genuine New England swamp needs no description of it. They who have not, cannot comprehend it. The swamp is amongst the most primitive of institutions.

" Hold on ! " the minister shouted, as they were both silently breaking their way through the dry reeds and grasses, and over the tangled, bushy hillocks. " The first blackbird's nest this season ! " as he pointed to a bird's-nest built in a sapling. " I always look at bird's eggs. I learned that when a boy. A red-winged blackbird," he said, as he lifted out a little gray spotted egg, " as I see also from the shape and work of the nest. There is as much difference between bird-builders as between men-builders; some are neat and show taste, and some are slovens and have no taste; and they all have their own mechanics, and their liking for certain building-material when these can be had. For instance, there is a striking contrast between a robin's nest and this, — with the difference in favor of this red-wing, who builds out of the cleanest stuff, and is a neat bird in her household economy. There is hardly more difference between men than there is between birds," he said. " I have observed, also, with some care, the reasons which lead these creatures to select their building-places, and I have always found them to have been wisely chosen, either for protection against the elements or the reptiles. This nest is set on this small sapling, as you see, so that no snake could wind around it and reach the young; and I hence conclude that the bird has a wise instinct or reason, or whatever it may be called, which often surprises me. I have no doubt many have wondered at the story of the swallows, read out of sunny-hearted old White of Selborne, how, when the nest of young had fallen down by accident, and a lady had set it in an open work-basket, and the cold wind came through to trouble them, the parents built up a wall against the wicker-work to keep off the wind; or at the still more surprising story of the English fly-catchers, who, having accidentally built their nest in an exposed place, where the glare from a white wall would inevitably have destroyed the young, hovered over the nest by turns during the hot hours of the day, and by the shadow of their wings, protected their offspring. And I fancy that birds and birds'-nests have a deep philosophy about them. If you choose to doubt that, you have only to read in the Transactions of a very learned society across seas what is said about the musical variations of the cuckoo's voice in a single season. However, as this swamp hummock is not the easiest of professors' chairs, I will leave philosophy and birds to rest a while : though I confess to have a liking for this blackbird of the swamp, whom men have made an outlaw, and put a bounty on his head, and in the old times compelled the settlers to furnish a fixed quota of these dead birds, to protect their harvests, until the bounty-man was besieged by all the urchins of the town with heads, and though he is always a rogue and gives the farmer much trouble. But he is still an outspoken, hardy, vigilant bird, and ready to grumble at any disturbance you make him in swamp or field, as though persecution had spoilt his temper; and I pity this Ishmael in black."

They came at last out of the swamp into a meadow.

" This is Goodman Barlow's meadow," Mr. Leverick said, " and he can't imagine how any man can spend his life and trample down his grass, trout-fishing. He likes salt codfish better for the eating, and as for pleasure, he finds more in laying a stone-wall or breaking a yoke of steers, and will look upon us, if he sees us, as two poor simpletons trampling down his grass. He, poor soul, like many another, lives always under a cloud that makes a narrow day, and sneers at another's sky as though he saw it. There is something fragmentary in a man who despises trout-fishing, you may be sure. There was a monastic order in mediæval Italy called the Brothers of Ignorance, the members whereof religiously swore not to know anything at all, and whosoever looks down upon the noble ordinance of trout-fishing is set down in my books as of that order."

They fished through the meadow, and Arthur had rare luck. And as the moss carpet beneath his feet was soft, and the meadow gentle, and the sky blue, and a wise friend near, he gave himself with increased relish to the sport.

" You have had a new phase of trouting in this meadow, Arthur, if I mistake not," the minister said, as, after fishing for some time in silence, they came where the brook-banks had been beaten down at a cart-crossing, and the stream broadened over its pebbly bed, to hide again in the thicket below. "A trout-brook is always changing its aspects and putting new problems to the angler's skill. I have always found this a meadow of limitations that contained a new lesson in ethics, and I have to work in the world, as indeed most men do, as I fish in this meadow. We have fished along carefully, and yet I fancy the best fish lie under the banks there still. The brook is so trammelled with the dead rushes of last year in its bed, and the bushes have so overgrown it here and there, that although one sets out to clear the brook of fish, after the best, most escape. And when one angles among men, to win somewhat to himself, or to help on truth, the dead weeds and rushes of bygone years so thwart him that he recovers from them only a tithe of what he hoped, until he learns to be content to bring home only a meagre basket after all his angling. And I fancy that the men who chafe under their luck, and try to force fortune, and despise the tangle that interferes with them, catch fewest fish, and a bad temper in the bargain. Life is a trout-brook, where we catch only a few fish, and have to be content to leave the rest behind. Yet so the men who come after us find their sport, or work, as you choose to call it, ready at hand.

"However, as a good trout-fisher is always ready to talk and to rest at the right time, and as the sun is well up, sit down here awhile, and take breath. This is one of the places where I always get a good look at the brook to study it. The wise angler never makes his sport work, and out-tires himself, but rather takes his pastime and holiday, as he should, leisurely." ·

"Well, leisurely then I take it," said Arthur, smiling; "and I suppose a good trout-fisher helps himself to the best leisurely, so here goes for a drink of this cool water, as it flows out from the banks here, cooler for its underground habits. And as I drink, I get a sight of the brook-bed you speak of, with all its shadows, from the whirl and eddies above, and all that moves in its crystal clearness, all floating down stream, — stick, dust, leaf, stone, or fish. Truly, this reminds me of the old microcosm, so vaunted by the alchemists."

"True," said the minister. "And mark how full of grace and ease this running water is in every motion, — nothing awkward, harsh, or angular, but all is circle, rounded, graceful. The motion of the brook, indeed, is music written in water. You remind me," he said to Arthur, who meanwhile had been scooping up water in his hand, " of Gideon's choice, — of whose men some fell down on their knees to drink in the march, and the rest scooped up the water with their hands, as you are doing. And he chose these last ; about which Lord Bacon says that Gideon was an able captain in doing this, since those who had no need of kneeling showed that they had more endurance than the others, who went on their knees to drink.   However that may be, rest yourself awhile on the bank here for a fresh start.   You would like, no doubt, to fish straight down through the woods, as I should, and as many a man in this life likes to go straight on to his mark ; but below there the brook runs through an impassable swamp at this season, overflowed with water, and we must have a tramp round it and strike the brook below.   And yet I should like to show you the brook as it keeps its own channel under the water, and beside, some of the finest trout keep there ; but the best things are the most diffi-cult, and I cannot show you my garden under the water to-day.   I brought a skiff up here last year, and had a sail over it, breaking my way at the start through the bushes and fishing down, and caught some nice trout ; but the brook-bed itself was best of all.   I think no words could describe it.   It was floored by what seemed wood-heather, only shorter and of an emerald color, deep almost to black, and the most delicate water-plants of a lighter shade creeping over it, so fragile, and all so exquisitely toned and shaded as no weaver could weave his carpet, surpassing even in its harmony of colors any wood-bank of mosses under the trees where is always a harmony of tints no painter can even imitate; and further on were the long, slender water-mosses, so exquisitely arranged, and yet a clotted mass when touched ever so gently, bent into shapes as graceful as a water-eddy, and of more brilliant shades and brighter colors, with all the hues of a sunset laid there, from which, as it were, the water had taken out the sunset passion and fervor; so that as the skiff glided along it was a perpetual surprise in colors, as if I were sailing over fairy-land which a breath might destroy. And I found there a certain subtle and soft beauty I have seen nowhere else, so that the voyage seems a beautiful dream when it is ended. And yet it is hid in a swamp, and costs bringing a skiff up here when one would see it. I confess to wonder sometimes at God's prodigality in beauty, — setting this fairy-land here where few can see it, as he sets sunset upon the sea where no ship cleaves it, or the most delicate Alpine flower on precipices where no hand can reach it. And I cannot show you fairy-land to-day.

" But come," he said, — " this catches no trout. New for a dash through the woods yonder, and to the trout waiting for us below."

And they went in under the pines again, with their white, dead branches below, and their green heads above, on through the solemn twilight of their shade, over the mossy, crumbling trunks of old trees, wind-mown scores of years ago, — on through the tangled brushwood beyond, pines and bushes in that disorderly order that marks our woods.

"I do not thank the Puritans or somebody else for this," said Mr. Leverick, as he halted for a moment on a hill-side, from breaking his way through a scraggy, thick growth of young wood. "Men neither improve nor adorn Nature with the axe anywhere. Good Parson Hooker, with his caravan, could march hundreds of miles, with their cattle, from the Bay to the Connecticut, without let or hindrance from the primitive forest, and here we are out of breath from these scrub-oaks that have grown up since somebody's axe levelled the old trees and let in the sun here for all this trash to grow. Under the pines there is pleasant going, but you see what this is. Nature, left to herself, kills all this out and leaves only the forest where one may walk without breaking his neck, and she makes a smooth floor and open glades for the wild grasses, and delights in great trees ; but when the woodman's axe is put to work, the next growth are pigmies jumbled together, and the majesty of the forest fails forthwith, and we have only brushwood. Our woods have degenerated beneath civilization, so called, as they always do."

And so they went on in their laborious holiday, chatting and fishing in that free way which belongs to the woods, fishing along the winding brook, in the fresh wood-air that gives such health and appetite, passing by the solitary houses in the fields, until it was high noon in Sandowne. Who analyzes a trout-fisher's satisfaction on a lucky spring-day, when all goes well with the sport? All is peace around him, and peace is at his heart.

They climbed at last out of the ravine along a hill-side, to lie down on the greensward under a wild apple-tree, and to eat dinner, with water from the brook, and the rest out of the fish-baskets. Sweet pastime for hungry fishermen is dinner on the May greensward under the trees. How pure the sunshine, the violets, the white-clover, and the apple-blossoms on the branches overhead! Then the old world seems a child again, to whom the Magi have borne fragrant spices and frankincense, and the Greatest has given the greatest peace.

" We dine here," said the minister. " Dinner in the fields is what no true trout-fisher neglects."

And they proved themselves of that order, by the appetites with which they disposed of the eggs and buttered bread which the housekeeper at the Parsonage had provided.

" This is always my inn when I come this way," said Mr. Leverick, " and it gives me such a dining-hall as no king has, except he lay aside his crown for a trout-pole sometimes; and I mean to lodge here for an hour or so for a royal after-dinner reverie; for in such a place as this I·feel as years ago I felt under quite other skies, that it is sufficient happiness to be allowed simply to live and to breathe in the air, and to be among the living things of the spring around me, as one of them, without passion and without effort of any sort."

And he laid himself down on the sward, looking up through the fresh green leaves of the tree at the sky beyond. Arthur did not disturb his reverie, but yielded himself to the silence in the *far niente* spirit of the place that allows thought to loiter beside all waters that be tranquil, and dreamed — shall it be said? — of Agnes Lawrence. What dream was it? Was it a pleasant dream? Do you who have dreamed in a spring-day such dreams, when it was spring in your heart, answer? Have you forgot your dream? If so, the winter that has followed your forgetting must be very deep. Nay, in true hearts memory runs back always to the spring to make the whole year not altogether night.

Arthur's reverie was broken in upon by the minister.

"I have been wondering whether ours are the only eyes that see this landscape, and maybe we see only a little of it; and how prodigal of blessings our Father is to provide this only for the few creatures able to consider it. For of most men, I fear the Egyptian tradition is true, that though every man has two pairs of eyes, the one given to look up with and the other down, most men have the eyes turned towards heaven shut, and look only down. And yet the fault cannot lie with Him who gave the eyes, but with those who use them. There are no such inequalities in possible happiness as men imagine. Men go grumbling that their work is heavy and their lot menial ; but it is themselves who elect their own destiny, whether they will be kings or serfs. The Great King would make all kings. This spring-day is over every farm and home in my parish, and if those who live in them would only take it and use it, they would be the truly rich and happy. A spring-day like this lies round every home, with histories, with splendors, and with riches ; and Isaac will drive his oxen, and Prudence will set the house in order, and lose it all, and then maybe complain in their innermost lives that they are not kings or queens, or at least the very grand folk they read of, instead of the very unromantic hirelings they make themselves, while a regality greater than Cæsar's stands just by every farm-door waiting to be put on. This apple-tree here, with its white blossoms, (and many another stands round these homes,) true Madonna of the fields, of purer robes than ever Raphael painted, what a blessing it is, — what a history it has ! Let these men ask where it came from, and how it came, and a thousand other questions, and the answers which they might get would lead them into a most wonderful land of the Heretofore ; asking with what merriments the Romans held the feast of their goddess Flora under its branches, or even

how that black life of the Emperor Domitian con-
nects itself even with this tree ; and there is hardly
another tree in our fields that is not equally rich in
lore.   Or, after all the talk of the parsons in this
parish for two hundred years now, one could get a
better idea of God's Infinity, say, by lying down on
the sward by their door-stones and looking five
minutes at the grass, than from all the sermons
preached.   I have tried it, and you may try it until
your head aches.   Try to count on any square foot
of this sward by you the blades of grass ; mark
how each is of different shape, and the cluster of
dead turf beneath, and then the grains of sand under, and how each has many colors and angles to it,
and then compute how many grains, with how
many shapes, are under them, and then how many
the shadows of these grasses are, and how these
shadows are never the same in any two moments,
or any two years, in the eternity which is around
us all ; and then multiply these by the acres and
fields of the earth's surface, and by the miles below
the surface, and I tell you your head will ache before you are through computing this shadow of the
Infinite fallen on a square foot of the sward.   And
I say that, while such things are under every man's
feet, if he find the world commonplace, or anything but the veil before the Divinity, it is his own
fault.''

Many other things, not to be repeated here, were
said of the same sort by the minister as they lay

there upon the sward. And so they spent pleasant moments under the white branches of the Madonna's tree, as Mr. Leverick called it, talking about many things, but especially of the signs of the Divinity, seen everywhere in a New-England landscape, as indeed in all landscapes, until the shadows of the pines in the ravine were creeping up the hill-side, black banners of the sun, flung silently upon the sward as he verges towards setting.

" Our day's trout-fishing is wellnigh over," said Arthur; " thanks to this enticing spot and the thoughts you have got from it."

" Well, then," was the answer, " bring out the trout. Let us count the game, as all true fishermen do. Lay out the fish on the greensward here, and let 's have a look at them. You fish for yourself now, I fancy, though a true trout-fisher, when he can, carries his trout home to his wife's inspection, with a pleasant story of the day's sport : that is the truest sport, when the true housewife at home shares it with you in the farm-kitchen, as the fish lie in cool spring-water in the pantry. But to-day we must tell over our fish by ourselves."

So they laid the speckled trout on the sward, and the minister scattered some violets and the purple swamp-pinks over them, and the wet mosses he had gathered from the ravine.

" Now there is a picture and a history for you," he said. " See the contrast of the white and the blue and red in it, and what artist paints such spots of gold and crimson with any brush ?   The trout is a true gentleman in all his habits, — so neat, so apt, so ready, so well-habited in his graceful robes, and he should have a fit shrouding of these flowers. He is the flower of the brooks, and their clearness and grace somehow cling to him.   I have noticed that the trout takes his hue from the part of the brook he frequents, — lying on the dark mud gives a dark color, and on the pebbles their lighter yellow color.   And men are like that ; and our New-England folk have taken into their lives somewhat of the granite of their hills, as the flowers do, and there is a certain austerity and granite purity in all.   The finest flavored trout are found in the purest waters, and where the stream runs swiftest, and gain a certain delicacy of fibre from their struggle with the stream.   The trout in tanks, like those near Heidelberg, are fat, gross, unpalatable fish ; and I have thrown a trout-line into the Reuss, on the St. Gothard Pass, which has hardly a foot of water not broken into spray or foam, and there are the finest trout in Europe.   And the flavor of the best lives comes from the spray and foam in them, and the wrestle with them.   And so with these flowers here.   In gardens the flowers are fat and heavy, though brilliant often ; but in the woods, where there is more struggle, there is more delicacy, until high up on the mountains, and especially on the higher Alps, both flowers and grasses have a delicate, spiritual look. And the little white flowers, the Alpine crocuses, maybe, that lie in the early spring among the snow-water of the passes, and wrestle there alone with storm and avalanche, have seemed to me like true saints or vestals watching there with the stars their brief hour of victory. And our New-England wild flowers, and especially the arbutus and the violet, seem to have in them the purity of our winter snows, and the saintliness that follows a successful and patient struggle for mastery over their foes. And everywhere in this realm, in men and flowers, are traces of granite and snow," he said, smiling.

So they went homeward.

"I have one specialty," said Arthur, as they reached the road which led to the village, "that your talk tempts me to bring out, and which I owe to a quaint question which my nurse once put to me: 'Why a hen went across the road?' and her answer, 'Because she could n't go round it,' which was a conclusive reason even to a child. And I have found a mystery in a road. Where does the road running by my house lead to if followed? To the Rocky Mountains, maybe, and ten thousand villages. What feet walk that road? Ten thousand feet on ten thousand errands, — trivial, weighty, on errands of shame or fame, of life and death, — and yet the road questions none and takes taint or harm from none, but gives free pass to all. And who owns the road that runs by lands preoccupied for generations?   None.   It is a stony democracy that grants no favors and allows no rank, and it is very old.   And who invented roads, and how?   There is also a mystery equal to most that you and I have found in a trout-brook to-day."

"True," said the minister; "I have just now two thoughts about New-England roads.   In the old time all our roads were found closed every now and then with gates that have now disappeared.   In still older days, at the gates of Rome, from whence started roads which traversed that broad empire, stood stone statues of the gods, worn with the kisses imprinted on them by the pilgrims who went forth in travel.   And whosoever starts upon a road should first salute the gods that everywhere upon the roads he may meet the gods."

Arthur left Mr. Leverick at the Parsonage.   As the minister went in through the door, a little head was beside the trout-basket, and a little hand was in it after the trout.   It was Fritz's welcome home.   But Fritz, truth to say, was to-day under a cloud.   The housekeeper did anything but smile upon him.   He had been caught trout-fishing in the water-pail.

CHAPTER XIX.

CHILDHOOD.

"Little children are nearest God, as the smallest planets are nearest the sun." — *J. F. P.* RICHTER.

"I would create a world especially for myself, and suspend it under the mildest sun: a little world, where I would have nothing but little, lovely children; and these little things I would never suffer to grow up, but only to play eternally. If a seraph were weary of heaven, or his golden pinions drooped, I would send him to dwell a month upon my happy infant world; and no angel, as long as he saw their innocence, could lose his own." — THE SAME.

PURE, gentle, faithful, sunny dream of childhood! We all dream it once, and it floats down the years, leaving behind an aroma which a soul seems to have caught from its one brief hour among the flowers that bloom upon the hills of God, and its echo is like forgotten music to the ears dulled with the wage and wrestle of our stormy after-life. Once every one of us stands by the golden gates, and through them flow in upon us water from the river as clear as crystal, and music from the unseen choir before the throne. Once only here, are hands clean and eyes clear, and our souls lie at peace with all, yearning to find in all One who is to souls the All. And once hereafter, when we stand beside those gates again, having cast off the earthly, and ready to enter in where there is beauty and life forever, it is as little children, with the old dream made plain. The cycle of life ends in a childhood that is eternal.

I should in nowise wonder but that the mystery which was named Fritz Maud was even greater than that of any meadow or hamlet in Sandowne. And yet Fritz was only a child like the rest of the elves and fairies who slept and dreamed in Sandowne, and were passed by of the great world as only children, as you will pass maybe the little ones in the street to-morrow, — only that Fritz happened to be an orphan at the Parsonage, and dreamed on its comfortable sofa in the parson's library. And the children of the abject poor dream also in their rags. Neither could one say just what was going on in the soul that looked out from the hazel eye in any hour of Fritz's child's work-day. You have read of " their angels who do always stand before the face of my Father who is in heaven," but do you know what angels work at a child's heart? You think that fancy, maybe. That which is truest is never proved, but felt. You think this little boy had no angel. I said he was an orphan.

Fritz had a passion for out-doors. When he was tired of books, or his great friend at the desk was busy, he would solace himself in the warm sunshine, lying on the grass with his face turned towards the sky, and as if asleep. Sometimes he would wander with uncertain, loitering steps towards the mill-pond, and watch at a safe distance its black waters amongst the rushes. Watching what? I do not know, neither did he, but watching somewhat, I plainly affirm. Most of all, he seemed to fancy the brook that ran down over the green hill-side in mimic foam and spray upon the brown stones, into the pond, — sitting near it in its noise and babble, listening. Listening to what? What does a child hear in a brook running over the brown stones, or in the sea, or in the storm? I cannot give it a name. Something that speaks in his little heart a name he will learn to know, not here, but after here. And then maybe he would come back again under the trees on the lawn, with some roadside flower, or a dry stick, in his hand, and inspect curiously the tree-bark, or have a look up into the branches, and then round about everywhere at everything in his field of travel, with a child-gravity, in a sort of aimless study, back with his sticks and flowers to the study. All for what? For nothing you can touch or taste. One might speak in riddles, saying that every little child is a Greek and a wandering Ulysses in search of home. In plainness, your little child strolling about with aimless feet to handle everything, is sent, — I say sent, so early, to begin his life-long lesson ; to find out beneath all shows a spirit which sometime he may learn to call Father. Can you say how blue the sky is to your little boy, or how fair the flowers are ? Bluer and fairer than to the man perhaps; for in them he feels at his heart a prophecy of skies that never cloud, and of flowers that never wither. You call that fancy, maybe. If so, then tell us, who were once children, what childhood means.

There were in Fritz's consciousness, if one could only have seen it, two lives that somehow united themselves in the outward signs which Fritz made of himself as the child who slept on Mr. Leverick's sofa. The life that looked out from the hazel eyes and went into the great gentleness of the child, which had ever a certain sadness in it, and which lay furtherest down in Fritz's nature, it would be very hard to analyze, much less explain. Indeed, it is true that there the child found a certain passive pain and sadness, never spoken, and only showing itself in a grave gentleness, as most sensitive children are grave and gentle. He seemed often listening for something, or at least trying to recall something, as he lay quietly looking out from under the long eyelashes, half-shut, with that dreamy, quiet look of his, very intent on something that cost him hardly an outward motion or expression of any sort. And at such times the minister would carefully abstain from disturbing him as he saw the little face so grave and thoughtful, and asked him no questions, but only looked over his way every now and then from his books to see when the dream had ended. And then oftenest a little child came to climb into the great man's lap and lay a little head upon his breast, nestling there closely, as if he wanted sympathy or protection from the silent man who kissed the forehead under the golden hair. What was his dream? He could not have told you then or any time this side the Hereafter. It was a dream half-dreamed,—a life fed only on faint memories, as it were; or shall we call them intuitions, wherein a child turns back towards the unseen Heretofore that somehow is always moving him with its subtle sympathies? Was it that upon the side of his soul turned skyward fell the shadows of celestial things within the gates, which moved his soul into desire and longing for the things themselves? Was it that a half-heard voice floated out therefrom,—a low, sweet voice with a mother's tenderness in it,—that called for him in the inner temple which no eye saw, to come to her? Or was it that an invisible Presence stood near him always, and, with invisible, spiritual sympathies so moved the boy unconsciously that he dreamed with the half-shut hazel eyes? I cannot tell. Can you, wise man, say just how the immortals touch mortality, whether it be in child or man?

The other life which Fritz lived was an outer life, which went into the more common tasks of childhood. It had its trials like most, its judgments and prejudices like most, among which was one against the housekeeper, a busy, bustling, loud-voiced woman whom Fritz avoided, mostly answering in his quiet way, in monosyllables, and under her rebukes, which were not wanting, looking out upon her with the hazel eyes in a most perfect silence. He shrunk away from many; a few he came to, as if he had for a long time known them. It was not his will that decided thus, but the sensitive, open nature of the child beneath. The man from whom a child shrinks away with inward disrelish, has lost, for the time at least, the best part in him, — the child. And yet Fritz had no general fancy for other children, — only for the more gentle of them, — and he stood by, oftenest watching with grave face the more noisy sports of the rompers upon the parsonage lawn, and acting sometimes as host, in aid of the great friend who was at play among the children. And yet Fritz was not without a certain fire, — as the housekeeper found when she somehow had violated Fritz's personality, — but it soon went out again in the old gentleness, and showed itself more in the flashes of the hazel eyes than in any words. You say this child was only diseased or sick. Not a strong child, perhaps, nor one whom you could fairly call diseased; only a child that God sends to men oftener than they imagine, with a soul of that ethereal fire which climbs out of the flesh sometimes to the kindred flame that holds all, or oftenest, when neglected, goes out in ashes.

Between Fritz and the minister there existed the most subtle and tender friendship, until at last they became indispensable to each other's happiness, and the one complemented himself with the other, so that a day became fragmentary to both when either was absent.   A true but strange friendship of equality between the grown man and the child, as the truest friendship is always in equality.   And the child gave the minister somewhat that he needed, and received back somewhat which he laid up among the treasures of his child-life that made him rich.   Fritz would have always gone with his friend when he went out-doors.   He silently made ready with his hat at the gateway, when there were signs of a parochial visit in the library, and went back very slowly, with a grave resignation, when his great friend said, " Not to-day, Fritz."   There was something in the grave look of the hazel eyes that made the minister careful of saying " no " to Fritz, so that very often the child trotted along by his side into the village, with a certain restrained aspect of perfect satisfaction at his good luck in being allowed a visit with his friend.

There were not so many words as one might imagine between the friends.   Love showed itself in the acts, the motions, the silence of each, rather than in any words, and above all in the gentleness of each, while the child lay in the minister's arms and the minister held him there, often without a word.   This was the favorite refuge of Fritz, when work was over at the study-table, just before candle-light, and when they two sat together in the twilight, each with his own thoughts, and there was silence in the study.   Sometimes there was a question, even then, from the little head that lay still on the minister's heart, — oftenest a theological question, for Fritz had long ago a confused theological consciousness, into which had fallen, with no great order, some things from the Sunday's sermon, when Fritz listened in his seat in the pulpit to his great friend's discourse to his congregation, — and other things entered there from other teachers, to him without a name. And Fritz had strange questions to ask, not easy to answer, — as a child's thoughts any day outrun our swiftest philosophies, though they have had four thousand years of practice. And the minister answered all as simply and as clearly as he was able, as though it had been a wise man who asked and not a child, not forgetting how a child is sometimes very wise.

There were two things about which, at such times, the child oftenest spoke. It was about God and his mother.

"Where is God?" said the child. "Up in heaven, where the stars are?"

"Yes."

"Is my mother there?"

"Yes."

"Did God want her up there?"

"Yes."

"But I want her more than He does, don't I?"

"What He wants He must have, Fritz, and we must let Him have it without a word."

"It's very hard," said the child.

With such questions, so answered, and others like them, did the child Fritz Maud betray his consciousness of the solemn mystery that lay round about his life and was casting a shadow in upon his heart.

CHAPTER XX.

FACEM, NON PACEM.

SANDOWNE had sunk down slowly into its former estate of chronic somnolency shortly after the events of the May Search, which resulted in nothing more important than furnishing staple for town's talk for a fortnight. Every day the farmers went to their work in the fields, and wives made themselves Marthas over the ever-returning, never-ended house-work, and the sun set upon the tired towns-folks out of the busy golden days, and saw daily somewhat done afield or at home. But the Eye in the heavens, that never sets nor shuts, saw, in all these workers, men and women who at nightfall had taken another step towards a quite other home than Sandowne, and had sown quite other seed than that which ripens afield. It can hardly be concealed from my readers that I, as historian, am not altogether in sympathy with the village life of Sandowne, having had my taste of it many years ago ; but I never am able to recall even its stolid, hopeless drowsiness and stupor without a certain awe, and solemn apprehension, and even reverence for the issues that are sure to come of it.

Strange as it may seem, the Sandowne consciousness was actually exposed to a new sensation the
very morning that followed the visit to Frenchman's Head. It came in the form of a calamity.
Sam Jones, at work in the fields near Bassett House,
saw it first. A little white cloud, lying just on the
tree-tops of the woods southward, when he first saw
it, and forthwith rising and surging up, white cloud
parting all ways into white billowy clouds, and underneath surging clouds of black lifting the rest and
rising higher and higher in the warm day.

" Fire in the woods!" cried Sam, throwing down
his hoe, after he had watched the cloud moving
above the trees. " Fire at Great Hollow! as sure
as the Devil 's a liar. There 'll be plenty to do to-
day besides hoeing, and nobody 'll get rich by it,
I 'm thinking." And he raised the cry of " Fire
in the woods!" on the spot, and his next neighbors
took it up, and it was shouted from farm to farm,
and the cry ran into the village, and soon through
every house and hamlet of it, and along the county
roads and the farms beyond; and it drove men out of
their furrows, and women and children out of doors,
until Sandowne became wild with clamor, and the
meeting-house bell rang out its sharp, quick peal;
and in a half-hour hardly an eye in the town that
had not seen the cloud rising higher and higher
over the woods southward.

Sandowne had not heard that cry for fifty years
before, and then the flame had been very cruel;

but when it came now, the townsfolk bestirred themselves with true Saxon vigor, and shortly the able-bodied men were pouring out of the village and the farm-houses amongst the hills, on foot, in wagons, — fire-wardens on horseback, bustling and dashing past the footmen, — while the cloud crept steadily higher, and the whirl of the black, angry mass beneath was clearly visible amongst the trees.

As the bustling, noisy crowd vanished into the woods, and the day went on, the excitement steadily increased among the groups of women and children and old men, gathered on the hill-sides and on the meeting-house green, watching the cloud in the south that had now spread over the sun, which shot through it only faint, yellowish rays. No one had come back, as yet, to report the damage doing beyond the hills, and each openly or silently made their comments upon the calamity which had befallen the village.

" The fire 's not so bad to-day, to reckon from the smoke yonder, as it was the year that old Parson Bent died, for then it swept everything clean to the shore, and drove the deer clear out of the woods, and two men lost their life afore it was done."

" P'r'aps it 'll come to that ag'in," said another man, less hopeful.

" There 'll be less taxes to pay, anyhow," said a third, who had very little to be taxed.

" It 's a retribution on people for their sins," said a godly soul.

" People 'll have to burn black wood for a year or two, which 'll make the womenfolk a sight of trouble, and my old man will make a dreadful litter with it in the kitchen," said Mrs. Sam, who had made her appearance with the rest on meeting-house hill. It is right, however, to say that before coming she had diligently scraped together all the edibles in the house into divers boxes and firkins, to be sent up to the hungry men fighting fire in the woods, — and every Sandowne housewife, having done the same, had nothing else to do but gossip and wait for news. Noon passed and there was no dinner for Sandowne, for its cooks were out watching the woods. It was hours past mid-day before news came from the fire. A wagon, with a dusty, begrimmed man in it, found its way off the hills, and crept very slowly — so thought the crowd that watched it as it came out from under the trees — down into the village. The crowd hurried around the wagon before it passed the meeting-house.

" What news? Where 's the fire? " shouted a dozen voices to the man.

" Fire 's in the thicket, back of ' the Hollow,' and it 's hot enough, I tell ye. Squire Howe's woodlot 's all gone, and I 'm afeerd the rest 'll go if the wind rises. The fire runs like mad in the dry leaves, and it 's coming down, right towards here ; and you 'll have it all in plain sight before twelve o'clock to-night, if luck does n't change."

" What are your men doing up there? " asked an old man of the newsman.

"Bless your soul, Father Bates, what can men do? We've got a line of them all along the sides, every one of them with a bush in his hand beating fire; but 't is n't no use. Fire's worse nor an Injun. It's creepin' about, and runnin' about, and we can't stop it. We tried it at the town road, and the men dug a trench afore it, but Lord-a-mercy! when it came down there it crossed it in a minute and drove us all out in a jiffy. And we 're all hot and hungry, and I 've ben sent after the men's grub, and I must be back afore long; and the men has got no rum nor water, and are choked to death for some. So bring out your grub here, and let me be off, quicker than Jack Robinson." And the " grub " was quickly brought and loaded into the man's wagon, and that for which the men were choking was not forgotten, and the man drove off again, leaving the crowd to discuss the news. Towards evening, stragglers from the woods brought nearly the same story, — how the fire could not be got under, — and were pumped quite dry of their information by the crowd that kept its place at the meeting-house; and as one by one the woodlots which had been burned over were mentioned, the spirits of the crowd became depressed at the loss, in which most were sharers. It was a black day in Sandowne.

Mr. Leverick and Arthur went up to the fire towards nightfall. Both had been busy all day, — Arthur, with Cloe's help, in packing provisions for the men at the fire, and the minister, in his quiet way, speaking cheerfully to the excited citizens as he came across them. And both carried with them in a wagon from the farm comfortable things for the weary men who were to pass the night in the woods. The cloud, blacker hourly since morning, had drawn its sable train over the evening stars from east to west, as the two friends passed in under the trees from the open pasture-lands upon the hill-range that lay southward from the village. None would have thought, who looked in under the dim green shadows of the silent oaks that fringed their borders, what frightful work was going on nearer the heart of the forest. Three miles of silent driving and not a man met all the way, and it became evident that they were coming upon the fire. Overhead lay the cloud; and now through the tree-tops they caught glimpses of clouds among the trees that surged, and fell, and rose again, and moved slowly on without a sound, with a certain angry restlessness that told they were hardly rain-clouds, and a sense of smokiness lay in among the trees. They came suddenly upon the path of the fire and a group of men sitting by the roadside eating their supper. All around the gray smoke was rising from the red embers under the black trees, where the fire had been and licked up with its red tongue every leaf and twig, and left only the burnt, black, desolate sod.

"Well, how goes it?" said the minister to the men.

"Bad enough, Parson," was the answer. "The fire 's been all round, to-day, as frisky as a young colt, and given us a sight of trouble ; and we have n't done much with it, anyhow, and it 's having its own way with us. We 've drove it in on the edges, but it 's been dodging about, and back-fires has done no good ; and I heerd the selectmen say, as they drove along just now, that they meant to try it down at the county road when it comes along. But we 're about tired out, no mistake, fighting fire. I hope, Parson, we shall never have hotter work to do than this," said the man, with a sort of grim humor, half-jollity and half-vexation, at thought of the day's work.

"I can't say," said the parson. At which retort a laugh went round the group sitting on the black ground, in the twilight, eating supper.

"If you want to see the fire, Parson," said another of the group, "you can take the blind road through the woods, just above here. It 'll bring you down where most of the men are who are waiting for the fire at the road. And it 's safe, I reckon, for the fire has been over it once to-day, and fire won't run in the same place twice, you know. First left, and then straight down to the place."

"I know the way, very well," said the minister.

"Nobody 's a better right, Parson, and I reckon you know about every road, hereaways, by this time. Good-by! Good luck to you!" said the group.

So they drove where the fire had been. On either side stood the black forest, smoky, with its red embers scattered about, and here and there a pile of damp brushwood burning slowly and lighting up the trees over it, but mostly silence everywhere. Farther in, the red glare against the night-sky showed where the fire raged hottest. And as they drove down the narrow road, under the black branches, they heard a low, muffled sound, like that of the sea in the distance breaking on its beach.

"That is the rumble of the fire," said Mr. Leverick, "and it only proves what was said the other day, that Nature always expresses by sound the work she is at. We are nearing the fire, evidently."

They came ten minutes later into the county road and the red glare of the fire; and all along the road, just in the bushes, was the line of men beating and trampling out the fire.

"Leave the horse here, Arthur, and let 's walk up to the fire. This is evidently only a side of it, and the head of it must be further in."

It was a striking scene, — the men flitting about the line of fire among the brush, and the green woods lighted up beyond, waiting its enemy, while further up the road was the thunder of the fire-head, and the gleam of the flame through the smoke.

"Hullo, Parson! have you come to fite fire with us?" shouted a burly, begrimmed man, wiping the sweat from his face with his shirt-sleeves, and standing back a moment from the fire-line, as the two came up to the men.

" Is that you, Sawyer ? "

" Yes ; all that 's not sweated out of me, thrashing out this fire, only to make it burn brighter," said Bill. " Hullo, boys ! the parson 's come up to see us."

His parishioners flocked about their minister, eager to tell him the adventures of the fire and not a few hair-breadth escapes from the same, looking to him, as it were through habit, for some comfort in even this novel and mundane trial of their tempers. And the minister distributed the provisions he had brought amongst them.

" Our supper 'll go to the right place this time, anyhow," said Bill ; " we 've got to make a night of it, and an empty stomach is no good for this kind of trainin'. If you just want to see the fire," said Bill, taking away a huge piece of beef from his mouth, " come along with me, and I 'll show you the creetur. It 'll beat anything I ever seed in Sandowne, all my days. I 've got no woods, and I 've put out my neighbor's fire long enough for this present train, and I 'd like to show you the fire and do a little shirking afore bedtime, anyhow."

Bill conducted them up the road — fire on one side and the green woods the other — till, at a turn on the edge of a pine-forest, they came upon the fire.

" It 's crossed," said Bill, " spite of the selectmen and all the rest. 'T won't stop here, anyhow, you see."

A group of men, evidently in anxious consultation, stood at a respectful distance from the fire as
the minister and Arthur came out upon them. The
fire had crossed the road, as Bill said, and had already fastened upon the thicket beyond. It was
truly a sublime sight that was before them. The
fire just now seemed to have gained new fury, as it
swept on through the green wood. It licked up,
with its ten thousand red, lambent tongues, every
branch and twig upon the ground, and ran along
over the dry mosses in its red, angry flight, and
smote down the tender shoots and undergrowth. It
ran up the dry tree-trunks and flashed out upon the
long mosses that trembled a second in its fiery grasp
and then perished into thin ashes ; it crept out along
the branches, to their very tips, and shrivelled in its
hands of fire the green leaves and shoots, and then
with sudden bound it leaped to the very tops and
danced over them a quivering, reeling, gleaming
dance, as if it were wild with passion, and it ran
from tree to tree, creeping, climbing, shooting, flash-
ing, racing, leaving only ashes in its track over hill
and through the hollows, over rock and stump and
frail grass and tree alike, hissing, moaning, smiting,
with its line of fire, that ran along the ground, as if
in charge, with its fire battalions overhead among the
trees that rose and sank and twined around the trees,
and flashed and gleamed and ate away the green
woods ; and over all rose the black, billowy smoke-
clouds, twisting and hurrying and soaring up into

the upper air as messengers of what went on below; and through the fire came the low, ceaseless muttering and rumbling of its gleaming chariot-wheels, as it swept on and on through the woods.

So great was the din of the fire, that Mr. Leverick came up to the group before-mentioned without being noticed. They were in eager consultation about the fire, and were evidently discouraged. The fire had swept across the road in spite of them, and many miles of woodland lay at its mercy.

"How goes it friends?" said the minister, in his quiet, cheerful way.

"Bad enough, Parson. The fire has got away from us again, and there's no knowing when it will stop. A smart rain might do it, but that's hardly likely, and it's seldom that a fire like this don't raise a wind before long that makes things worse."

"I should n't wonder but that the wind had changed now," said Bill Sawyer, as a shower of fire-flakes and hot ashes fell down suddenly on the group. "That's a warm welcome for a feller, anyhow."

Just then a man came running up from the party below. "We must get out of this, men," he shouted. "Don't you see the wind has changed?"

And for the first time they all noticed that the wind had changed and was every moment freshening.

"Pick up your traps, men, and be off!" was

the cry. " Sooner the better. With this wind the fire will run down the road like a horse, and the quicker you are in clear land the better." And the men, rapidly gathering up their spades and hoes, ran in a crowd down the road to the wagons.

It was, indeed, high time to be moving. The wind had changed into the worst quarter and their retreat was in danger.

" Move on men, with your wagons ! " shouted the fire-master. " The fire will sweep everything clean to the open land." And they crowded themselves into the wagons and drove rapidly down the road. There was no overwhelming danger, provided there was no delay, but the clouds of smoke, and the cinders that the wind drove down upon them, every now and then, gave warning that the enemy behind was not to be trifled with. The fire threw its red glare on the hill-tops and over the trees that were now bending and moaning under the fresh breeze ; and then again the fugitives stumbled along, as best they could, in the Egyptian darkness of the wood-hollows through which the road led. And there was hard driving and heavy hearts in the wagon-cavalcade that hurried along under the dark trees. All knew that with this wind there more trouble ahead. The fire was sweeping down with a power that rendered resistance useless, and in its present course was sure to sweep bare the whole Sandowne forest. It was moving certainly towards the Neck. The Neck was a narrow ridge

16

of wood between open fields that united the woods on the south and east by a narrow peninsula of forest, and once across that, the fire must certainly sweep to the sea.

" If we had somebody at the Neck, to set a backfire carefully, we might stop it there," said Mr. Leverick to the party in the wagon with him.

" Yes," said several, " but it 's too late. It 's too far round by the road, and no man could find his way across the fields in season. We 'll have to take what comes, this time, Parson."

Every eye was instinctively turned towards the Neck as the cavalcade came out into the fields. It was utterly dark. " If we had supposed the wind would act in this way, we would have had a fire at the Neck six hours ago, but it 's too late now," was the inevitable conclusion of each ; and yet they hesitated to go townward, as if they hoped against hope to do something yet to stay the fire.

" What 's that," said Bill Sawyer to his neighbor, suddenly, " over at the Neck ? Is that the moon or a star there among the trees ? "

" Can't see it," said the neighbor.

" I 've poor eyesight," said Bill, " but there is something there as true as gospel."

Every eye was strained looking towards the Neck. There was certainly something there, as Bill said ; a light, at any rate, or what looked like that. It was a moment of intense anxiety to the whole party. The able-bodied men of the village were there in the wagons, and the shift of the wind had been too sudden for any to go from the town, and a back-fire at the Neck seemed too unreasonable to be true.

" Hoorah ! " said Bill, breaking the painful suspense ; " there 's a fire at the Neck, as sure as my father's name was Job. Don't you see that, men ? it 's acting just as it has been all day, up above."

And sure enough, just then a flame of fire was seen to run up a tree and out over the top, and then another and then another. There was clearly a back-fire at the Neck. But who had set it ? Nobody could even guess.

" That fire works well to windward," said Bill, who seemed himself called upon to justify, in all essentials, the fire he had discovered and vouched for. " The man 's no fool who has that fire in hand. He 's driving it straight up to where it 's wanted, and keeps a good lookout in the rear."

" We must move further out from this," said Mr. Leverick, as a shower of ashes and cinders fell just on the edge of the woods. And they moved further out into the pastures and then stopped to watch the end. The fire at the Neck, as has been said, was steadily working to windward, up towards the hills, and those best acquainted with the ground felt sure, as they watched it, that it would stay the conflagration. But the other fire behind them ! That was a spectacle for even Vulcan. It ran before the wind like a living thing, and it swept over the forest and it ate down into the green trees on the

wood edge, and it swept on, mile after mile, broadening and wasting and swaying, fire-billows, smoke-
clouds, altogether in the strong wind, — capping the
trees with flame and hurling spark and ember broad-
cast into the restless air, — a fire-sea in its most
stormy fashion of the woods. It swept on angrily
and swiftly to meet, as it were, its rash foe creeping up towards it from the Neck; and a long hour
they marked its onset, nearer and nearer, until the
two fires rushed together and fought together among
the tree-trops until the flame seemed fiercest; and
then slowly the fire sank lower, lower, until it
seemed to be hiding itself under the black, charred
trunks of the wasted and shrivelled woods.

It was daybreak as the tired company of townsmen reached the village. Who had set that fire on
the Neck? was the first question. No one could
tell.   But the dark, withered band of the forest
along the borders of the green pastures, from whence
rose silently slender columns of gray smoke in the
clear daylight, showed where the fire had been.

CHAPTER XXI.

CHILD LOST.

"Black hearts are like black eyes, — when closely observed they are found only to be brown." — J. F. P. RICHTER.

ARTHUR was waked from the first heavy sleep into which he had fallen after the night's fatigue by a loud knocking at his chamber-door.

"Who 's there?"

"It 's me," said a voice which Arthur recognized to be Sam's. "Get right up! The parson's boy 's lost in the woods, and you 're wanted."

Arthur hurried on his clothes and came out with only a confused, half-waking sense of the great calamity that had befallen his friend.

"How did this happen, Sam?"

"Can't say," said that now excited individual. "Don't know nothing about it. What with the fire, and this, the Devil 's round here, sartin. I only know the boy 's gone, and the parson has sent over for you." And the two hurried into the town.

The meeting-house bell had already rung out its sharp, unwelcome peal, and the townsfolks were flocking out of doors, supposing that the fire had broken out again, until the news spread rapidly of the new calamity. All pitied the minister, and were flocking to the parsonage as Arthur came up. There was a sober crowd upon the lawn around Mr. Leverick, who was listening calmly to the suggestions and the reports of his sympathizing flock, and every now and then giving a new comer the little information he had of the child's departure. The housekeeper had missed him late in the evening, and her inquiries in the village had come to nothing, and she had no idea how or why the child had gone off. A dozen people had seen a child, or fancied they had seen a child, in a dozen different places, but had paid no attention to it, thinking it a neighbor's going home, and the excitement of the fire had so confused their recollection that their testimony came to nothing. It was only plain that the child had been lost since last evening, and no one could say where he had gone.

"My friends," the minister said, in a low, firm voice to the crowd, who were proposing a hundred things about finding the child, "we must scatter ourselves at once over the fields, and search carefully in every hollow and thicket up and into the woods. The child cannot have gone far, but unless we search carefully we may miss him, and God help us all! If we find him safe we will blow the horn three times; if we find him otherwise," — here he paused, as if struggling with that thought, — "then once."

And the crowd — this time women as well as

men, every woman thinking of her own little ones at home — hurried off into the fields and along every path and lane where the child might possibly have gone. There was one terrible thought in the minds of all, — so terrible, indeed, that no one spoke it. What if the child had wandered away into the woods and been caught in the fire? There was indeed a sad, anxious company in the fields to-day, searching for the parson's boy.

Arthur and Sam Jones went with Mr. Leverick. " We must go towards the Neck," said the latter, briefly, and they hurried along in silence. The same bitter thought was in the mind of each, — " If the fire," — and only the minister finished that sentence in his mind calmly, firmly, and the others shrank away from the sickening horror. They separated into the fields as they came out of the town without a word, and began their search. Did you ever go out for a lost child in the fields? Can you remember the heat and weight at your brain, — fire and lead, — and with what thoughts you looked down into the clear water, dreading to find a white face underneath, and a little form among the dank water-plants, — or searched under the solemn trees that would not speak to you, fearful you might find a stark body with little hands laid on the wet leaves as if in sleep? If never, may God forefend you from that experience. The minister had taken that way because he remembered that Fritz had a strange longing to know what lay over the hills, as the child called the place from whence he had sometimes seen the sun rise up.   Over the hills, he knew, was fairy-land to Fritz, and he judged from the questions the child had sometimes asked him, that beyond the hills where he could not look he had an indescribable sense of a wonderful realm, where was — What? Nothing the child could name, but something dreamed or fancied, that had often made him ask his great friend about what was " over the hills."   And this was why Mr. Leverick went that way.   Meanwhile the search went on ; eager men and women over all the fields between the woods and sea, searching every wall and clump of bushes and along the wood-roads, after the child. And they had found nothing.   And the minister? Outwardly calm and silent, hurrying on with his firm, decided ·step, — a little paler, perhaps, and the lips a little more firmly set than usual, — but with- in ?   " How strange it is that I should be searching here for my little orphaned boy, — that Fritz should have left me so !   How dreary it will be at home if I must miss the golden hair and the low voice ! And yet is not He over all when we are the most helpless?   And he hurried on and saw nothing, not even the day or the sea, only the phantom of a child hungry and wasted, calling to him out of the woods for help.   He stood, before he knew it, on the edge of the burnt woods, close to where the back-fire at the Neck, which had stayed the confla- gration, had been set.   And he hastened along the

edge, peering under the bushes for some vestige of
the child. There was nothing. As he ran on now
with a wild excitement which increased at every
step, his foot struck against something. It was even
a relief to stoop down to see what it might be.
Perhaps something to tell him of the boy. It was
only a rough stick or cudgel, shod at the end with
a sheep's marrow-bone. He had not found the boy,
but he had solved one mystery that had perplexed
him. A shout from below startled him. It was
Sam swinging his hat and beckoning him. He ran
down to where Sam stood in a sandy gully, which
the heavy rains had washed out in the pastures.
He looked where Sam pointed. There were marks
of little feet in the sand:

"We 're on the trail, Parson, as sure as fate,"
said Sam; "he 's crossed here, you see. And
there, on the bank above, somebody 's been pullin'
up May-flowers. I should make a good Injun, I
reckon, huntin' up folks. He 's on a-head somewhere, or my name ain't Jones."

Sure enough, the little footprints pointed over
the hills, as the minister had somehow foreseen, and
they hastened on with quickened step after the child.
They had reached now the top of the hill-ridge that
lay eastward from the town, and beyond and before
them was "over the hills" of the child's dream.
It was a wild spot, that sank away to a deep glen
between its woody hill-sides, and beyond were
patches of open land, and then the forest.

" The other side is old Treeman's hut," said Sam, " and maybe he knows something of the boy." And they went down through the brushwood towards the glen. " Hoorah, Parson, here 's the youngster ag'in ! " shouted Sam, as he held up from the scrub-oak, where he had found it hanging, a little cap. The child had certainly gone this way, and the men broke down the hill-side to the glen.

" The boy 's not crossed the brook, Parson, for there 's no tracks in the mud," said Sam, as he examined carefully the soft edges of the brook that ran in the glen ; " let 's keep to the path that turns sharp to the left and we 'll be soon upon him." And the three hurried down the path again.

" We 're coming to the Cross, directly," said Sam, " where the murder was, and to think the boy went such a way, in the dark, perhaps, poor creetur ! It 's bad enough for grown folks in daylight, lettin' alone children."

It was, as Sam said, a gloomy place, quite shut out from the rest of the world by its dreary slopes of low bushes, mountain-laurel, and scrub-oak, that make up the dreariest part of our forests.

A child's life was depending on how they went, and the men pressed on as though they knew it, without a word. A moment more and they were out upon the open spot, and on the other side stood the cross where the murder had been committed. Good God ! seated under it was old Treeman, holding in his arms the child !

The old man started to his feet as they came up to him, still holding the child, whose golden hair lay on the old man's shoulder, and who seemed to be on the best terms with his strange protector.

" I found your boy," he said almost gruffly, " running about in the woods here, and I have brought him back so far. Here he is, Parson," and he gave the child to the minister with an air of half-concealed impatience, as if he were anxious to be rid of the matter that brought him here. "I have n't hurt him, and since I 've found him I have taken care of him, — at least such care as an old man like me could give."

" I am very grateful to you, Treeman," said the minister, " for your care of this little boy, and we all owe you many thanks."

" I want no thanks," said the man, " and I won't have any. The townsfolk think, perhaps, I would eat a child if I found one in the woods, like a wolf; but you, Parson, know better than that, and I told you that the other day, when they were after me as though I were a mad dog. You have n't misused me, and I have shown you that I am not a wild beast. So we are quits. But no thanks. And as I have something else to do, and have no further business here, I must be going." And he turned sharply round in his tracks and went away through the brushwood down the glen.

" Is he gone away ? " said the child. " He was very good to me, and gave me a piece of bread when I was hungry, and I want him to come back with us home."

"Will you go home, Fritz?" said the minister to the child, who lay listlessly in his arms, as if very tired.

"I am willing," said the child.

"Don't you want to go with me, Fritz?"

"I want to go with my mother."

"Your mother is n't here in these woods, child."

"Yes, I saw her," said the boy.

The minister troubled the little boy no farther: "Home now, friends!" he said, and they went back with lighter hearts townward. And the child lay as if half-asleep in his great friend's arms, with those dreamy, half-shut eyes under the golden hair, with a bewildered, careful look in them to-day, pale, un-resisting, silent, as the party hastened up out of the ravine to the hill-ridge which they had crossed.

"Now for good news!" said Sam, as they came in sight of the Sandowne fields. And he raised the tin-horn that he carried to his lips and blew a blast. The searchers in the fields who heard it stopped short and listened eagerly. Once, — twice, — three times. Thank God! the child is safe! And the townsfolks hastened homewards with light hearts, eager to hear news of the boy's recovery. Parties of them joined Mr. Leverick on the way, anxiously listening to Sam's story, until a thankful crowd at-tended them through the village as they came to the parsonage. Old Treeman had found and saved the child, — that was the story, — old Treeman, who was such an outlaw and bugbear in Sandowne. The crowd were surprised almost into silence when they heard it. That old Treeman should care for anything or show gentleness to any one seemed past belief. But the minister said it, and Sam had seen it. Sam, indeed, was very emphatic about the matter.

" I tell ye, neighbors, the Devil 's never so black as he 's painted ; and I vow I wish all my cakes may be dough, if I call any man hard names again, as long as I live ! " said Sam.

But still the neighbors wondered. And why ? Was not old Treeman somehow a man ? Had he not once a mother as other men have ? Had he never been a child as all once were ? Can son of human mother turn to be altogether brother of the brutes that perish ? Do women bear devils, think you ? O, Pharisee ! judging in your comfortable home your brother of shame, know that beneath the foulest sins God still keeps his sanctuary in human hearts, and that to the most erring come sometimes the fairest angels of love, of prayer, of memory, and casting over them the mantle of a divine compassion, whisper, " Brethren in the Love that died for all, come now in a new life unto Him who is the Lord of all." And these weak ones struggle and agonize and reach up again towards heaven for pardon with some well-meant deed or charity. And One judges tenderly, for that One hath borne the burden and felt the thorn.

CHAPTER XXII.

ONLY ABOUT A CHILD.

WHEN the child had been brought and laid in his customary place in the library, he forthwith fell asleep, as if worn out with the exposure of the past night. Mr. Leverick watched anxiously the sleeper, as he slept an uneasy, restless sleep, in which, every now and then, the child would turn with a quick, nervous motion, as if something troubled him, and mutter to himself, as if he were talking with some one, — what, the minister could not make out at first, as he watched the pale, anxious face, until it was plain to his great friend that the recollection of his last night's adventures was following him in sleep.

It was the late afternoon when the child awoke. He looked round him and towards the minister, who sat by him, with a painfully bewildered look, and asked, " Where am I now ? "

" In the library here, with me," said Mr. Leverick.

The child answered only with a disappointed look, while slowly the recollection of what had happened seemed to come back to him, and then the sweet, gentle look again, and the hazel eyes raised to the minister's.

"Take me!" said the child, reaching out his hands. And his great friend lifted him up tenderly into his arms, where he lay without a word, with the old dreamy look, as if he were waiting or listening for some one.

As the child roused himself by degrees from the fatigue and confusion into which he had fallen, in his recent adventure in the fields, the minister very cautiously set to work to unravel the mystery of his going; and gradually, from the child's strange and not altogether coherent narrative, the truth disclosed itself. There was, however, Mr. Leverick found, one great difficulty in dealing with him. The child did not appear able to distinguish between his waking and his sleeping experiences, but took all with the like certainty for truth. It seemed to the minister, as he listened, to be mostly a dream, yet he could not altogether content himself with that conclusion.

"Why did you go away, Fritz?" the minister said, quietly, when at last the child lifted himself up to put his arms round the great man's neck, in the old affectionate embrace.

"Because *she* called me."

"She? Who?"

"A very beautiful lady, all in white."

"Are you sure you saw a lady in white? Perhaps you were asleep, and dreamed, as little boys sometimes do, you know."

" I am sure," said the child.

" Tell us all about it then."

" Well, when you and Mr. Bassett had gone away, (was it yesterday you went?) I was very lonesome, and Mrs. Barlow had left me here, and I got up into your great arm-chair to look out at the window to see which way you went. And I thought you had gone over the hills, and then I was sorry you had left me at home, and I wanted very much to go along with you. And I began to be tired looking out, and it was so still, and you were gone, and I was afraid all alone, and I cried. And then *she* came and said, ' Don't cry, Fritz! come with me over the hills; there are many pretty things there, and I will show you where the sun comes from, and the red birds with the sunshine on their wings, and the pretty flowers with wings that eat the other flowers; and I will give you pretty stones and all kinds of flowers that grow under the trees there, if you will go with me.' And she kissed me and put her arms round me, as you do."

" Who is *she*, Fritz? "

" I don't quite know," said the child; " but I am sure I 've seen her before somewhere, and she seemed to know me; and I wanted her to take me up, as you do, but she only patted my head and smiled so kind I 'm sure she loved me very much; and she said so."

" How did she look, Fritz? "

" Very beautiful," said the child, " as the sun-shine does when I am out-doors and the birds sing; not like Mrs. Barlow; and she 's shorter than her, and is n't so red as her, and did n't talk loud like her; but white like, with black eyes, and I thought she was a child, too, only she was larger than me; and she said so kindly, ' Come, Fritz,' that I could n't help it."

" And so you went away ? " said the minister.

" Yes; I went with her over to the hills, and I was n't tired; and she was very kind and said, ' Don't go this way, Fritz,' and ' Don't go that way, Fritz, for there are briers there; ' and when I stopped to pick flowers she said, ' Those are pretty flowers, Fritz,' and I showed her them in my hand; and she was so beautiful a lady that I told her I wanted to come and live with her, though I meant to come and see you very often; but I could n't help it, she was such a good lady and I loved her so."

" But was n't you afraid when the dark came, Fritz ? "

" No," said the child; " for I could see her, and she showed me the way through the bushes; and when I wanted to go up where there was a great light and very pretty things among the trees she said, ' Not that way, Fritz,' and I did n't go. And when I was tired and sleepy she said, ' Now, here is a nice bed, Fritz, I will stay with you,' and I lay down on the leaves. And I said my prayer, —

'Now I lay me down to sleep,'—and the lady said, 'That is right, Fritz;' and I knew she would let nothing hurt me while I was asleep, for she said so. And I thought about her asleep, and how she carried me over the hills to a great house where there were ever so many lights and a great many beautiful things I never saw before; and she took me by the hand and led me in where there were a great many folks that I have seen somewhere, I know, and she said, 'Here is your home, Fritz; and here I shall always be with my little boy, and you shall have flowers and go out into the fields and hear the birds sing, whenever you like, and nothing shall hurt you here where I am.' And I felt all the tired was gone away, and I could go everywhere and was not afraid. And in the morning the sun waked me up and the beautiful lady said, 'Come, Fritz! over the hills where the sunshine comes from is where we are going.' And I went along with her among the trees until we met the old man, who did n't see her, and when he came up to me I wanted to go with her. But she said, 'This man has come. Not to-day, Fritz. But to-morrow I will take you with me over the hills where the flowers are, I told you of. Be a good child and wait,'—and she went away down under the trees. And when I cried, the man said, 'What are you crying for?' and I said, 'She has gone away and left me;' and I told him about the good lady in white. And he took me up and kissed me, and said, 'You are lost, child, and are tired. Let us go back, home.' And he brought me back to you. And I don't know where she has gone, only she said she would come to-morrow. When is to-morrow?"

"I cannot tell you that," said the minister.

"I wish it would come," said the child.

"What! and go away from me, Fritz?"

"I will take you with me," said the boy, brightening at that thought; "for I know the good lady will say ' Yes,' if I ask her, and we will be together over the hills."

"Dear Fritz," said the minister, "you are a little boy, and there are a great many things which you do not understand yet."

"But I have seen the good lady," said the child.

It was evident that the events of the child's wandering in the woods, whether dreamed or real, had sunk deep down into his life, and the minister avoided the whole matter with him henceforth, and tried to interest him in the more cheerful affairs of their daily life at the parsonage. He showed him again his favorite pictures out of the old books, and made the attempt to amuse him with his favorite specimens out of the museum, where the squirrels, and bird's nests were kept. He brought him spring-flowers, and was constant in endeavoring to restore its elasticity and vivacity to the child's mind. But somehow the attempt utterly failed. He seemed to have lost interest in former things. He made no complaint and listened patiently, but it was plain that his thoughts were on other matters; and Mr. Leverick judged that they were busy with the beautiful lady in white who had led him almost over the hills. And he lay quietly in his place while the library-work went on, as if in a profounder dream than that which aforetime had looked out through the hazel eyes. Shortly it became plain, also, that his health had been seriously endangered by his exposure in the woods. At first he suffered as acutely as his slight frame allowed, until it was clear that, at the best, the child must be lame for life. But, beyond any disease apparent to the medical attendant, there seemed to be something else that was rapidly draining the fountains of his life. Day by day he grew weaker without any apparent cause. It seemed, indeed, as if the ethereal soul of the child was knocking at the gates of the frail tenement of dust which held it, demanding egress into a wider liberty. And as the child grew weaker he became also happier and gentler. And when, sometimes in pain, he uttered that low, plaintive cry, which sounded to Mr. Leverick like the wail of a soul for some half-remembered sorrow, there was something in the sound that seemed weird and mystic to the minister, until the child became to him a more solemn mystery that was clinging about his heart; that was clinging — should he say it? — around another heart which had revealed itself to the child through the beautiful lady in white.

The child held closer to the minister every day.

Agnes Lawrence and the housekeeper were constant in their services, and even Mrs. Lawrence had come over to see her child and to exercise her old influence upon him. But he turned away from all to the minister again. From his hand he received everything with the same sober patience and quietness. He called for him when he woke up at night or morning, and was uneasy if his great friend was for a moment absent. And the minister noticed that at such times, when he had been dreaming, he always asked to be taken in arms, and laid his head on the minister's breast, awake. And through the long night-hours the minister watched the sleeper, and came instantly when the child moaned or awoke. It was evident to Mr. Leverick that the child's illness could end in only one way. He had asked himself, "What way?" and answered himself calmly, with the truth. The apprehension that, from the start, had been coming upon him, had some time since become certainty to him, and he had said in his inmost soul, "Fritz must go." And it only made him a little paler, a little gentler, a little more silent, as he passed about the study in his tender nursing of the child. Had he no tears? That which is wept is washed out in tears sometimes, but that which is behind tears — never. It was not that he had no tears, but rather that the agony at his heart smote down his tears with its great bitterness, and made his heart dumb before men, that he might open it and weep out of it before his God. And besides, he had not now for the first time suffered.   So the angel, who was over-shadowing with his wings the dreamer, was drawing these two lives closer together before he led away the little boy into a realm without a shadow, and the minister knew that ; — perhaps the child, also.

It was a fortnight, maybe, after Fritz had been rescued by old Treeman, towards the close of a soft June day, that the child awoke from what seemed, by the half-smile upon the pale, wasted face, to have been a sleep of pleasant dreams. The great friend came to him instantly and said, "Well, Fritz, you have been asleep?"

"Yes," said the child, "but I have seen the beautiful lady again, and she says, 'To-morrow has come,' and she was so glad I was going with her over the hills at last."

The minister said nothing, but an expression of pain passed for a moment over the calm features, and then all was at rest again. The children were play-ing their evening plays before the parsonage, and their merry laugh entered the old library where the wasted·child and his great friend were.

" Let me look out of the window at the children."

The minister lifted him from the sofa, and wheel-ing his chair to the window held him in his arms.

" I should like to be out with the rest," he said, as he saw the little merrymakers at their sports on the lawn ; " and I should like to walk round to the brook there and see the water as I used, only there is no time now, for to-morrow is come."

" You are lame, you know, Fritz, and could not go out."

" Yes, but if I had time I might go out with crutches, that Mrs. Barlow told me about, now that the birds and the flowers have come."

" You are very weak, Fritz."

" I am very weak," said the child. " I should like to go to sleep. Are you sorry for that ? " he added, quickly, without the languid air with which he had been speaking, as he detected something in the minister's face that seemed to trouble him.

" I should be sorry to have you die, my child."

" What is it to die ? " said the child. " If it is going away with the good lady in white, who has come for me, I am sure nothing could hurt me ; and the house over the hills that I saw asleep is so very, very beautiful."

The minister answered only with a kiss on the golden hair above the white forehead.

The setting sun was just throwing its last beams on the fresh, green leaves of the trees around the parsonage as the child looked out on the scene. He watched it a moment carefully, and then said, with a half-uncertain air, " I think I have seen all that somewhere, when I was asleep. I think she must have told me about it. But I am tired now and want to go to sleep." And he laid back his head upon the minister's breast. " I shall see the beautiful lady to-night," he said.

And the minister watched the sleeping child, listening to the low, irregular breathing through the long hours; watched while the evening shadows deepened on the pale face; watched till the night drew its black veil over the golden hair; watched, they two alone, in that silent library, — with what thoughts of Long Ago and the Here and the Hereafter one cannot say, but which the angels read, — and moved not; child in the strong, gentle arms, long after the stars came out and the night was deepest.

It had been several hours now when the minister bent down his head, close to the sleeper's face, and listened. What did he hear? Could you have looked through the night, as God did, you would have seen that what he did *not* hear had only made that calm face paler; and the lips were set firm together, and outwardly — nothing more. Within? Let us leave that to Him who pities — as man does not sorrow — infinitely. The minister rose up slowly from his place at the window and laid the child again carefully on the library sofa; and then knelt down beside him with his arms about him, as if in prayer. It was morning when he rose up again, and the morning light fell upon the worn, pale face. Sunlight or pallor, there was certainly a placid smile upon it. Whatever foes had wrestled with him in the darkness upon his knees, he had conquered all,— conquered through the Conqueror for all.

And the child? He had gone away with the beautiful lady in white to the home beyond the hills!

CHAPTER XXIII.

ASPHODEL.

"It is right, my friends, that we should consider this, that if the soul is immortal it requires our care not only for the present time, — which we call life, — but for all time; and the danger would now appear to be dreadful if one should neglect it." — THE PHÆDO OF PLATO.

THE child had been laid asleep with a simple prayer and hymn in a service which had drawn together the townsfolk to the parsonage library; and the lawn was dark with men who crowded the doorways and entry of the old house, in a grave, silent gathering that offered sympathy to the mourners. The chief mourner read, as his duty was, the hymn, and gave the prayer. One remarked only in him that his face was very quiet and his voice a little lower than usual; but, besides that, there was outwardly nothing more. He went through the service, and his voice never once faltered; and when he said, "Let us pray!" there were some who remarked there was a placid smile almost upon his countenance. And his prayer was especially of little children: and he gave thanks that God had given these little ones to men and women, to brighten and purify their lives by that eternal message of childhood

that bids us to become again as little children; and
that sometimes God called home his little ones before the feet were weary and the vestments dusty
in the way and wrestle of life; and that in their
heavenly home there was never the wasting sick-
ness, nor the tears of sorrow, nor the stain of sin.
And he prayed for the children that grow up and
into the common strain and burden of the life of
this world; that their merciful angels might lead
them unto the Life above the world, wherein the
Great Friend reveals Himself; and also for those
with whom God leaves their children, how that they
might be worthy of so great happiness, and might
learn therefrom of the Infinite Parent, " so that a
little child might lead them."   Was it pride that
held back his tears, that made him pray with lips
that never once faltered, though the child of his
heart lay cold and stark before him?   No; it was
the calmness of the man who had suffered long ago,
and found the strength of sufferers to lie in Him
whom he addressed.   It was the testimony of a servant before the people to the Master who had
opened to all disciples a way through death to Life.

Strangely enough, as it seemed to some, the child
was laid asleep in the graveyard, near to the spot
where the young girl was buried, whose fate in shipwreck had attracted so much sympathy from the
Sandowners twenty years before.   This was Mr.
Leverick's wish, and the reason he gave was simple,
— " I wish that.   One day I shall be buried near

there. The place is vacant and I have no other." And the matter attracted no great notice. When the company had left the child in the graveyard Arthur read the inscription on the headstone, which had lately surprised the townsfolk. It was a simple red sandstone, and the legend ran thus: — "MARY. BORN INTO LIFE TEMPORAL, JUNE 6, 17—. BORN INTO LIFE ETERNAL, SEP. 12, 18—. NOT THE HERE BUT THE HEREAFTER." As he was reading, a man came up from under the tree where he had been standing apart from the company which had gathered around the grave.

" Is the child dead ? " said the man.

" Yes."

" It is very young to die."

" Yes."

" And is buried here. Well, not all of him, — even such a heathen as I believe."

It was old Treeman.

The congregation that met together, on the Sunday which followed close upon the burial, assembled in the meeting-house with more than usual quietness; and the shadow which had fallen on their minister, in their real sympathy, seemed resting also on them. There was utter silence as the minister came in alone, and walked slowly up the aisle to the pulpit. Rain or shine, the child had always been there with him; and even the more indifferent marked the change with a sense of pain. He walked up the pulpit steps to his place and looked round on the congregation. A little child had always before looked down with deep hazel eyes upon the company. But now ? How life often drives its thorn through the commonest things into our hearts and fastens together the temporal and the eternal !

The text to-day was that old Scripture, " I am the resurrection and the life, saith the Lord." " The question of life and death," the minister said, " is the most solemn that God sets before us to consider. It is very right that every now and then we should ask ourselves again, ' What is life ? ' and ' Whither is life ? ' and find the answer somewhere. He that is indifferent to this matter cannot rightly discern the main problem of our existence. ' Do we rise from the grave ? ' is a question which graves all around us are asking every day, and which our own graves, so near to our to-day, put also. At first sight the answer seems not so easy. Everywhere about us is death. The leaves die ; the tender flowers of the spring die ; the grasses die ; the oaks die ; the beasts of the field die ; all flying things, all creeping things, and the fish that swim in the sea, die. Everywhere is wasting away : the granite rocks of the hills waste ; the mountains are crumbling slowly into fine dust ; and we have no knowledge that the life of such things is ever renewed. Our friends die ; and friends and foes through the whole earth die, — the old, the young, the weak, the strong. From every fireside some

are gone; no house of this parish but is vacant of
some that lived and wrought and laughed and sorrowed in it. They who have gone out from here
to their last sleep are more than gather here: those
who loved you and lived for you. And yet they
never come back to you, nor speak to you. You
have some time prayed them for a sign, — a single word, a whisper, a touch, a wafture of the hand.
And in all these years no sign. The dead never
come back. Do they forget? Are they asleep and
cannot be waked by even the strong petitioning of
love? If you search in the graves, only black
dust and ashes. In the whole world around us —
nothing.

" So far, then, the case seems to have gone against
us. We are, after all, but black dust and ashes, as
the rest are. And we look around for proof to
ourselves that we do not perish, as the plants and
the beasts do. I know that some men lay great
stress upon the fact that men in all time have said,
' We live beyond the grave.' No doubt they wished
that as we wish it, but to desire is not to prove. I
have looked through the speculations of men for
four thousand years, about the nature of death,
so far as known to me, and I have often found
happy guesses, earnest hopes of immortality, but
hardly certainty. Their great sages, like Plato,
prove nothing, except that they hope to live again,
beyond the dust and waste of graves. But at the
end of their most confident conclusions they seem

often to me to add sadly, ' Perhaps.' Antiquity proved nothing, except that antiquity dared to hope for immortality. Men answer, indeed, that where there is such general expectation of a future life the doctrine must be true. But men have had other general expectations that were not true. Why, then, these? There is, then, nothing within us or around us that proves our wish. The dim light that hovered round the problem of the grave in all the ancient world was simply a pale, lingering ray from that ancient sun of revelation which, at the start, was given a new race for guidance; and men had grown almost deaf and blind towards their only guide. The whole world, through all ages, when mourners out of white lips had asked, ' Do the dead live again?' had answered, ' It may be:' but Christ, ' It is.'

" Immortality, then, is a revelation. The whole matter rests on this simple question, — ' Do you believe in God?' If not, the matter ends. You are only dust and ashes. If yes, the rest follows. But we only confidently believe in God, as to what he is and how he is, on that testimony we call Scripture. Do you believe that testimony? And Scripture declares our immortality. So great is its confidence in it, that it even assumes it often as admitted truth. But still men say, ' We rather know that, from the strong desire which our souls have for immortality.' Even infinite desire, I answer, friends, cannot prove the most finite fact. And we must go back to God for comfort

"You call Him Father, — infinite, compassionate, eternal. You, then, are children. Would you suffer your child to perish if you could help it? No. Then God, who is infinitely more than you in the love that pities, gives his children immortality. You may say, We are made for that; we mean that in our very structure; we should not be men without that. I answer: Reckon as we may, there is only one thing sure, God gives us that. Freely we should give him our hearts for that.

"But where is that other life? you ask. Beyond the stars? There is no beyond to the stars. Upon the stars? Think you that any star is more beautiful than our own? that it has sunnier skies, or greener fields, or gentler waters than our own? Must you place the other life far off, so that the translated look through almost infinite spaces to us? Or do you think that a soul has nothing to do with space, and that far off and near are the same to it? I do not deny that, I do not affirm that. But how is that other life? The Scriptures tell us, in images of the most beautiful things, that it is a most gentle life, — stainless, painless, tearless, — a life where labor wearies not, and rest palls not, — aspiration without pain, and content without sloth. Do souls know each other there, in the house of many mansions, where millions upon millions of those we call the dead, live? Do souls remember the earthly there? Do you think the mother forgets her child? Then she ceases to be mother. Ceasing to be a mother, she would cease to be, which is annihilation; and annihilation itself is blotted out of God. Do the dead look down upon the living and know their ways? Do you think heaven would be beautiful if the mother therein must utterly give up her child on earth through many years? You say the mother is changed in immortality. If so changed, the change would be annihilation. Do you say, if the dead looked down on the world's wrestle and sin, their pain would blot out heaven? Do they not see the end, and the hand of God's salvation working to ends that we cannot see? No friends: we are tired, but they are never tired; we sleep, but they never sleep; we are absent, but they are never absent. In dark rooms, where we cannot see, they see; in stormy days, in sunny days, in happy days, by the hearth, by the altar, by the graveside, they are present, though the storm hurts not, and the grave pains not these blessed immortal ones.

" And the little children? Was not Christ once a little child? And does he not know their wants? Are they never lonely? He giveth his angels charge concerning them. Would they turn to weep for their mothers? Shall not, then, angels comfort them and point them to their mothers? Do they need instruction? Are not the angels teachers? Are they lonely? Is there not much company of the child-like within the gates? ' For of such is the kingdom of heaven.' No, friends! God

guardeth them that are his, better than we can think
or wish.   And when the storm is round our home,
their home is stormless; while we sin, they sin not;
while we wrestle, they wrestle not ; while we weep,
they weep not ; while we waste, they waste not ;
passionless, stainless, sorrowless children in their
beautiful home.   And we give them up, that in his
own time God may lift us up to them. 'And a
little child shall lead them.' "

18

CHAPTER XXIV.

UNDER THE ELMS.

ARTHUR paid his usual visit to the Lawrences after the meeting.   The solemn silence that death brings with it had entered there before him, and the little chair by Mrs. Lawrence's side this Sunday afternoon was vacant.   The recent loss seemed somehow to bring back and magnify all that had been sorrowful in her past, and the new shadow to have deepened the old she had so long without hope allowed to darken her life.   She went back forthwith to the old theme.   " This has been always a fatal month to me," she said ; " this month, thirty years ago, *he* was brought home murdered; and every year something just at this time is sure to happen.   I wish I could always sleep through it and forget.   The flowers are always to be made up into wreaths for somebody, and when they come I say to myself, ' Who next ? '

" I had a dream the other night," she went on, in a half soliloquy, " and it was a very strange one ; and I knew then something was about to happen ; and the dream always comes first.   I thought I was in the meeting-house again, and sat in father's pew, and all those I knew when a child were there, whom I half remembered were dead long ago, and *he* was there again, just as he used to look ; and the same psalms were sung by the young men and women whom I played with as a child ; and I thought the old times had come back again ; and the parson was saying something about our all being dust and ashes, though I could not make out what he meant by that ; and while he was speaking, though it was the morning service, it seemed to become twilight all at once, so that I could hardly see the parson's face, and his voice sunk into a whisper, though it still went on about dust and ashes. And I saw that all over the house they were skeletons that sat in the pews ; and they were skeletons in the singing-seats, who had sung the psalms just now, and skeletons in the pew with me, though somehow they each had something of their human looks about them. And in the pulpit the parson's skeleton arms were stretched out as if giving the blessing, and he was whispering something, as though to dismiss the people. Then they all rose up, though I could not stir, to go out. And I heard the bones rattling together in the pews, and in the aisles, as they went on past me in the twilight, as though they were all rushing somewhere in great haste ; and I could still hear somebody whispering, ' Dust and ashes ! ' until they had all gone out and left me in the church alone. And I could not move or speak, though I seemed to sit there as through days and years, and though I felt that the dust had fallen an inch deep, over all the pews and on the pulpit-cushions; and that the rot was eating down and into everything, and the beams overhead were falling slowly out; and the meeting-house had rents in its sides, and was crumbling piecemeal into ruins. But I could not leave it, until at last I knew I was to be buried under the dust where I sat, and this was to be my grave, and I was not to go out with the rest. And then Agnes here woke me, and said, I had been sobbing in my sleep. Ever since, I have known that something evil was going to happen."

It seemed strange, no doubt, to Mrs. Lawrence that she should be troubled so with such dreams as these. Dreaming or waking, the thoughts of our hearts that follow us so long are always the penalties, or the prizes for our attitude towards God's dealings with us. The old shadow that had fallen into Mrs. Lawrence's life was meant of God to have been like the clouds under which the flowers grow,—fleeting; but she had held it firmly overhead in spite of Him, and her life withered. O women, who hold to your hearts the cloud of a great sorrow, and will not let it go as God wills,—under God's clouds, that move across the sky and vanish, the beautiful flowers of life grow, but under the cloud kept over you by wilful or faithless hearts, — the desert. That is not Fate, nor God, — it is yourselves.

Agnes took the child's loss as Fate, to be received

and borne with fortitude. She saw neither the hand behind the cloud, nor the heart that moved the hand to be that infinite Love which merited from His creature, not fortitude, but the gentle acceptance of a willing soul. Arthur perceived only the child was dead in a solemn mystery that saddened his friend at the Parsonage. It was only the cloud he saw. When one sees only the clouds, the heavens are only a surging, billowy, unplanned waste, though above be the infinite deeps of blue, and the eternal shining of the stars. So is it that often God's providence, which has but one immutable lesson of peace, is turned about by our hearts to mean many other things.

Arthur went away early that evening from his friend's with the sense of a new burden resting on him. Perhaps it was Mrs. Lawrence's ghostly conversation that had made him gloomy. Even Agnes, that night, seemed to lack something. He was certainly in his inmost soul poor and needy. The rest he did not understand. The way home led by the graveyard, and he halted by the gate a moment to look over among the graves, where there was sleep without dreams. Over him and on either side of him stood two elms which from time almost immemorial had kept guard at the portals of this God's Acre where the Sandowners slept. And he looked up through the branches that were towering aloft with the aspiration of the elms, to the silver stars that shone through their rustling leaves.   How many have passed under those elms, he thought, asleep or in life! How many tears they have seen; how many sobs they have heard! In winter under the snow, in summer under the flowers, men are laid almost in their shadow; and their roots are fed on the ashes that waste below — life out of death! A new grave this week in the ground, and a new summer for the elms. Shall it be always thus, he thought. And the stars through the leaves should have taught him "always thus." Thus are we always made immortal.

Arthur's revery was broken by a sound from among the graves. It seemed as if some one had struck his foot sharply against a headstone, or fallen. As Arthur looked, he saw the form of a man just disappearing in the darkness towards the spot where the child was laid. He remembered that, once there, the form must disclose itself against the evening sky. He watched until he saw the form again as it moved straight thither and disappeared. Something told Arthur that in the darkness one was kneeling down in prayer. He waited over a half-hour under the elms for the return. A half-hour later he saw the form passing silently among the tombs towards the Parsonage. The walk revealed it. It was Mr. Leverick!

CHAPTER XXV.

AIR CASTLES.

Tous les riens immenses d'un amour naissant.

O EVERLASTING, holy mystery of Love; dream, prophecy, aspiration unto God through the Beloved; crowned queen and stainless child in Thy regality and purity! We call Thee Love, and Thou art — Love. Here Thou art forever the ineffable. Yesterday ten thousand hearts, kindled of Thee, rose into the new beatitude; to-day they are but ashes. To-day ten thousand hearts beat with the new life from Thee, and to-morrow — ashes. And again beyond to-morrows Thou makest in hearts the same old melody, and archest above them the same old heavens without a cloud to hide the serenely shining stars, and scatterest around them the same old spring of the unfading flowers, and repeatest the same old legend of happy lives, as though in Thy sunny realm there had been never night nor winter, and men could neither change nor die! The ancients fancied Thee a child forever young. They should have made Thee a garland, Love, of asphodel. Thou art immortal!

Thou bringest us fairy gifts, and we are happy;

Thou makest new heavens and a new earth, and we possess them; Thou buildest us fairy palaces out of the morning clouds, and we dwell therein with peace; Thou callest us out into the arena, and we wrestle in Thy great championing for masteries, and lay our prizes down at Thy feet; we follow Thee, and the fire burns not, and the stain reaches not, for Thou art a child in innocence, and makest us of Thy pure kingdom; and though we forget, and sorrow, and sin, and age, Thou art the same. Thine is the one holy dream of manhood and of womanhood. Pure angel of the best in us, for this receive our thanks!

Arthur Bassett loved Agnes Lawrence: that is the present conclusion of rambles in the fields, and reading Æschylus. How he had come to love her, he could not have answered himself or you had he been asked. The stream that had borne him down to fairy-land had no ripple nor eddy in it from which he could have remarked the sunny, bewildering voyage he had just taken. There is no Why? in love. Can one say why matter has weight or suns light? God made them so! Why does a man love? God made him so. There is no other answer known to our philosophies than that. To Arthur his love was the revelation of new heavens and a new earth. The old eternal legend had been read again by him, and the new life began. He, too. had learned what that saying means, "Transfigured and glorified by love." It was sufficient for him to breathe and live in the new sunlight, asking nothing more. A new beauty was on the flowers, a new voice was in the trees, a new meaning was writ upon the land and sky. It was new to him; but to the hearts who throughout time had once known the sunlight and heard the voice, it was very, very old. Is not our angel crowned with asphodel?

Arthur's passion had reached down to the fountains of his life and unsealed them. The new waters that flowed forth into the world about him were pure and clear. The angel that had knocked at his heart and entered in had built a new throne there, and a queen sat on it. Henceforth she ruled there with a benign sceptre that appointed him to new and beautiful offices of life. What was earthly and low-born fled away; only what was fit for her remained. What right there had she? One could not say. And yet she ruled there as unquestioned as though her dynasty had been older than Time. Self was annihilated. Henceforth he lived the ever broadening, all-embracing life of those who love. Agnes Lawrence had called him out and on to a man's work and wrestle. Henceforth he thought it is mine to be worthy and bring beautiful gifts of a heroic life to her. I must be worthy of her; and she is a queen: she must have a queen's gifts. Did not the ancients guess sublimely that Eros or Love built the universe? And Love builds again the most beautiful universe for all true souls.

One could not well overstate the influence of Arthur's passion on him. It made him first of all religious. In Agnes Lawrence he loved the Eternal. And his love for a young girl was leading him, unconsciously perhaps, but surely, nearer to Him out of whose heart all love flows. He said his prayers again as a little child; only a new angel stood by him when he knelt, and a new name was lifted silently on the holy wings of the supplication, and he felt a new tenderness towards all. True, what seemed frivolities and even littlenesses lay on the outside of Arthur's sentiment. Trifles with her were very grave affairs. Things light in others, in her would have demanded serious balancings and questionings. He lost his old zest for argument with her. Disagreements pained him. The happiness of being with her sufficed him. There was rest enough for him in that. Whatever seemed to separate them, though but a word, was full of pain. The reason is plain enough. He had narrowed the universe to her. Apart from her, and there was nothing left. He loved her then? Not her, but rather a beautiful vision that he had made of her, which had neither stain nor lack in it. He had lifted her among the immortals. Call it delirium, or what one may, it was still real to him; and he dreamed that one beautiful dream, in that one stainless day, given us mortals, which sometimes moves on to a most holy fulfilment, and sometimes ends with the night winds that blow across the ashes on the altar where the fire had been, and left henceforth the world chill for us, but which is never quite lost out of the most inconstant heart. What did Arthur dream in the sunny days that followed the revelation in Agnes Lawrence? You who have dreamed like him in the sunny days of the years long vanished, know well enough. The others have no claim to know. Shut the temple; conceal the mysteries. Let the profane stand afar off from the holy portals!

How did the divinity herself receive the homage? Did she ever plainly ask herself the meaning? Had she guessed the new life in the young man who read to her out of the old books? Did a true woman ever altogether miss the truth? Did she feel the new power given her? Did Arthur seem to her abject in the silent submission and reverence that he gave her? That thought, at least, let her and every woman dismiss forever. In love, it is the crowned heart that bows the lowest. If Dante, of all mortals, bowed lowest in his love for Beatrice, it was because woman had never so royal lover. Imperial passion, imperial reverence Dante's was, for his diadem was kinglier than any Charlemagne's. Was it in Agnes' heart to despise the homage? Oh, women, whose right it is to choose, choose as you will, but know, the whitest offering this side the hand of God is always a true man's love!

CHAPTER XXVI.

THE HANDWRITING.

A RAINY week followed the Sunday when Mr. Leverick preached from his pulpit on immortality. A damp gray week of moving clouds, broken in upon at long intervals by a momentary sunshine, soon overcome of clouds again, and wet days sinking into still more dreary nights ; rain soaking the curt house-mosses on the roof, and running down the water-ways, and slowly dropping in great drops with a sullen, constant patter from the eaves of the old mansion ; rain falling down upon the moist ground from the green leaves of the elms around the house which presented a gloomy silence in the dank mist that covered all, — rain everywhere.

The rain shut Arthur up at home. Despite the books in the library and Agnes Lawrence, time hung heavy on his hands. He made the tour of the house again. The fascination of the garret so far overcame him as to cause him to spend a couple of hours there one morning, when he in this wise fell upon a discovery. In his leisure rambles he remarked again, that on one side of the stack of chimneys a wood panelling had been built up into what might possibly be a room. There was no appearance of a door, however, and Arthur had heretofore passed it by. To-day an impulse, or something else, made him halt as he came that way, and examine more carefully the premises. He struck the panels with his hand. They gave out a hollow sound. He searched over the surface in the cross light that came through the little square garret-windows. His hand, by accident as it were, or good luck, found a keyhole so smoothly cut in the partition that he had not before observed it. There must be a room inside.

The door, however, resisted all attempts to open it. He went down into the kitchen for an axe to force it. It appeared that Cloe herself had never known of this room, or had forgotten it. " What for the axe ? " she said, as Arthur came back past her with that implement.

" To break open a room in the garret, Cloe."

" Deed, Massa Arthur, there 's no room there as sure as I'm alive, never since I knowed nothing, least aways."

" Come and see for yourself, then," he said ; and the old crone followed him slowly up-stairs. The door yielded to the axe. It was utter darkness inside. Arthur went cautiously in a little ; there was certainly a floor under his feet ; he reached round him with his hands in the darkness, and touched nothing. It was certainly a chamber of good size ; and that was all he could make out. He came out again. " Bring a light, Cloe," he said ; and Cloe went waddling down-stairs after a light.

"Lord a marcy," she said, as she came back, and saw the open door of what was a good-sized room under the caves. "The debil 's made that, sartin. I never know'd that afor, tho' I'se allus been on the farm. Curus, sartin that is."

"You may go down now," said Arthur, as he took the light from her and went in.

It was a queer place, certainly, and could not have been opened for a very long time now. It had a mouldy, earthy smell like a crypt or vault long out of use; not even cobwebs in its corners, nor sign of any living thing there; and the walls were damp and discolored with the rain that had crept through the roof. It was a chamber slightly arched and finished with considerable care, and had evidently been used by several persons for very diverse purposes, as appeared from the medley of things collected there. It might have been at first intended as a hiding-place from the Indians, in the early bloody border-warfare between the whites and savages; or as a place for concealed arms in the days just before the Revolution. And Arthur's researches afterwards led him to both conclusions.

There were shelves with rows of vials on them, half full of something that had been liquids, but was now only dry dust. There were also quaint old implements and green glass wares, that looked like crucibles and retorts extemporized by some old dabbler in sciences, gracious or sinister, which Arthur afterward supposed to have belonged to some one bent on solving the mysteries of alchemy, and the Black Art even. At the right was a chest of drawers, and in them he found what had once been new clothing, but eaten away now by moths and mice; and the kit of some old seafarer, with its tarred twine and sheath-knife, and what was once a ship's log, and bills of invoice and of sale to foreign ports in some ancient colonial venture; and there were ship's clearances, with the king's broad seal to them, and many other tokens of their owner's calling, laid away ever since their owner had given them up, when he went on his last voyage, in through the gate, under the two elms by the town yonder.

There was one drawer locked, which resisted Arthur's curiosity. The axe broke it. It was filled with old papers, thrown in there in great confusion, as though some one had been hurried in his last disposition of them, and was suddenly called away. Arthur, spreading them on the floor, by the light of his candle examined their contents. There were many things which had long ago lost all interest to any one, even to the men who owned them, and were laid back again in the old confusion. But Arthur soon fell upon something of quite another sort, — writ on stray sheets of paper that seemed to be parts of a connected narrative, and to treat of vastly more human matters; and, as he read some of them, he speedily became much interested in the search. At the very bottom of the drawer he came upon a package that appeared to have been laid there with more than ordinary care, and tied with what was now a faded ribbon. It seemed to be an older portion of the same narrative he had fallen on among the loose papers. He gathered these all together and hastily examined them. He could gain from the writings themselves no clue to their authorship. They seemed to have a certain unity of plan, and yet there were wide intervals of time, as it seemed, in the story, and the strangest things were jumbled confusedly together. The writer, or writers, if there were more than one, seemed anxious to preserve a strict incognito, and to have succeeded. There was, indeed, a certain impersonal air about the whole transaction, that afterwards, on more lengthy deliberation, increased Arthur's uncertainty still further. The manuscript itself was made up of paper of different sizes and years; some with its watermark of old English manufacture of long ago still on it, and yellow and stained with age. And much had evidently been lost.

The handwriting was also another riddle. It had a certain unity about it, if carefully examined, and yet, at first sight, it seemed to have been written by at least half a dozen different persons. The larger, and evidently the older portions are in one style: a plain, sharp, angular, precise, positive, but cramped hand, as of an old person, and bears a striking resemblance to the penmanship of a late celebrated New-England statesman, who won the highest honors of the state. But the rest seemed to have been written out, as has been said, by several hands, and yet the writing bore certain marks of having been made by one scribe, but one scribe, perhaps, in several very devious mental moods. Some persons who have examined the later portions of this MSS. have decided it to have been penned by one and the same person, in different states of mind, though they too have confessed to a certain sense of impersonality, before mentioned, that pervades the earlier parts especially ; and a few have gone so far as to point out just where the penman had a mind perturbed by some strong passion, and have named parts that one had written in anger, or in pain, or in sadness, or in weariness, and also traces of more genial moods. Certain it is that in its pages there is dash and haste, there is youth and age, and many other things, if the handwriting itself reveals anything accurately. The editor of this narrative has been promised speedily a facsimile of several representative passages in this important document, which he will publish. Then a careful public will judge this vexed question for itself.

Arthur himself was so absorbed in the study of these papers, that he forgot everything else for them, until the candle, quivering and flickering in its socket, reminded him that he had been at least a couple of hours at work. He gathered together the papers of the quaint handwriting, and went down-stairs.

CHAPTER XXVII.

AUTOBIOGRAPHY.

THE editor of Arthur's MSS. hastens to confess two things to the reader: first, that the MSS. itself came very legitimately into his hands some time ago, how, he does not feel called upon to say; next, that he has bodily suppressed many parts of it as irrelevant to matters at present in hand, and more, because it is best that the thing narrated should quietly perish, as the actors have perished into thin dust and ashes. There were certain griefs and scandals of long ago, that concern nobody now, which he has at present under lock and key, not quite certain but that he ought to consign them to the fire immediately, as the only proper disposition of such wares. Certain hints and reflections upon matters which he supposes relate to the practice of the Black Art, he has, for like reasons, wholly suppressed. The most painful paper of all, however, he conceives to have been written shortly after the delusion of New-England witchcraft had come to an end among the Puritans hereabouts, wherein appears, if the statements be not altogether prejudiced, which the editor is not prepared to deny, a very sad spectacle of private animosities and family feuds, at the bottom of foul persecutions that cost several innocent persons, and women amongst them, their lives. The prime actors themselves have long since been sent up to God for judgment, and the editor is not disposed to tempt any to reopen the question of His equity again. He would also further premise, that whatsoever brief headings appear in the following excerpts are his own, though he will not affirm their appropriateness to the subject-matter of the MSS., since he himself is by no means sure that he quite grasps the main drift of the writing, if indeed it had any, and that he offers his reader only those parts which quite obscurely, but, as it seems to him, truly, have reference more or less remote to several persons who are presented in this book for judgment.

The first excerpt which he presents the reader he has called " Life," though upon consultation with Arthur Bassett, some time since, the latter, for whose opinion he has a high respect, inclined to the heading, " Long Ago." It is written in the angular, cramped handwriting before mentioned, and, without date or name, begins abruptly thus : —

" What a strange thing life is ! It has not changed its essence even in the wilderness, only its accidents. How it begins and how it ends, is alike mystery. I myself have no knowledge of when or how I came here, nor how I can ever pass off from here, though I have a sense of years, and time alters everything, even our profoundest emotions. I have busied myself with watching life for a long time now, and I hardly know whether to laugh at it or weep with it. In the wilderness here what strange things have come to me. I have seen these green fields around, when they were black wastes fretted with the black stumps, out of the fire that smoothed, after the axe had levelled the old woods, and then the corn out of the blackness. How eagerly, long ago, did the emigrants husband the yellow ears, that stood between them and famine, when their other storehouses were three thousand miles away, across seas; and what fear in the house when the frost came too early and ate away the corn! They have plenty now, and forget how close for many years the fathers stood, every year, to gaunt famine in the wilderness: only God in the land between them and that. I have seen the Indians with their squaws and children filing down past here to the fishing-grounds, looking gloomily on the black cornfields where the oaks stood, and scowling at the white children in the porch yonder. I have known the time when, up among the hills, a black smoke told of where the tomahawk and fire were at work; and the mangled carcasses of whole households were brought down afterwards, and laid, without memorial, in the graveyard yonder. I have seen the time when the windows were nailed and boarded, and the doors barred below stairs, while white faces gathered around him who offered the evening prayers in a low voice, as though, any moment, the savage yell might break in upon them, and the fire-arrows flame out on the dry roof; when, for weeks, they slept with matchlock by the pillow, and every morning went to the house-top to reconnoitre before the good man opened the house-door below. And I have seen men go out pale and grim to the woods, and come back sometimes pale and faint, and sometimes with a graver look, as though there had been cruel work in under the old woods as indeed there had been, back to their prayers again, and the silent, steady, Puritan life of Gospellers. Must everything be built on sweat and blood? The quiet life here-abouts is certainly built on that. New England had its fire-baptism, and the flame was very sharp."

.   .   .   .

" All that changed long ago. What jollity in corn harvest! What comfort in the long winter nights, when all came around the huge fireplace, and the burning logs in it; and the women knitted, and the young men made ox-yokes and axe-handles, by the bright light, or went down cellar after cider and apples with a lighted pine knot, flaming and guttering with its black smoke; while the elders told of the Indian warfare, and how it fared with them in dear old England, when they were children. Alas! there were many hearts that fell away to ashes in the wilderness, that remembered till death the swelling Kentish hills, and the cottages among them sheltered under their orchards from the stormy sea that had beaten and foamed so long against the chalk cliffs, at Dover and at Deal. Self banished, that a nation might people a continent. When all history is writ, should one call life comedy or tragedy? It may be both."

. . . .

" One sometimes thinks life a masquerade. Are all men by nature actors in a private way of their own? They are always personating, sounding through their masques, something to some one ; but the men themselves, who penetrates to them? It is my good fortune, more than most, to have done that. I have known many intimately. They do not think it worth their while to keep up appearances with me. Men and women are as far apart as heaven and earth. I prefer the women. They have more courage than men, and courage I like. Men run away from their sorrow. Women take it bravely. Womanhood is endurance from cradle to grave. Manhood, escape. I fancy self-contained people. Womanhood, I say, is silence ; though you may laugh at that, professing to know the world. I tell you I have known many women here, and seen their hearts break with their lips shut. That which belongs to everybody, women are talkative enough about, but what is hers as woman, never. I told you I had seen several things in my time. I have seen two young girls (and I thought them beautiful) lie in one another's arms through a long night, and neither slept for the same love they two had for one, a matter of life and death to both, each knowing that of the other, and in the morning kiss as friends and go down the hall-stairs together, without a word of that between them. I did not laugh that morning. I wished well to both. Why not?"

. . . .

" Life is a medley. Has it any order in it? Sometimes I think I catch glimpses of an order in it more iron than any fate. And straightway its confusion and litter come back again. What a strange jumble have I seen hereabouts. From the same nail hung the shroud and the robe of marriage ; perhaps both meant marriage. Let the parsons settle that, it is not my matter. I have seen many little children grow up. I heard their first cry ; I heard their last sigh. And between the two were — Well, never mind. I am tired thinking of this old riddle they call life. It should matter not a nail to me, and yet something draws me back again to it. Nonsense ! If Master John's son chooses to make a wedding in the very room where almost yesterday Master John himself lay in the coffin, what is that to me ? Nothing. It is only a little quaint to me, who saw both. I am only a spectator at the play. Let the actors look to their parts."

. . . .

CHAPTER XXVIII.

LIBERTY AND LOVE *vs.* LIBERTY.

"As public conflagrations do not always begin in public buildings, but are caused more frequently by some lamp neglected in a private house, so in the administration of states the flame of sedition does not always rise from political differences, but from private dissensions, which, running through a long chain of connections, at length affect the whole body of the people." — PLUTARCH.

THE excerpts which follow are also in the hand-writing of the earlier MSS. One notices and must pardon a dash of real Toryism in the rather confused vaticinations of the unknown writer, who seems to have fallen into some excitement therein.

"There is a new uproar in the land, worse than wild Indians or witchcraft! Men talk of being free. I do not see that they are not free. Men damn themselves by bandying words they do not understand. Words have cut many a man's throat, and will cut many a nation's throat before the panto-mime is over. When they become free, what then? There is a new regime hereabouts. The king's arms have gone from the walls, and yester-day his portrait was hid under the stairs, and not a

Bassett stirred in his grave, in the graveyard yonder. I miss many of the old comers here. I suppose they have quarrelled over these accursed politics, perhaps. They prefer old wine below stairs, why not old friends? I like to take a hand I know the lines of. Then I know there is nothing sinister about it. They pledge new names at table, I see. Who is this Pitt I hear in everybody's mouth? Slaves and fools show which way the wind blows. What if the whirlwind — ?

" They say they will make war on the king. The clamor and the conversation below stairs now mean that. What do all these gatherings from the neighborhood by day and night mean? Even the children sing liberty-songs, and the women wear the new colors. Women and fools, and then — the storm. New letters have come to-day from headquarters, I suppose, and the Squire is after the minute-men. I do not say nay to the king. I have had all my rights from him. Oliver Cromwell is at the bottom of this. I never liked the man. This is the beginning of the end of Puritanism. Will they stop at the king? If they give up the king, what will they find? Anarchy? Men are too fast. The new is very good, but the old is better. A horse you have backed, you know; but a wild ass out of the woods, bah! Patience! Without the king you are out at sea, and what port next? The last port may be Tyre. The prophet Jeremiah tells us what sort of a market Tyre is. Long live what is! I cannot stomach this everlasting 'shall be.' I stick to the king."

  . . . .

" A pleasant scene in the porch this morning! A neighbor came early to the Squire. They had been boys, and played together in the orchard, there. ' We have been friends these fifty years, Squire,' the man said, with a voice that choked, ' let us remain so.' ' No Tory is friend of mine,' answered the Squire. I saw tears in the man's eyes as he went away in silence. Bravo, Liberty! Bravo, Absurdity! The play is comedy to-night. Prepare to laugh. Stop a little. At the fifth act is time enough. Long live the king!"

  . . . .

" I had always a fancy for young Mary Hastings. She and I have been fast friends together ever since she came here as a little girl and played with her dolls in the nursery with our girls. I dare say she never knew my fancy for her ; for one like me even has fancies they can't well help. I think I must give up Mary ; only it is so much the fashion nowadays ; and I don't like the mode.

" There was a scene in the parlor down-stairs to-night. I hope it will be the last in Bassett House. Mary Hastings had a hand in it. Young Wareham came over here this evening, and asked for Mary. All her folks were at tea here, talking politics as usual. Everybody stared at one another,

when Cloe said, ' Massa Wareham wants Miss
Mary.' What did he want here ? This is a Whig
house, at least the folks are, and he a Tory. Nobody
guessed but I. I had private information from
several sources. I always knew he was in love with
Mary. He is a brave, dashing fellow, the strongest
wrestler hereabouts, and sticks to the king like a
true Englishman. His blood has n't grown thin in
these parts, or else he would have been a Whig.

" I heard the conversation. Why ? I could not
help it. I wish I could. I would never hear dis-
agreeable things, if I could help it. It is my lot to
always hear. ' Do you treat me coolly like the
rest, Mary ? ' he said, as she came in with a courtesy
and a ' good evening, Mr. Wareham.' ' Is it coolly, William Wareham ? I did not know it.' ' You
think it strange that I come here, perhaps, and ask
for you, Mary ?' ' Yes.' ' Well, other people
do. I see it in everybody's face when I come
here, and yet I have been as a brother to the young
men of this house, and they know who has broken
our friendship. Not I. I have come to you, because I cannot endure this any longer. These are
wretched times, and cannot last; better or worse
they must be. I cannot bear this coolness between
friends. Our families have always been, before
these politics, the best of friends ; now they are
something else. I have lost most of my old com-
panions. Why ? Because I chance to defend the
king. I have always thought one thing. Mary

Hastings will not go with the rest. We have been children, and played together; we have been friends as young folks together, and she, at least, knows I am not a coward, nor a villain, though I am not a Whig. The times will not come between us two.'

" Has Mary Hastings not one word to say to this? I wonder she chooses to harass the young man with that silence. Not one word; she, then, has altered too.

" William Wareham, if you have anything to say, or do, go on.

" ' Mary Hastings,' the young man said, with increased excitement, ' I have come here to say one thing to you. I did not mean to say it for a long time yet; but suspense, and these times, I cannot endure. I will know the worst. I love you; I have always loved you; I loved you from a child, when we played together, and I love you now, when these times are breaking away my life from every one. I turn to you. You are good, you are kind; you do not despise me because I am a loyalist. You can understand what I cannot quite say.'

" There is no answer from the young girl with the white face now, sitting opposite him.

" ' I will give up everything for you, but what you would not have me give, — my honor. Home, friends, everything. I will go to the Provinces, or England, if you choose, and make a home for you,

and a name also. I am not a pauper, as you know.
And I have brains. Everything but the king.
My family have been loyal for five hundred years
at least, and never lifted a hand against the crown.
The crown has bestowed favors on them. Why
should we change now? They must preserve their
traditions. If I give up the king, whom shall I
honor? Good men are on the other side; but the
men who will rule in revolution are never the best.
Remember the revolution when King Charles died.
No, Mary: the people around you tell you the king
is a tyrant, and we must resist him, and you,
because you are a woman, and love justice, believe
it. Mary, there is another side, that men will see
after their passions cool. They may be very slow
to see it; but time will prove it. Everything but
the king I will give up for you. And I will give
my life to you, only to call you wife.'

"Will Mary Hastings speak now? I think, yes.
I always knew Mary had fire enough when a thing
struck her heart a blow. The white lips say slowly,
in a low, firm voice, —

"'Arthur Wareham, this can never be.'

"'You would have never loved me, whatever I
might have been,' he answered, sharply.

"'I do not say that at all. I do not know; but
as you are, never. You are for the king. I do not
blame you for that. I pity. I am not. My father's family are not. My brothers are going out to
the army, to give their lives against the king. You
say truly, these times have separated you and

yours from your old friends.   I am only a woman.
Which side would you have me take?   Against my
friends, against father and mother and brother?
I cannot leave them.   I do not hate the king.   But
I love liberty, and the men who die for it.   I may
wish these times otherwise.   I have no control over
them.   I accept what comes of them.   They have
separated us two.   We have been friends, — let us
remain so, though we never meet again.   For the
rest, as you wish, — Never!'

"I said, I do not like some words.   I hate that
word *never* as I hate the grave and the mould and
the dust.   It has no mercy.   It is too long.   Mary
Hastings, I hoped better things of you.   I forgot:
Eve was your mother."

.   .   .   .

"I said, or wished to say, I did not like scenes.
What is the use of disagreeables?   I have taken up
a strong liking for Arthur Wareham.   I have
a secret of his in my keeping.   I saw him pick up
a liberty rosette on the door-steps, when Mary
Hastings had closed the hall-door behind him, as he
went away with a reverent adieu to Mary.   What
did he want with it?   Did Mary miss it from her
bosom?   I know she never found it.   She went
back to the family gathering in the dining-room,
and finished her tea.   There were no questions
asked.   Her face was very pale.   And William
Wareham?   I have seen many men go out from
Bassett House on several errands.   Never one I
pitied more than him."

CHAPTER XXIX.

DEATH IN LIFE.

THE reader finds here a last instalment of the
MSS. The editor judges it to be altogether a later
writing, with a new hand on the pen. The penmanship itself shows a perturbed mind. It has
haste, passion, and several other things in it.
Some have pronounced the chirography that of a
man in years. Parts, the reader will notice by the
periods, are wanting in the opening and at the end.

.   .   .   .

"I cannot live much longer with this cursed
weight bearing me down. It is strange I have
lived so long. Some men do not seem to know how
to die. I am one of them. I sometimes fear I am
growing too old to learn. I suppose every man
must have something to fret him. Every man I
ever knew wore a boot that pinched somewhere;
but not pain like mine. I curse the world sometimes. That is a coward's business, though I am in
a different mood to-day. I do not intend to whine,
however: only to set down what this agony of mine
is, that somebody one day, when it is over, may read
and pity, not me, but the world that judges me.

" The pain is, that I should have been, and might have been, something very otherwise than what I am. I say, ' It might have been,' a hundred times a day. I am something else than — what I do not like to think. This cursed masque over my heart, it is nailed on it. I did not wish it. It was nailed on me long ago; and my heart is almost perished under it. Thank God, not all of it. I am an outcast. I should have been, and meant to be, as other men are, honorable, honored; and be buried, as other men are, with their kinfolk. My heraldry is smouched with blood; and my carcass must have a dog's grave, perhaps among the paupers. I should have had children come about me, and call me father, as other men have. And the children run away from me. I never had any to call son. The poor devils that starve in their holes call over that name as carelessly as though it meant nothing. But I was not always poor, and did not always live in a hole.

" The thing I did, I did it in hot blood, as every man would have done. I murdered no one. I did not hate the man; but he smote in on my very heart, and the hot blood fired my brain. It was a fair wrestle. He lost: and I ? I won, — what they do not always find down in the pit yonder. One blow — I did not mean it, and I would have recalled it; and for that I am this wreck. I am an outlaw. There is some wrong somewhere, besides in me. If the whole world says nay, I say yea. I wished to be something else, and strove for it, and I am this. They wronged me at the start. They tabooed me as though I had been a mad dog, from the start. That maddened me. Why was I a dog? Because I stood by my colors. They had been my fathers' colors for a thousand years, and I would have no others. Was that like a dog? Curse the fellows. They stamp down a man in the dust, and then grumble if he grows dirty. The trampled-on are seldom friendly.

" I took arms against them, I know. I had the king's commission though. I gave them trouble; they had troubled me. So far we were equals. But they began by damning me; and I could only kill, which was much less. They told it in their newspapers how I killed in cold blood. One of their lies. I never killed but in fair fight; and my blood was always hot enough. I know it was a little rough on the borders often; and I had Indians sometimes. But war is savage all the way through. I kept these savages from scalping. When they were out of sight — I do not know. I do not like blood, and never did. But they, they had no mercy for me. They destroyed everything. The answer was, You are a Tory! The scalping-knife would have been mercy to what they have used upon me. Well; they and theirs will write history, and we — are Tories."

.   .   .   .

"I am bad enough, but not so bad as they paint. If I were, I should not suffer so. The worst have seldom heart-pain. On the battle-field the mark of a mortal wound is absence of pain. I sometimes thank God for agony. It assures me I am not a brute.

"The worst is, I am so near to her, and yet so far away from her. And she thinks of me like the rest. No doubt I have done a great wrong to her, but I did not mean it. And she, thank God, does not know it all. I have spared many, for her sake, whom I might have sent to their graves. Would she have done as much as I, had she known as I? I have forgot happiness, not her. There is some spot in my heart where I keep her likeness. The rest is ashes.

"If I were God I would make a new revelation. I would say to men, 'Judge no man; for you are men. Leave that to me.' I believe, however, that somewhere that is revealed already. Then men have misprinted their Bibles."

 . . . .

CHAPTER XXX.

CRANBERRIES.

SANDOWNE had one holiday of its own. It was called "Cranberry day." Its origin was on this wise. The neck or cape of land that stretched out into the sea, northwardly from Sandowne, had belonged in olden times to the Indians, that is, to nobody, and had in due time, whether in due or undue ways, one cannot say, come to be the common property of the town. On this property, among its sand-hills, were almost innumerable patches and snatches of cranberry meadow, where long ago the Indians and the birds had gathered the berries at will. With true Puritan thrift and order, one day had been set apart in the Fall, when every householder in Sandowne, with his household, might gather these berries on the Neck, free of any charge. This was "Cranberry day." It had long since come to be a holiday. It was foretold by the marvellous bakings and brewings of the Sandowne matrons, who at this season, for several days beforehand, were thus accustomed to spend themselves in preparations for the frolic. It was a day anxiously anticipated for a long while by the younger members of the borough, and had been from time immemorial, so to speak, a day of jollity, frolic, and good-humor. It was a feast-day that had occasioned much good-fellowship among the townsfolk, and, to the certain knowledge of persons curious in such matters, more than several weddings. It was in fact the one pronounced holiday in the Sandowne calendar.

The cranberry meadows on the Neck were accessible by water. The town, at such times, stowed itself away in innumerable boats and scows and dingeys, that composed the Sandowne fleet of all sorts. It was, therefore, a motley crowd that assembled itself at the town-wharf, where the boats were moored on the " Cranberry day," whose incidents form an integral part of our story. The tidy, well-habited folks were there, as they are in every proper place. And " the scraggy folks " turned out in force. They furnished the grotesque element in the picture.

" The scraggy folks " are well known to the careful student of any New-England town, and merit a moment's notice. They are mortals of retiring habits, who have hid themselves all their lifetime away from the common life and progress of the age. They have grown distempered with a certain ineffable sluggishness of intellect and feeling, that antedates them in all essentials of a true New-England citizenship a couple of centuries or more. They are queer people, living among the hills, who

creep down sometimes to have a taste of human society, and then go back again to their lairs in silence.
People must inquire for such mainly in the tax-book,
and among the gravestones. Very often these folks
have grown distorted with huge excrescences on their
personality, as warty trees in the woods are, and
are "knotty sticks of timber," the townsfolk tell
you. They shun the meeting-house: that is too
public and outside their line of business, and require
the minister only at burials and at weddings. They
pay perennial visits to the village grocery, with a
timid or a very loud air, as it may chance, as one of
the very few pilgrimages they ever make on earth.
They swarm at town-meetings, where for an hour
their vote gives them a political importance, which
ends with the closing of the polls. They are great
on funerals, if one of their class is buried; when they
gather themselves outside the house, a grave, rumi-
nating crowd, in very conservative coats that seem
for a score of years or more to have known no
development, like their wearers' minds, and everything about them wears a finished look, as though
the whole man had stopped short in every sort of
progress. They have their politics not writ in
any book; their religion, maybe, not writ in any
catechism; are grumblers against society often, and
serve as cog-wheels upon the general march of mind,
these scraggy folk. The country parson knows
them well. They give him occasion. He is not
their favorite.

These scraggy folk mustered in force on "Cranberry day," and gave a picturesque and ancient air to the crowd assembled at the wharf. They were armed with pails and firkins, of every age and pattern, and the kitchen-furniture of Sandowne seemed to have emptied itself into the boats. The Sandowne dogs and children had also a holiday, and were well represented among the noisy, good-natured medley of men and women that bestowed themselves with an indefinite amount of joking and disorder on board the boats that were putting off for the Neck. Arthur and Agnes, with the minister, went with Sam, who garnished himself to-day with Mrs. Sam, and held an appointment from the town as Cranberry warden and overseer of the festival. On such occasions the Sandowne parsons had always accompanied their flock, from the old times when the entertainment opened with prayer, and Mr. Leverick only followed custom.

It was a very pleasant sail to-day on the blue water, for the happy multitude, that shouted to one another from the boats, and trimmed the sails, and laughed and frolicked, and told stories, and cracked their homely jokes, and sailed over to the Neck. It was a pleasant jaunt across the beech-sands to the sheltered spots among the sand-hills, where the crowd settled down among the crimson berries to gather them.

It was a busy overseer that Sam Jones made, with his assistants, in allotting to every party their place, and keeping up some sort of order in the picking. It was a happy company that gathered and chatted in the yellow autumn sunlight, a little noisy, maybe, some a trifle rough, but this time intent on frolicking. It was a pleasant dinner that they ate at mid-day, under the bushes: family groups, grandsire, sons and grandson, with the good-wife to purvey the Sandowne cookery to her hungry family. Even the dogs, who lay waiting among the beech-grass for their morsel, seemed happy. One remarked how some, who had nursed their wrath a year's time against a neighbor, thawed out to-day under the general good-humor, and chatted again as friends; and how a thousand devices, traits and shades of character displayed themselves in the passing festival in a way very instructing and very salutary to the observer; and the ineffable happiness of the country swains, picking the berries alongside their favorites, or strolling with them among the sand-hills in a silent, aimless ramble, that somehow very likely one day brought the two lovers to the parson's, was also noticeable. The minister had entered into the innocent sports of his parishioners in his quiet way, and had the good things of a score of dinners pressed upon him, and gave a kind word to all. Arthur and Agnes had disarmed the democratic jealousies of the townsfolk by picking cranberries with the rest. Not "mighty stuck up, anyhow," was the reward they received from the Sandowners. "Mighty thick together,"

said the groups to Mrs. Sam. " When will it be ? "
For once that lady was non-committal. " Don't
know," said Mrs. Sam. " I 'm afraid to ask him."

It was a little world, mimicking the great outside
world, that disported itself to-day among the sand-
hills of the Neck. Alas! progress is everywhere.
" Cranberry day " has now for several years been
given up as vulgar. The town rents the Neck to
pay the taxes. And that is progress!

The day was wearing itself out, and the well-tired
pickers were gathering their berries together, to go
home. A sky, threatening rain, hurried them. A
cloud had been for some time gathering in the
north, which the old sea-dogs of the party, after
watching it for some time, took their clay pipes out
of their mouths long enough to say, meant mischief.
The beech was even now growing deserted, and the
boats, with their white sails, were already making
their way home. As Sam Jones was overseer, he
stayed behind to see the rest off; and when he had
sent off the last boat-load, with injunctions to carry
all sail before the weather became rough, and had
left all snug at the Neck, it was apparent to every
one that the storm was close at hand, and night was
fast overtaking them. They must either spend the
night on the Neck, or face it. When Sam's boat
pushed off, the sea already wore a black, angry look,
and the gray storm was rapidly drifting down upon
them, while the white houses of the town looked
out from the answering gloom to leeward, calling

them home. But Sam had a crew of men who had smelt salt-water long ago, and they silently set themselves to trim the boat, looking to see every rope in place, and to windward where the gray mist was driving down. "All taught, Captain, forward," said the man in the bows to Sam at the helm. Sam took a squint at the cloud to windward. "The women-folks had better keep close under the thwarts, afore the rain comes," said Sam, "and keep their shawls over their heads, for it 'll be hard weather for young chickens afore it 's through." And the women, wrapped in their shawls, were stowed away under the lee of the thwarts, Agnes amongst them. "Now, parson," said Sam, who, with Arthur Bassett, was in the stern sheets near Agnes, " keep quiet, and take what comes; for here it is." And, as he spoke, the cloud fell down upon them with rain and sudden darkness; and the mist went drifting over the sea to leeward, shutting out the land ; and the black waves rose higher and higher, capped soon with white foam ; and the boat sprung forward over the sea before the wind, as if, with a consciousness of danger, it were trying to escape from the furies behind. " What sort of a boat have you got," said the minister quietly to Sam, who was keeping the helm steady and the boat close upon the wind. " Capital," said Sam ; " clean, taught, and not a rotten plank in her. I 'd risk going round Cape Horn in her. But that's not the trouble," speaking lower: " I 've got no bearings, and the Rock is ahead." "I know," said the minister, quietly. There was not a sailor on board that did not know that somewhere ahead in the storm that had swept past them, between them and the harbor, lay Dead Man's Rock, where in the old times many a crew had perished in the storm. Even Mrs. Sam, who ruminated on all evils, saw fit to say to the women round her, that the young girl in the graveyard, of whom so much had been said lately, had been wrecked on the Rock, and all knew the danger.

The men came aft to the helm. "Well, Captain, what will you do? Lay to?" "Lay to? It's a pretty kettle of fish we've got to cook, anyhow," said Sam, "but layin' to won't do it. The storm may last a week, and we'll drift ashore in the breakers, or starve long afore then. We've got to run for luck, anyhow." "What's the course," said an old sea-dog, just a little nervously. "I calculate about South-East by South," said Sam. "Do some of you strike a light for a look at the compass, for I don't exactly like to risk my corporation on guessin', and I'm not ready to buy a coffin just now, afore corn-harvest." A man struck a light with the flints, under the gunwale, and looked at the compass. "Two points off your course, Captain," said the man. "Three points northerly then, maybe, 'ill put us by the Rock, countin' for currents settin' inshore. What do you think, neighbors?" "Three points northerly 'll do it, if the guess is good." And they sat down silently to wait for what comes in the storm, as sailors who have seen rough weather always do. The night was intensely black, and one heard nothing but the ceaseless clamor of the sea, maddened of the blinding storm. And the boat plunged on and on into the sea, and rose and fell upon the black waves, and was hastening on — to the Rock, or port? Which? No one could say. "We must be near the Rock, parson," said Sam to the minister: "a few minutes will settle all, and maybe some of us 'll be past prayin' for." The minister looked round him into the storm, but said nothing. He had learned several things from that rock before. All were waiting for what might come. "Down with your helm! Down with your helm! Hard down: we 're close aboard the Rock. Light ahead!" shouted the man in the bows, starting up with a cry that rang over and far beyond the boat into the storm. "Aye, aye;" and the helm went down with a run. The boat came up to the wind, until the sails shook in the wind's eye. "Steady! Don't lose headway; a little off will do it!" shouted the lookout forward. And the boat, caught by the wind, again swept on its course. It was high time for that. Just under the lee, waves were breaking into white foam along the steep sides of Dead Man's Rock. A moment more, and the boat would have been beaten in pieces against its granite. As the boat swept by into the night again, all eyes were riveted upon the rock. On its summit, close to where the waves broke over it, a man was standing, enveloped almost in the mist, swinging lustily what seemed a firebrand or lantern, they could hardly say which, until all had disappeared into the night again. That light had saved them. All felt that, and all breathed freer. "Hard up the helm now!" — "so, Captain;" and the boat went round into the smooth water behind the Point.

It was an anxious crowd of men that waited at the wharf in the rain for the boat as it came in. "Thank God!" broke from several lips as the boat rounded to, and a rope was thrown from it into the crowd. "All right! Pull away!" And the boat swung up to its moorings at the wharf. "Who was over at the Rock with a light for us?" was the first question asked. "Light? we saw no light." "A light on Dead Man's Rock saved us, sure as there's a God in heaven," said the lookout. The crowd stared aghast. It had several theories about the matter, not one of which was right. The company went home through the rain, and Arthur left Agnes at her door. An hour after, he found himself before the comfortable wood fire in the library, watching the red embers, and awaiting supper. And outside, with wail and shriek and the muffled roar of breakers, the angry sea was beating for three days to come upon Dead Man's Rock.

CHAPTER XXXI.

TREEMAN'S COTTAGE.

BILLY TREEMAN, who has appeared in several remarkable aspects in our story, lived up among the hills. On his first appearance in the town he had taken lodgings in the ruins of what had been an Indian hut or hovel, and had kept them ever since. It stood among the scrub oaks that overgrew an Indian graveyard of later times, with a patch of garden behind it, among the oaks; and apparently the old man had repaired it into some sort of comfort. Here he lived by himself, and had no callers. Sometimes he would disappear for weeks together, and rumor had it that at such times he became, in distant parts of the country, a vagabond medicine man or doctor, curing with herbs, and even making pretensions to surgery, in which, it was sometimes said, he had wrought wonderful cures. He came and went so quietly that he was seldom missed, and never welcomed back of any. Only one thing was clear: he seemed to have a strange antipathy to the townsfolk, who, on their part, showered upon him anything but blessings. People shunned his hovel as though a ghost dwelt there and practised incantations.

Mr. Leverick one day, shortly after the events of the "Cranberry day," went up to Treeman's hut. In doing so he went round by the way where the fire had been checked in the Sandowne woods. The reason for this conduct will immediately appear. When he knocked at the door, Treeman opened it. There was a start, and even a flush on the old man's face as he confronted his visitor. Then he flung the door wide open, and said, "Come in." The minister went in. "You are the first person that ever came to see me, parson, so that I have the trouble of only opening the door for myself. Sit down," and he pushed a bench, of an indefinite order of workmanship, towards him, and the minister sat down. It was a narrow room without a floor; and the ceiling was built of black smoky boards, through which at the further end was some sort of trap-door by which its occupant evidently ascended on a rough ladder against the wall to his dormitory. Over the huge fireplace hung a fowling-piece and powder-horn, and the sword which he had worn at the May Search; and in it, on a pile of stones that served for andirons, a fire of brushwood was burning. A few chairs and a table, all made out of the woods around him, comprised its furniture. The old man seated himself opposite the minister, and was evidently waiting for him to explain the object of his visit.

The minister went at once to his business. His instincts told him that was the safest way with the

man before him. " I have brought back," he said,
" this cane, which I found at the fire in the woods.
It is yours, you see. It was you who kindled the
back fire, and saved the town from much loss.
You found my little boy, and brought him back.
The other night you saved our lives at Dead Man's
Rock. I come to you, as one man should come to
another, to thank you for it. I am ready to be
your friend, as you have been mine. It is your
right." The old man interrupted him abruptly.
" Who knows this, or thinks this, besides yourself?"
" No one," said the minister. " You say you thank
me for something you suppose I have done, which
has served somebody. I admit nothing, and you
know nothing. You only suppose. If you are
my friend, keep this matter to yourself; that is the
only way you can do anything for me." " But
why," the minister said, with a half-expostulating
air, " do you wish this so? Why should not the
townsfolk know who it is that has been their bene-
factor, that they too may feel the pleasure that I
do in making some return, — thanks at least." The
old man interrupted him sharply again. " Stop,
parson. I will not have it. Let that go. I mean I
do not want it. I mean no disrespect saying it so
bluntly; but I talk so little, I have forgot how to
talk very long about a thing; and what I mean is,
it would be no pleasure for me to have thanks from
anybody." The minister stopped.

" I can't tell you all about this, parson, between

them and me. They think I am a scarecrow or a beggar, or something worse. Let them go on thinking that. I shall not go on being that. If I am something else, as you think, it is nothing to them. They judge according to their kind. They can give me nothing. I have this hut, and very few wants. I want to be let alone. Every man has his story. I have mine. Those folks in the town there, they and the dead have made mine what it is. What it is, is my matter. Nothing would be gained by making it another's. You have been kind to me, parson, and I thank you for it. I am not indifferent to your good opinion. Our lives are too far apart to ever come any nearer together than they are this moment; for the rest, nothing. Good-bye, parson." The old man went with the minister to the door. There he shook hands with him as a man shakes the hand of his friend. For a moment, Treeman's manner had fallen back into a strange gentleness, and Mr. Leverick, as he went away remembering the expression on Treeman's face, felt that somehow a new life, or a very old life, had come back for a moment to that man's heart. "After all," he thought, "it was only my fancy." Fancy? — in this life it is a kind word, a human, manly sympathy, like Mr. Leverick's, that brings back a new life to many, many hearts.

CHAPTER XXXII.

CORN HUSKING.

ARTHUR BASSETT felt himself to be proprietor on Bassett Farm. It had been an old custom of his predecessors to make a corn husking for their neighbors in corn-harvest. So Arthur made one. His was like the rest. Everybody was invited. A sense of the rights of a country democracy required it. None were slighted. His invitation put everybody in good-humor. The old folks recalled with pleasure the husking-suppers and the dances at Bassett House when they were young, and had their stories to tell about them; and the young folks anticipated. The last proprietor had been an invalid, and therefore there had been no husking-bee at the Farm for several years. Arthur called in Mrs. Jones to help out old Cloe with the supper. And after a couple of days' baking, that was ready. Arthur awaited his guests.

The lights in the old house under the trees shone cheerily as the guests from the town came over in noisy groups to the husking, and merry voices in hall and barn rang through the moonlight with greeting and rustic raillery, in a general happy confusion of tongues. There was only one thing that seemed incredible about the visitors. Mrs. Lawrence was one of them. How she came there, no one had the slightest knowledge but Agnes; and she hardly understood it. It had seemed an impulse which had brought her here. When she heard of the husking at Bassett House, she had said, suddenly, "I should like to go to that house once more. I think I will go to-night." Agnes looked at her mother in astonishment. It contradicted all the poor woman's habits for twenty years or so. And she only said, "I shall go to-night," and came. A woman's impulse? Maybe. The astonishment at Mrs. Lawrence's appearance at the Farm was universal. Arthur received the unaccustomed visitor at the hall-door, and led her into the old parlor of the house. "It has not changed much," she said, —"only something older than when I last saw this room: as we all grow older in twenty years." The poor lady had not come for corn husking; but only to enter again the house where she had once been a wife and young. She wished to be left with herself in the parlor, while the young folks enjoyed themselves over the corn; and she watched the company go in and out to the husking.

The husking was in the floor of the barn. There the corn had been gathered out of the fields for this festival. Who shall describe the bustle and merry-making and bantering and love-makings with which they husked the corn, — children, young folks, pretty girls with rosy faces, and young gallants in cowhide boots; and the old folks telling again how it went when they were young; and the young folks hoping that it all would come true again; modest huskers of the softer sex unfortunate over red ears of corn; attentive sympathizers of the rougher sex helping them dispose of the same with peals of laughter that rang through the barn; beaux and blushes, and the heap of the golden ears steadily broadening upon the floor.

Supper was served in the farm-kitchen. By ancient custom it could be served nowhere else. Cloe had a levee in her quarters not altogether to her liking, when the merry hungry crowd came in to supper. The company were not ashamed to eat. The supper was fit to be eaten. It was of the olden times, with doughnuts and Indian puddings and salt beef, and the hugest beets and carrots and cabbages off the farm for garniture, like an old-time supper among the Puritans; and none despised it. After supper, as was meet for people of Puritan blood, they sung this harvest-hymn that had been written by a former parish minister.

THE HARVEST-HYMN.

I.

Let us sing a song of the Ages
In praise of our mother Earth,
In the light of her smile rejoicing
With our jocund harvest-mirth.

Let us sing a song of thanksgiving, —
The dead now in graves once sung, —
A song of the husbandman resting,
Which through ancient homes once rung.

CHORUS.

For the golden corn is gathered ;
The wealth of the fields is treasured ;
The gifts of the Giver are measured ;
The Harvest Moon shines bright.

II.

Let us raise our pæan, shouting
That the work of the year is done ;
That our garners are graced with its fruitage ;
For the days of our rest to come ;
For the promise of Spring-time answered
By Summer's favoring heat;
For Autumn's generous bounties,
Which the patient workmen greet.

For the golden corn is gathered ;
The wealth of the fields is treasured ;
The gifts of the Giver are measured;
The Harvest Moon shines bright.

III.

For the Spring is the time of sowing,
And the Summer days are ours ;
And the golden grain is gathered
From the light and the cloud that lowers ;
And the harvest is always waiting
In the Fall of a true man's life ;
And the rest of the Autumn's fulness
Is the boon of our manly strife.

So the golden corn is gathered ;
The wealth of the fields is treasured ;
The gifts of the Giver are measured ;
The Harvest Moon shines bright.

After supper came dancing. A half-breed Indian from the woods, seated on Cloe's settle in the chimney-corner, played the fiddle; the rest danced. Even old Cloe was found in the buttery with her rheumatic feet going through the passes of an African war-dance, or some other sort of pantomime. She could not resist the fiddle. Neither could the rest, albeit it had been so often declared in that parish by the parsons to be the Devil's instrument to lure souls to their ruin. The fiddle had beat the parsons on their own ground. Mr. Leverick had always let it alone. If it was not the fiddle, it would be something worse, he thought. And so they danced dances, as they wrought in the fields or kept the house, vigorously if not gracefully, and were tired in the whirl and chatter of the dance, while the half-breed in the chimney-corner fiddled.

A new entertainment called them out-doors. Some of the youngsters had kindled a fire in the orchard out of the corn husks and dry weeds there. And the company, ready to be amused at anything, went out under the moonlight to see the fire. It was, moreover, a chance for some of the younger to be romantic, and play coquette with the white handkerchiefs over the smooth brown hair in the moonshine. Agnes had left her mother in the parlor for a moment, to go out with the rest to the fire. She came back shortly, to the room half-lighted with the moonlight, to her mother. Old Cloe was standing over her, rubbing her temples!

"She's clean fainted, Miss, I guess," said Cloe, as Agnes knelt down beside her mother. It was true. It was some time before the poor lady came to herself. When she did, her first words were, "You must take me home." And they took her home without disturbing the dancers in the kitchen, or the group around the fire in the orchard. A brain fever was the price the poor lady paid for her visit to the Bassett House. When the delirium was on her, she was always raving of the picture that seemed on fire, and calling to her husband. Long after, when she had come back to health, she told Agnes the story how, when she was sitting in the parlor, after her daughter had gone out, her husband's picture suddenly seemed to be on fire, and she fainted. She did not tell her also how, when the flaming picture had terrified her, a voice she thought long since stilled in the grave had spoken distinctly in the darkness. This is what it said: "Mary Hastings, it has never, never been."

And the dancers in the kitchen? They, too, went home, tired, happy, — young men and women chatting in the moonlight, — some time before the daybreak.

CHAPTER XXXIII.

DEAD LEAVES.

THE leaves were dying in the autumn forest; but before they fell through the dun air, they flashed out in those brilliant autumnal hues which make a carnival-time among the hills, as the last flush upon the cheek precedes the deeper pallor that follows the last sleep in mortals. Everywhere was gold, vermilion, crimson, fit for a queen's mantle, or the colors of a king's crown; and underneath, all was desolation.

Arthur Bassett went out with Agnes Lawrence for a walk among these fairy colors of a fading landscape. This time it happened that these two went up among the hills in the wood road, where they had first met, and talked about the sea, last springtime. Now it was quite another matter that filled Arthur's heart and brain. There was a conversation, too, fitly spoken amid falling leaves from which the glory wasted; for this time it seemed as if the light and glory were fading out of Arthur's life, and leaving only dead leaves. It had come to this; he had told Agnes Lawrence that halting story with trembling lips, told of men so often in moments that count as years, told her of his love for her; how she had entered into everything with him; how she had found him with uncertain aims, and had given him the fixed aim of living for her a true, noble life; how he felt himself a better man for her; and how he would wrestle to gain fame for her, so that he might win her to him, and honor her.

Agnes heard him through without a word. Her face expressed both surprise and pain. She even delayed to speak, as though the words were hard to say, and she was forcing herself to say them. But when she spoke, it was with a certain hopeless speech that seemed to admit no appeal. " This cannot be. I must follow my destiny. It is impossible." " You do not love me, then ? " " I am too much your friend to be anything but frank with you. You would not have me say what I do not feel? No." " I do not ask you for mercy," Arthur answered. " I do not even ask you to wait and let me prove what I am, before you answer finally to that. I have only told you half; the rest is your right. I would have done several things to win your love to me, all that man should do. And you tell me you could never love me, then ? It is very, very strange. It is very hard." " I do not say that at all," she said. " It might have been very different. I do not know. You have forced me to answer, and I have answered so. I am unspeakably pained at this. I did not expect it. I must somehow be to blame for this. And yet I am only a young girl, with no one to speak to, and I have meant the best. You may blame me if you choose, and may think me heartless. I did not mean to trifle with your heart. I mistook, interpreting your heart by mine. I aspire to know certain things, to lead a certain life among books. You could help me, and I found pleasure in your society. I did not think of marriage, only of friendship; and that I prized in you. It may be friendship is not possible between two persons as we are. If so, mine is a sad mistake. I am your friend; but I am nothing more."

The whirl and blindness in Arthur's brain, under the young girl's words, made him for a moment unjust, even ungenerous. " Agnes Lawrence, you are stone to speak so. I mistook." " You wrong me, Arthur Bassett: I am anything but stone. You do not understand me. You pain me more than I can tell you. I am not even indifferent to you. Can you look at my face now and think that? I am only trying to do what is right: and you call me stone! Think a moment what my life has been. You know my mother's story: a life crushed out under a blow upon her heart. I cannot tell you why, but somehow, ever since I came to know her pain, I have had an indescribable fear of suffering like her. Something in me has been always saying, ' Marriage is not for you. You belong to her.

You must do your work with her, and the happiness that others know, in a sunny life, you must give up.' I do not know what the future has for me. I count on nothing in it, only to do the tasks it brings. I believe God will do well with me. You may think it unwomanly or vanity, but I have sometimes thought that God had dealt so with me, that I might not lead the life of other women, but, giving myself to the study of what they call the Good, the Beautiful, the True, might do something or say something, or perhaps write something, for Him beyond what is the wont of women. That is my dream for a long time now, and I must follow where it leads. What you have said sounds strangely to me. That you should care for me as you say, I cannot understand. My heart has never looked that way. Blame me, if you choose, despise me. But I could only say what I have said. It is the truth."

"So, then, this is all," Arthur said, slowly, as if speaking with himself, and as though he was trying to realize the agony that came with Agnes' words.

"All, Arthur Bassett. But I am not heartless as you think me. God knows that. You do not. I shall be wiser henceforth for this; better even because of this sentiment of yours. I shall think he has been my friend, and he will say sometimes, in the years to come, she was unfortunate with her friend, and made mistakes, but still meant to do right with him. I can never be indifferent to anything affecting you. I shall rejoice in your fame, when you win it, as you will. When I hear of it, at this life-work of mine, with these townsfolk round me, you may be sure one heart will be glad and proud of it, though you are not by to see it, and I should not speak of it if you were."

"Anything but pity," Arthur Bassett broke in, impetuously. " Anything but that. I do not need that ; I shall be strong enough without that."

" I do not pity you," she said. " I know you better. I am a woman, and have more need of it, and am not too proud for it. This is a painful matter to us both. Let it die out with both of us. It will be best it should not be spoken of again."

" I will never speak of it again," he said.

Never, Arthur? Yes, he meant never. That which was deepest in him had been touched — his pride — and he said, " Never."

They went home together in the twilight of the frosty evening. " Good-bye, Miss Lawrence." It had always been before, " Miss Agnes."

" Good-bye." He watched her as she went slowly up the steps and entered through the house-door, and then went home to Bassett House. The October air was very chill. Alas! a sadder chill ran through all his life.

And Agnes Lawrence? She of the heart of stone, as Arthur thought her, she of the pale face, and the compressed lips now, went quietly up the hall-stairs to her room, locked the door, sat down in the chair before her study-table, and, laying her head upon it, sobbed like a child, until the Æschylus upon it was wet with tears. That a heart of stone should weep!

CHAPTER XXXIV.

FROST AGAIN!

FROST everywhere in the forest, upon the leaves that lingered on the branch, and on the leaves that fell; frost in the dead grasses of the bare fields, and on the yellow corn of harvest; frost in the swamps and on the hills; frost in the graveyard and in the dooryards of the Sandowners; frost on the barberry, and on the fern, and on the pennyroyal, and on the oak, and on the pine; frost on the wood-nuts, where the squirrels found them under the trees in morning; frost in the ravines, upon the brook that flowed, and the springs that welled up from the pure sands; frost on the sea-shore; frost round Bassett House, on the elms both branch and trunk that stood in the autumn wind around; frost among the dead garden-flowers of summer, and in the woven spider-webs upon the dry leaves blown into winrows along the garden-walls, and rotting in corners; frost under the door-stone and round the sill; frost in the mosses upon the roof; frost on the window-panes and in the chambers; frost every-where.

Arthur's dream was ended. The fairy palace, which he had built as air-castle in the spring-days, had faded out into nothingness, as the golden and crimson clouds of sunset, built into cloud palaces along the west, fade swiftly away into the night. And his night seemed without stars. After the pride the pain. He had received the blow, that stunned him, as one does when his pride is wounded, and he feels called on to play the man. He had supplicated no one, he felt; he had asked what he had a right to ask, and had been denied what there was right for denying; and he had only to accept what had come to him. He went home confused, stunned, with a weight upon his brain, — only conscious that a great calamity had befallen him. He came to himself a moment as he stepped on to the broad door-stone of Bassett House. He was wading among the dead leaves that the night-wind had blown there. Then he went in, with the pressure on his brain, straight to his chamber, and slept — shall so homely a fact be noticed? — slept ten hours.

The pressure was on his brain when he woke next morning, and a certain indefinite sense of a great evil somewhere surprised him, until last night's events came back to him, and then the pain. He rose and dressed himself with especial care that morning, and went out to walk. That morning's elaborate toilette was the only sign he gave of the one burning thought that rose from his innermost heart. "I will conquer my love for Agnes Lawrence, and put it under my feet. She wishes it."

Conquest, Arthur, and of that sort too, is not so easy, as many a man could tell you, who has gone down that road before you ; but conquer, if you are a man. And he tried it like a man. The first thought was, that he could not realize the blow, nor what caused the weight on the brain. It was several days before the truth stood plainly before him ; and then he looked it fairly in the face, and took the measure of it, — not in haste, thrusting it away in cowardice because it pained him, but deliberately, to know the worst in it, and then steadied himself to bear it, and conquer it. He found no short way to that. If he could have despised Agnes Lawrence, it would have ended all his pain. If the young girl, whom he had made his saint and worshipped, had stood before him as unworthy of his homage, of very common flesh and blood like other unworshipful mortals, and he could have despised her for an instant as unwomanly or base, his love for her would have perished instantly, and left him free again. But even in that which had given him this pain she had appeared to him a true, pure woman, of instincts loyal to what she thought duty, and she was still the beautiful vestal of whom he had dreamed and prayed in the spring-days that had now brought his heart only these dead leaves for flowers. He must find some other way.

He went over the dream again, with all its en-

chanting imagery and prophecy of future things, —
with all he had hoped and planned and aspired to.
It was only a dream. Wreck was all around him.
It must be buried. He tried to bury it. Love he
would ignore. He would not read of it, nor think
of it, or her. He shunned every book that spoke
of it, and every place that might recall it; and
when the dream came back, he said, "Away!" —
and it went away again.

He was not quite successful. The vestal looked
out again upon his heart from the books around
him which he had read with her, — from the trees
and hills where he had walked with her, and from
a hundred places where he had dreamed of her.
He could not bury love. Will not some one tell
Arthur the secret and say, "Use your love to lift
you to a beautiful life with God, to whom all wise
love tends, through the temporal to the Eternal"?
Stop a while. Arthur must go his way alone, till
some other than we mortals teach him truth. Us
he will not hear. There is some one near his
heart to speak when time is.

His instincts came to him first. I must go away
from here and her. I must work, wrestle, endure,
until release come. Something tells me it will
come one time, if I have patience. I am beginning
to see how invisible hands are shaping my life to
ends I cannot see. I will have faith and wait.

CHAPTER XXXV.

CONQUEST.

"Thou art to me all I desire: make me to be what thou desirest.
O thou the most Merciful of the merciful." — MOSLEM PRAYER.

"Come, Creative Spirit, visit the minds of thy faithful servants.
Finger of the hand of God, thou dost enrich all lips with eloquence.
Kindle light in our senses, that by thee we may know the Father and
acknowledge the Son, and that we may ever believe thee to be the
Spirit of the one and of the other." — HYMN TO THE HOLY GHOST,
ATTRIBUTED TO CHARLEMAGNE.

ARTHUR BASSETT went abroad, across seas. He
could do it, and he went. He surprised all but two
in Sandowne doing it. Agnes Lawrence's intuitions
saw it at once. Mr. Leverick more than guessed it.
Mrs. Lawrence was too absorbed in her own suffering to think much about it, and only expressed
a faint surprise when she heard of his departure.
And for the rest, it was not in any wise their matter. Arthur had spoken frankly but briefly to his
friend, the minister, about the reason of it. " Miss
Lawrence and I have differed about some matters
of our own. She has acted her part, like the true
woman she is, and is not to blame for anything.
You can do nothing for me. I have only made a
mistake, and must pay the penalty. That is all."
And the minister guessed the rest for himself.

22

Agnes Lawrence, quite unconsciously perhaps, had put herself of late in some sort of silent antagonism with him, as Arthur's friend, who might know his secret.

Arthur went abroad to an old university town of Germany, by the river Neckar, where it moves sluggishly between the Odenwald and Schwarzwald towards sunset and the Rhine. It was a place venerable with the dust of more than a thousand years, and memorable for the feet that had trod its streets, and for the scholars that had adorned its schools. The ducal castle, that looked down upon it from the hills, with its silent, tenantless, roofless halls, and its stalwart stone giants guarding its gateway, through which now passed neither knight nor courtier, though kings had aforetime entered, — with its courtyard where no child played, and its broken palace-windows through which no fair lady looked, — seemed the fleshless skeleton of that mediæval life which, for hearts worshipful of antiquity, is so full of music and pathos and beauty. Everywhere on its hill-tops, where the founda-tion-stones of ruined monastery and chapel were draped every spring-time with the sympathetic myr-tle, in its streets and bridges and warehouses and inns and halls and churches, were the traces of a Heretofore more wonderful than any romance of Troubadour or Minnesinger; and a certain calm-ness and peace of Long Ago fell silently into the heart of the young man who had found a home in

this ancient realm of men. His life grew silent
first among the libraries of the University, wherein
were gathered the thoughts of his elder brethren of
the imperial dynasty of scholars, who, sufferers in the
one Solemn Passion of human life, had left here for
him thoughts out of their innermost hearts for
solace. And then, after a time, when his soul had
been soothed by the solemn antiquity of the place,
came to his heart, as the angels come, in a silent
mystery, the presence and the peace of One who
is never old and never young, and whose message in
wilderness or city is always the same. And His
coming brought Arthur peace. A letter which he
wrote Mr. Leverick after a twelvemonth's absence
explains it well enough.

" . . . I have found a new life here, or rather a
new life has come to me from God. I have had my
struggle, and I have won. This new life in a man,
— how strange it is, how blessed ! Before, I under-
took to do things in my own might, and gain
things for my own aims. I lost all, and in losing
all I found all. When my life was waste, He entered in with His fulness, and I am satisfied. Now
I say in all my wishes and aspirations, 'If God
please to give me this.' I lost all because I held
things in my own right. Henceforth, when I have
a friend or thing, I say, 'God gives me this in trust,'
to be recalled when best. Can I lose it, then, if
he recalls it ? No, nothing. I held it only at his

good pleasure, to be given up. It is all I bargained for or wished. With God nothing is lost. Does not this abolish for a heart all death, and loss harder than any death, so that we conquer life through Him?

"Once I tried to do my own will: now His will. Once I centred my life in earthly things: they perished and the old life with it. Now — shall I say it, dear friend — I have centred my life in God, and as he cannot perish, life also for me is the imperishable. Whosoever grounds himself upon himself, goes under, one time when the storm comes. But when he grounds himself on God, he stands upon the Rock, and conquers. I am coming home to work for Him.

"Your friend,

"Arthur Bassett."

CHAPTER XXXVI.

THE POOR-HOUSE.

" A nature with any nobleness in it never forgets that once it loved, and once was happy in that love. The generous heart is grateful in its memories." — GOETHE.

SANDOWNE poor-house stood a little way off from the village, at the end of a lane that stopped short in a hill-hollow. Public charity had provided it as a resting-place for the poor and needy of the town, until they were borne out to their last home, where there is no need nor wretchedness. The house itself partook of the character of the misery alleviated in it. It was a large, black, weather-stained building, without pretence to any thrift or comfort outside, with its board fence fallen in pieces, and its front yard choked up with weeds. Its steep sunken roof, on which the younger paupers in their leisure hours, of which there was no stint, had lodged innumerable pieces of broken earthen-ware and bricks, ran down behind almost to the ground, as though the very house itself was chary in its hospitality, and inclined to entertain the fewest lodgers possible, and gave an air to the house of being perpetually engaged in falling backward to the ground again.

Its out-houses, of which there were several, had been very fitly built from the timbers of decayed vessels, or of salt-houses long out of use ; and the rust that ran down in streaks upon the boards, from the holes where the iron bolts and nails had been, lent them an especially dilapidated and cheerless look. And all around the place were piled the skeletons of bygone carts and cartwheels, and a score of other carcasses of things which had once their use, but which now, like the human beings in-doors, seemed to have drifted down round the poor-house, as the only place where they could, with any degree of fitness, be taken care of. Even the apple-trees behind the house were gnarled and stunted, with great holes eaten into their trunks by the rot, — as though life had also dealt harshly with them, because it had been their misfortune to belong to the poor-house. The only comfortable-looking thing about the place was the fat wood-pile beside it ; and that, too, every spring had melted away into chips and splinters on the ground, as though there was an irresistible proclivity in everything hereabouts to waste and poverty.

The people in-doors had always this same dilapidated, dreary look, as of slowly rotting and falling away in sympathy with the waste and unthrift outside. They, too, had been wrecked in life, and what was left of them was only the drift and rubbish that had drifted ashore just here awhile. Many had started from the tavern, and had found, at the end of the drunken frolic they called life, only this harbor, which for forty years perhaps they had been steadily making, without a thought of it. Some had been unfortunates, wrecked of others' sins, before they came into life; and idiots, because their progenitors had been worse, had lived all their lives without sin, as the beasts live without thought or hope. Some had been in company with men who had not been husbands except in an old certificate of marriage, and after wrecking a woman's life by their shiftlessness or worse, had left them in their age to the poor-house charity. As one saw these unfortunates sunning themselves on the south side of the poor-house in a fall-day, silent between themselves for hours together as though there was nothing to say, and keeping their motionless attitudes with a certain animal instinct for warmth and comfort, or watched the stragglers crawling along the town-road, intent on nothing but an aimless peregrination somewhere, in their bygone patched coats and homespun woollens, he thought of nothing so much as the rotting hulks in the beach-sands, that waste and part under the tides from month to month, till they sink away and leave no sign; or of still nobler craft, that had been burnt out of the very fires which, governed well, should have borne them proudly across seas to quite other ports of recompense, but now with their very hearts eaten out of the flame and passion which had been their ruin. In short, if one would study the immutable laws of Life, when they come to judgment, and exact their inexorable payments, he should go nowhere so soon as to the poor-house.

It is one of these immutable laws of life which leads our story there. How, the reader thereof shall now be made to see. The fall has deepened into the winter, frost into snow. The winter has come to one life at least in Sandowne, for which in this world again there will be no spring. Last week old Treeman had been found, on a frosty morning, insensible in the wood road that led to the town. Exposure to the season and the paralysis which had smitten him, were evidently making haste with him. He had been brought, therefore, to the poor-house for shelter. There was no other refuge. He had been there a week or more when the events that follow, happened.

It was a dreary winter night, — with the snow drifting high along the fences, and shutting up the roads, with the wail of the storm through the trees, and the snow beating against the panes, and the roar of the sea outside, — when a messenger came to the Lawrences from the poor-house. "There 's a man near upon dying at the poor-house, who wants to see you, marm," the man said to Mrs. Lawrence when he was ushered into her presence. "Me?" said the poor lady, bewildered at such a message; "and in such a night as this, too? You must have mistook your house. It must be somebody else in the village. What name did he give you when he sent?" "Your'n, marm." "Mine? Impossible! Who is this sick man?" "Old Treeman, who like to have froze to death in the road last week, and, the Doctor says, is dying." "Treeman, Treeman," she said, — "who is he, Agnes?" Agnes told her the little she knew about him. He was a strange character who had for some time now inhabited the old Indian hut upon the hill.

The man who, during Agnes' explanation, had been fumbling with his wet mittens in his coat-pocket for something, broke in now with, "Please, marm, I forgot how the man sent you something here, which he said as how you 'd know and p'r'aps come when you 'd see it ; " and he handed her something wrapped in a wet piece of dingy paper. The poor lady of tears could hardly believe her senses. She took the package, however, and opened it almost mechanically. It seemed only a bunch of faded ribbon, with some sort of gold device in the centre of it. She held it nearer to the light beside her to examine it. One close enough might have seen the initials *M. H.* engraved on the small gold button in the centre of it. Mrs. Lawrence turned deadly pale, and the ribbon fell from her hand. Agnes sprang to her. • "Why, mother, what has happened?" There was no answer for several moments, and she only held her hands to her brain, as if something had struck there and stunned her. "Nothing, child," she said, then, "nothing. Only," speaking in a low, deliberative tone, "I must see this man who is dying." "In such a night as this, mother? You forget yourself. It is impossible." "Nothing but God must stop me, Agnes," she said, with a certain positive, imperious, and almost passionate tone, that Agnes had never before seen in her mother. "Come." And she started up to go. Agnes had one recourse. "Let us send at least for Mr. Leverick to go out with us in this storm." "Anybody, so that I go. But quick. — Go to the parsonage, man, and tell the minister I need him instantly. It is life and death, remember." And the man shuffled out of the house into the storm. Mr. Leverick came in haste, and with some surprise at the strange summons. Agnes had hoped he would be able to persuade her mother out of the strange excitement which seemed to her insanity. But Mrs. Lawrence went straight to him when he came in.

"Come with me," she said, "to the poor-house. A man is dying there whom I must see." He turned to Agnes for an explanation. "Do not stop, but come. It may be too late. I must see him. Then you will know." And she was even going before them out into the storm in her strange impatience.

The storm was at its height when they went out into it, moaning, howling, smiting, beating down around them with its blinding snow. The man from the poor-house led the way with his obscure lantern as they toiled on through the snow, that deepened and drifted every moment deeper, higher, all around them. Not a word was spoken.

The poor-house door opened to them, and the red-faced, bustling overseer holding the door ajar, and the flaring candle behind it from the storm, received them. "This way, marm, this way," he said to Mrs. Lawrence, as she came in before the rest. "This way to where the man is," as he led the way up-stairs with the vulgar, heartless air of a showman whose business it was to expose the rags and wreck he managed. "We'd no other room, and so we've put him to the top of the house."

The overseer led them into the sick man's chamber. It was a long low room under the eaves, of unpainted, unplastered walls, and littered up with chests, and rags, and the common wreck of garret-furniture, full of dust and of things which had wasted or burnt out. In a corner, on what was meant for a bed, the sick man was lying. A pauper, with a dripping candle, sat at the head, watching. The sick man turned himself slowly from the wall as the party came in, and, with some difficulty, raised himself to receive his guests. Mrs. Lawrence went straight to the bed before the rest. " You wished to see me ? " she said, abruptly, almost fiercely. " Where did you get this ribbon ? " holding out the missive she had received from him.

The sick man made no immediate answer. The company came silently round the bed, and Mr. Leverick noticed how a great change had come upon the man. He was haggard and wasted indeed, and very weak, and the eye was strangely lighted up, but the face had, what the minister had seen so often in the face of the dead, a look of childhood in it, as though the soul under, had gone back to fresher days, and become childlike again. The sick man, under the inspiration of death in him, had risen up to the stature of a strong man again, as if he were laying aside with the flesh the stain and weariness that came through it. He seemed trying now to recall something, or steadying his brain to say something in answer to Mrs. Lawrence's question.

"Yes, I did send for you," he said, finally, turning to that lady, as though he remembered now. "I sent something, and you got it. I wanted to say something. Do you not know me, Mary Hastings? I am William Wareham." "William Wareham, — William Wareham!" ejaculated the bewildered lady, "he is in his grave long ago, and you are not he. He spoke to me out of his grave this very year, and he said what he and I only know. You are much older than he." "No, I am not in my grave, only going there, and I could not go before I had said something I must say while I can speak. Mary Hastings, it has never, never been. That is what I heard from you once, and it blighted my life : you heard it from me at the house last fall. You hear it now again from me, this wreck you see. Are you not satisfied ? When you said 'never,' you sent a man to worse than his grave; to this I am. Mary Hastings, I, too, have said 'never.' I never forget. I never change. You and your race made me an outcast. Why? because I befriended the king. I am an outcast still, and I am still the king's liegeman. I shall be that in my coffin. Let that pass. One thing more. You and yours made me an outcast, and wrecked my life. You may say you did not wish it, or it was your right to do it. I do not wish to blame you — only to show you your handiwork in me, a pauper. Mary Hastings, my hands are not white, but red. I own that to you, as I have owned it to myself a hundred times. I have wrecked your life, and I did not mean it, and there is no help for it. You were a wife, and" ——

Mrs. Lawrence, who during the sick man's monologue had looked him steadily in the face, as though a word or motion should not escape her, broke in impetuously, "I *am* a wife, William Wareham."

"Well, then, I wish to speak of your husband."

"Go on, then. What of him?" (imperiously).

"This. They had made me, as you can remember, an outlaw in the woods. I was no murderer. I was only what they called a Tory, and yet they hunted me as though I were a dog. Your husband came out on that errand. He had been my friend. We met face to face in the ravine. He was armed. I was not, just then. He had forgotten our friendship: we met as enemies. He would have laid hands on me. We had tried strength as boys together, and were well matched. Had it been as a boy, or a friend, I would have yielded. He would have seized me by the neck as a dog. I said, 'Stop. Let us save this. Let me go away.' He said, 'No.' He taunted me with several things, and said sharp words that bite a man's heart. He was your husband, and I forbore. He charged me with base things, as though I had attempted to steal something from him as a rival underhand. I forgot. I answered roughly, — what, I do not know now, — and he struck me in the face. I grappled with him. I do not know what happened. My brain was blind with hot blood. I did not see, nor know as we struggled there. We fell together, and sprang to our feet together. There was a gun between us, and we strove for that. I do not know how it was. I did not mean it. Maybe I did not do it. It might be accident; but your husband fell — shot through the heart. I stood above him, and could do nothing. Perhaps I was a murderer."

It would have been hard to analyze the thoughts which were in Mrs. Lawrence's brain, summoned thus suddenly in such a place into the presence of one she thought long since dead, and whose life had once come so strangely in contact with her own, while she listened to Wareham's story. Pain, surprise, bewilderment, all together, until, as he went on to the story of her husband's death, all else in her nature seemed to sink down before the overmastering

passion of her love for him, thus wronged and blighted, and her life crushed out by one who had been her
friend. Everything gave way before the one great
sentiment of her woman's heart. It was no longer
a dying man, a friend, an unfortunate before her:
it was her husband's murderer. She said, " Was
this love, William Wareham? Was this a man to
crush a woman's life as you have crushed mine?
Was this your honor, that you should smite me
down so, in a foul damning murder? No, no,
William Wareham. This life of mine, with its years
of sorrow, rises up before God, and cries out against
you. He may forgive: I never can; I never will."

" You may leave that to Him," the man said,
calmly. " I am going very soon to Him. I cannot
suffer so much again as I have before. You say
well; ' Let Him judge.' You have no mercy. I
do not pretend to have a right to your mercy, and
I never had it, and I do not ask it. I am dying, as
you see, now. I have thought many times, ' Now it
has come at last.' But no. My blood is on that ribbon of yours; and I thought then, when the ball
sped so well in battle, ' Now it is come; ' but I lived
through the battle to die here. I came back, when
I could not die, here, where I had been wronged so
and had injured so, where I had been young, and
was an outlaw; and I have lived, as you may know,
an outcast. Mary Hastings, this should be enough
for you." There was no answer. " Well, then, to
God. Mary Hastings. Good-bye. It has never,

never been," — and he turned himself slowly away from the company toward the wall again. The woman's soul beside his bed had been frozen through with her lifelong grief. She had misused the pain, and it had refused her peace. She left the chamber without a word.

The minister remained with the sick man when the rest had left. The storm was moaning outside, and beating upon the roof above them with its sharp, angry sound. The man turned to the minister with a smile. " Parson, I feel easier now. What a strange thing this life is, that a man should come to this," pointing to the bare walls around him. "I am glad it is almost over. Suppose God were to speak to these townsfolk about this life of· theirs and mine, would n't there be one soft word for even me. And she had not one. — Parson," he said again, beckoning him, " good-bye. You have judged kindly ; and the rest are — Whigs." And there was no more talk that night in the poor-house garret, until a soul went out from there to judgment. And when it went, the drifting storm was round every home in Sandowne. And above the storm were stars that never set, and beyond the stars, and through them, and through all the earth, a Love moved on that never fails, on, on forever. And the man in the rags, out from amidst the wreck, had gone forth to that for judgment.

They buried William Wareham in the pauper's graveyard under the heavy snow. He had requested it of the red-faced overseer, and it was granted. Mr. Leverick wished otherwise, but Wareham was to be laid there. The man dug the grave among the stunted locust-trees, with only the thought how cold the weather was, and was stopped short by the hard iron pan of earth that refused a lower grave, — as though the very earth begrudged the pauper a grave like other men. It did not, however, for it was not human.

But when they buried him in the dreary fields among the locusts, in the ravine that ran down by their side, some tufts of green grass showed here and there through the melting snow, as though God had not forgotten, in His winter, spring. Let us hope that what William Wareham found beyond the snow was also spring!

23

CHAPTER XXXVII.

LACTANTIUS'S Y.

THE Latin poet Lactantius has a saying some-where, derivable, he says, from an earlier age than his, that every man's life is like the letter y. For as the man comes forward into action and passes once for all through the point where the y divides itself, he passes on to life or death, to weal or woe. Two lives are about to pass through that point now.· Whither?

Arthur Bassett had come home again to San-downe. He came back a calm, strong, patient man, with the old impatience and self-will dead in him, ready to work. He had thrust down the idol from its throne in his heart, and a King reigned there instead. Not that he had forgotten Agnes Law-rence, for a true heart never forgets how it once has loved; he had only subordinated her in his affections to what one may call his sense of the duty God had given him and every other loyal man to ascend to the battle and the conquest of what is base and false in this world. Once she had been to him a life, now she was a memory, — grateful, maybe, but with an undertone of sadness running through it. He thought, " Her I cannot win, having lost her altogether. One thing is mine. I will show her, in this life of mine, that I am not unworthy of her, nor of my love for her." So he came home to work.

His love was absorbed in another love. He had passed on through the temporal to the Eternal. The Beatrice of his dreams had led him unto the Throne from which the white-robed, immortal lady herself was not altogether absent.

And Agnes Lawrence? How had it been with her in the year of absence? Had she gone on realizing her dream of a woman's life, solitary with truth alone, above the common needs and nature of woman's heart, to grasp her Ideal of some sort of woman's work above that which in this life has come to most women? Did the life above woman's susceptibilities and woman's great supremacy and reliance — woman's love — satisfy her? Had she forgotten Arthur? Had the old readings, and the old companionship, faded away from her, and left no voice behind? Were there none to speak to her of Arthur? She had grown more gentle and more silent than of old, and went about her daily tasks with greater assiduity. She never spoke of him, nor asked of him from Mr. Leverick, whom she divined, as a woman will, had heard from him. No doubt she had forgotten. That is her woman's secret, not to be disclosed, unless she choose to speak of it.

This is a book of surprises, maybe, but Life is also that. Arthur Bassett had been home two days now, — and Agnes Lawrence did not know it. She had gone out in the spring-day again, to walk. She went up the wood road, where she had first met Arthur and talked about the sea and other matters. Arthur was also out among the hills: by accident, of course. I tell you there is only One in this Universe who should ever dare to say "Accidental." He is God, and he never says it. After Him the wise say " Providential." Arthur may turn down a dozen other wood roads home, and they may never meet again. He goes to-morrow to the city to spend several years, to fit himself for the calling he has chosen. Then through which limb of the y will his life pass on? Listen! Lactantius forgot one thing. For the true heart, at the point where the y diverges, always stands God to denote the choice. Then whichever way, is best. He passed on (though no man saw it) once and for all through the diverging point, down one wood road, and stood face to face with Agnes Lawrence. Only two young persons met again. The blood rushed to Arthur's brain, as if a blow had been struck on it, and then back to his heart again. It created an old pain there, and perhaps something else. A moment's embarrassment, and then he steadied himself in his new strength, and went forward to meet her, as a man like him should, with the frank, respectful greeting of an old friendship. She

seemed to receive him without embarrassment, as
though they had parted only yesterday with nothing
especial between them: she was a woman. She
asked him about his life abroad with a friendliness
and interest that reassured him. He told her of it,
and something made him very frank with her, when
he meant to be guarded. It was, maybe, the old
sympathy with her still lying down below, in some
remote chamber of his heart. But he told her, as
a man would tell his sister, of his studies at the
University, — and how he had found a new life of
peace there, — and how he had come back to work ;
he hoped it would be true work ; and how he had
come to feel that it was only left for him to accom-
plish his work for God, that so he might suffer no
loss or disappointment. He supposed, honest soul,
that in all this he had never for a moment betrayed
the secret that had wrought all this in him ; and
yet behind all he said, rose up one fact from which
all else started. Could Agnes Lawrence see it ?
Had his love for her perished then, and a new life
been built upon its wreck, and Agnes become as
other women to him ? Perhaps. One more self-
possessed than Arthur Bassett would have remarked
several things. He only noticed that she was something paler, and more quiet. He did not notice
that somehow she seemed to have given up the
old intellectual antagonism which he always came out
of over their books in their very diverse theories of
them, and also that she was more ready to avoid

differing with him than of old. Mere trifles, no
doubt, but, for him who would get at a woman's
heart, something. There was one overmastering
thought in Arthur's mind. "I have promised
'Never,' and I must keep it. She meets me upon
the only condition of being friends, and in my innermost thought I will keep a man's faith with her."
So when the old thoughts came back, he said in his
heart, " Away, it is impossible ! " — and they went
down under his will, and only his lips were pressed
closer together. He thought, " this meeting is a
trial that I must go through as a man should. I
should not find it well to have many such." He
avoided looking at her face, and, with his heart
forced down under his will, he went on talking with
her, striving to make her impersonal to him, and
only half succeeded. He was not in a mood to see
anything very clearly, but keeping his own honor
in the interview clear and whole.

And yet there was a certain enchantment which
held him unconsciously to prolong the interview.
Was it the delirium of the moth that flutters about
the consuming flame, and perishes in it as though
it were sport? Something led him on, in a half
pleasant conversation, to speak of many things ; and
Miss Lawrence was giving him a true sisterly sympathy. There was the pain again ! How pleasant
it was to find that his affairs had any sort of interest
for her ; and she was entering into all his plans, in
a delicate womanly way, applauding the manly in

them, and hoping much for him in the old spirit of
a pure unselfish woman. Dangerous ground is
this for any man.

The sweet charm of this interview was not dimin-
ishing for Arthur. Illogical it was, dangerous no
doubt, wrong on any theory but one, namely, that
he had a right to it, and the heart under the will
was rising up, asserting its right to be heard again.
And Arthur struggled with it so. This interview
must end. Only pain could follow. And yet he
went on blind and struggling with himself. Could
he not see ? What was it that made her so gentle ?
Why was it that she went back with him to some
old things, to reading Æschylus, — and she a woman ? Why did she stay here talking with him ?
As a woman, why did she hesitate to command to
vanish anything connected with Arthur's love for
her, as she could by a single cold word or tone,
such as are in every woman's keeping ? Had she
changed too ? Arthur Bassett, you are very blind,
as all proud men are, put on their honor before
women. If Agnes Lawrence loves you, and has,
after all her struggle, come to that, that she, too,
would give her life to you, will you have her tell
you that ? Put away your pride and look. And
Agnes Lawrence did not tell him that, nor speak
one word of that, and yet she showed him that,
out of her true, delicate, womanly heart, without a
word or sign : only that sign which the royal Master
of Love puts on in a tone, a look, silence sometimes.

And Arthur saw again that Agnes Lawrence loved him. True sphinx is woman; life's immeasurable riddle. No: the sphinx is of the passionless, unmeaning face, cut out of stone; and she is only the riddle we call — woman. And Arthur's love under the will rose up again, clear, constant, purified, and went forth into the world once more, and the fairy palaces were built again, this time of fabrics that could not waste; and the spring was at his heart again, and overhead were the same old skies of the unfailing stars that arch themselves above all lovers, and over all was God.

Two happy hearts went slowly down the road together, talking of the future. The past had been explained; how that one had found all love to be used for God, and the other how woman, sovereign as she is in life, reigns queenliest, not in wisdom, nor in policies, nor in great performances, but when she bows to crown herself with a pure human love. Two lives had flowed together in one, with peace and a new life begun in each, and yet no spring-flower whispered it, nor wind spoke it, nor tree rustled it with soft green leaves of spring; and the earth moved on as ever, though two had come together in the holy sacrament of love.

Let the spring crown them: as the spring has crowned so many like them in the same old beatitude of souls. Agnes Lawrence went home again. She brought out the Æschylus that she had hid away months since, and laid it on her table as of old. And then bowed down her head in silence. Was it a prayer or anthem that swept through the young girl's heart? Both. Her destiny has passed on through the divergences of the y to happiness.

CHAPTER XXXVIII.

THE SPRING AGAIN.

THIS is a chapter of fragments. The excuse is, that most lives can only be represented in fragments. Something that William Wareham had told the minister on the night when the latter had watched with him, led to a search at Bassett House. It revealed the fact that a secret passage-way led around the chimneys of the house from garret to parlor. It was supposed to have been contrived in the Indian times as a place of refuge from the savages. There were several strange things brought to light in it, which are very likely to be narrated some time in a book of greater historical accuracy than this. It was clear that William Wareham had been often there. The passage opened into the parlor by a movable panel, just behind the portrait of the man who fell in the ravine. That will account for several things. Why William Wareham frequented Bassett House was a mystery to some, while others thought it part of that awful fascination which had brought him back to spend his life in the scenes of his former ruin, crime, and sorrow. It was supposed it was he who had set up the cross on the spot where his victim fell, and every spring hung May-flowers on it, with some dim sense of making atonement, or at least yearly repentance for the fatal deed. Many other facts about him remain unsaid.

The careful reader may also observe how, in some way, the life of the minister connected itself with the story of the girl who died on Dead Man's Rock. I should in no wise wonder if, of the two lovers standing beside the sea at even-tide, as writ in the opening chapter of this story, Mr. Leverick was one.

There was a wedding in Sandowne meeting-house. Several persons, whom the readers of this book know, went to it. Among the rest Mrs. Lawrence, who, in her own way, took a kind of pleasure in it. Also Mrs. Sam. The old bell rang out a merry peal, and the country folks turned out in force to see it. As a thing unusual, it may be noted here that the bride was thought to look sweetly. She wore a wreath of May-flowers over the brown hair that also looked sweetly. Mr. Leverick performed the service; it was very short; and the village-choir ended it with an anthem, as was proper; while the gentler songsters thought of another wedding they hoped would arrive one day when they should be below-stairs. A new mistress went in under the elms at Bassett House, — a happy bride for many, many years.

There was a gay company which danced on the

wedding-night in Bassett House, and Cloe danced in the kitchen. The old house was one blaze of light. The minister came in the early evening, and the bride took his arm and set him by her in the post of honor at the supper-table. Mere trifles, some one is sure to say; but these trifles are writ down for those who like them. Let something else be written. The minister in due time went away from the supper-table. Home? No. In under the two elms, to kneel down beneath the stars between two graves an hour or so. One was the girl's grave who had died on Dead Man's Rock, and the other was the child's of the hazel eyes, called Fritz. O Death, angel of God, stronger than the flesh, weaker than Love, who comest with graves between our hearts and our beloved, thou thyself diest by faith, and we live with wife and children still! O Life, stronger than death, who weavest thorns for some and flowers for others, angel of God, to try us as with fire, thou, too, yieldest us the palm by faith, and we find peace. Ye two are one; for the Ineffable shines through both!

The rest is history. Mr. Leverick found a second home at Bassett House. He had also several christenings there. There were some girls among them who had eyes very blue.

A strong wise man, purified of sorrow, made that house famous as the home of one who had served his age well in literature and life. A gentle woman, wise as her sex is, strengthened that man's hand,

and gave him good courage and direction in many difficult matters that affected the common weal. A new life floated in on Sandowne from Bassett House. Last spring-time, some persons in that venerable township had passed on from there, — Mr. Leverick among them, — on where was no sea, and many friends ; — two that had seemed to sleep together in the spot where the minister had so often prayed. But one, no stranger in that township, saw young men and women go out of Bassett House, and a happy couple, gray-haired now, sat at evening in the doorway, under the elms, and talked of long ago. It was a spring evening without a cloud. Life had brought them to this peaceful haven. But the same solemn mystery of Being beats to-day in hearts innumerable, with storm and cloud and day and fire inexplicable. But the sea that tries us so, if undergone in trust, brings all, one day, to a life where there is no sea. Gratias !

THE END.

NEW BOOKS

And New Editions Recently Issued by

CARLETON, PUBLISHER,

NEW YORK.

418 BROADWAY, CORNER OF LISPENARD STREET.

N.B.—The Publisher, upon receipt of the price in advance, will send any of the following Books, by mail, POSTAGE FREE, to any part of the United States. This convenient and very safe mode may be adopted when the neighboring Booksellers are not supplied with the desired work. State name and address in full

Victor Hugo.

LES MISERABLES.—*The best edition*, two elegant 8vo. vols., beautifully bound in cloth, $5.50; half calf, . . $10.00

LES MISERABLES.—*The popular edition*, one large octavo volume, paper covers, $1.75; cloth bound, . . $2.25

LES MISERABLES.—Original edition in five vols.—Fantine—Cosette—Marius—Denis—Valjean. 8vo. cloth, . $1.25

LES MISERABLES—In the Spanish language. Fine 8vo. edition, two vols., paper covers, $4.00; or cloth, bound, . $5.00

THE LIFE OF VICTOR HUGO.—By himself. 8vo. cloth, $1.75

By the Author of "Rutledge."

RUTLEDGE.—A deeply interesting novel. 12mo. cloth, $1.75

THE SUTHERLANDS.— do. . . do. $1.75

FRANK WARRINGTON.— do. . . do. $1.75

LOUIE'S LAST TERM AT ST. MARY'S.— . . do. $1.75

A NEW NOVEL.—*In press.*

Hand-Books of Good Society.

THE HABITS OF GOOD SOCIETY; with Thoughts, Hints, and Anecdotes, concerning nice points of taste, good manners, and the art of making oneself agreeable. Reprinted from the London Edition. The best and most entertaining work of the kind ever published. . . 12mo. cloth, $1.75

THE ART OF CONVERSATION.—With directions for self-culture. A sensible and instructive work, that ought to be in the hands of every one who wishes to be either an agreeable talker or listener. . . . 12mo. cloth, $1.50

Mrs. Mary J. Holmes' Works.

DARKNESS AND DAYLIGHT.—*Just published.* 12mo. cl. $1.50
'LENA RIVERS.— . . A Novel. do. $1.50
TEMPEST AND SUNSHINE.— . do. do. $1.50
MARIAN GREY.— . . . do. do. $1.50
MEADOW BROOK.— . . . do. do. $1.50
ENGLISH ORPHANS.— . . do. do. $1.50
DORA DEANE.— . . . do. do. $1.50
COUSIN MAUDE.— . . . do. do. $1.50
HOMESTEAD ON THE HILLSIDE.— do. do. $1.50

Artemus Ward.

HIS BOOK.—An irresistibly funny volume of writings by the
immortal American humorist . . 12mo. cloth, $1.50

Miss Muloch.

JOHN HALIFAX.—A novel. With illust. 12mo., cloth, $1.75
A LIFE FOR A LIFE.— . do. . do. $1.75

Charlotte Bronte (Currer Bell).

JANE EYRE.—A novel. With illustration. 12mo. cloth, $1.75
THE PROFESSOR.—do. . do. . do. $1.75
SHIRLEY.— . do. . do. . do. $1.75
VILLETTE.— . do. . do. . do. $1.75

Edmund Kirke.

AMONG THE PINES.—A Southern sketch. 12mo. cloth, $1.25
MY SOUTHERN FRIENDS.— do. do. . $1.25
DOWN IN TENNESSEE.—Just published. . do. $1.50

Cuthbert Bede.

VERDANT GREEN.—A rollicking, humorous novel of English
student life; with 200 comic illustrations. 12mo. cloth, $1.50
NEARER AND DEARER.—A novel, illustrated. 12mo. clo. $1.50

Richard B. Kimball.

WAS HE SUCCESSFUL?— A novel. 12mo. cloth, $1.50
UNDERCURRENTS.— do. do. $1.50
SAINT LEGER.— do. do. $1.50
ROMANCE OF STUDENT LIFE— do. do. $1.50
IN THE TROPICS.—Edited by R. B. Kimball. do. $1.50

Epes Sargent.

PECULIAR.—One of the most remarkable and successful novels
published in this country. . . 12mo. cloth, $1.75

Miss Augusta J. Evans.

BEULAH.—A novel of great power. 12mo. cloth, $1.7·

A. S. Roe's Works.

A LONG LOOK AHEAD.— A novel. 12mo. cloth, $1.5c
TO LOVE AND TO BE LOVED.— do. . . do. $1.50
TIME AND TIDE.— do. . . do. $1.50
I'VE BEEN THINKING.— do. . . do. $1.5
THE STAR AND THE CLOUD.— do. . . do. $1.5
TRUE TO THE LAST.— do. . . do. $1.5
HOW COULD HE HELP IT.— do. . . do. $1.50
LIKE AND UNLIKE.— do. . . do. $1.50
A NEW NOVEL.—*In Press.* do. $1.50

Walter Barrett, Clerk.

OLD MERCHANTS OF NEW YORK.—Being personal incidents, interesting sketches, bits of biography, and gossipy events in the life of nearly every leading merchant in New York City. Three series. . . 12mo. cloth, each, $1.75

T. S. Arthur's New Works.

LIGHT ON SHADOWED PATHS.—A novel. 12mo. cloth, $1.50
OUT IN THE WORLD.— do. . do. $1.50
NOTHING BUT MONEY.—*In Press.* do. . do. $1.50

The Orpheus C. Kerr Papers.

A COLLECTION of exquisitely satirical and humorous military criticisms. Two series. . 12mo. cloth, each, $1.50

M. Michelet's Works.

LOVE (L'AMOUR).—From the French. 12mo. cloth, $1.50
WOMAN (LA FEMME.)— do. . . do. $1.50
WOMAN'S PHILOSOPHY OF WOMAN.—By Hericourt, do $1.50

Novels by Ruffini.

DR. ANTONIO.—A love story of Italy. 12mo. cloth, $1.75
LAVINIA; OR, THE ITALIAN ARTIST.— do. $1.75
VINCENZO; OR, SUNKEN ROCKS.— 8vo. cloth, $1.75

Rev John Cumming, D.D., of London.

THE GREAT TRIBULATION.—Two series. 12mo. cloth, $1.50
THE GREAT PREPARATION.— do. . do. $1.50
THE GREAT CONSUMMATION.— do. . do. $1.50
TEACH US TO PRAY.— do. $1.50

Ernest Renan.

THE LIFE OF JESUS.—Translated by C. E. Wilbour from the celebrated French work. . . 12mo. cloth, $1.75
RELIGIOUS HISTORY AND CRITICISM.— 8vo. cloth, $2.50

Charles Reade.

THE CLOISTER AND THE HEARTH.—A magnificent new novel, by the author of "Hard Cash," etc. . 8vo. cloth, $2.00

The Opera.

TALES FROM THE OPERAS.—A collection of clever stories, based upon the plots of all the famous operas. 12mo. cl., $1.50

J. C. Jeaffreson.

A BOOK ABOUT DOCTORS.—An exceedingly humorous and entertaining volume of sketches, stories, and facts, about famous physicians and surgeons. 12mo. cloth, $1.75

Fred. S. Cozzens.

THE SPARROWGRASS PAPERS.—A capital humorous work, with illustrations by Darley. . . 12mo. cloth, $1.25

F. D. Guerrazzi.

BEATRICE CENCI.—A great historical novel. Translated from the Italian; with a portrait of the Cenci, from Guido's famous picture in Rome. . . 12mo. cloth, $1.75

Private Miles O'Reilly.

HIS BOOK.—Rich with his songs, services, and speeches, and comically illustrated. . . . 12mo. cloth, $1.25

The New York Central Park.

A SUPERB GIFT BOOK.—The Central Park pleasantly described, and magnificently embellished with more than 50 exquisite photographs of the principal views and objects of interest. A large quarto volume, sumptuously bound in Turkey morocco, ... $30.00

Joseph Rodman Drake.

THE CULPRIT FAY.—The most charming faery poem in the English language. Beautifully printed. 12mo. cloth, 75 cts.

Mother Goose for Grown Folks.

HUMOROUS RHYMES for grown people; based upon the famous "Mother Goose Melodies." . . 12mo. cloth, $1.00

Stephen Massett.

DRIFTING ABOUT.—A comic illustrated book of the life and travels of "Jeems Pipes." . . 12mo. cloth, $1.25

A New Sporting Work.

THE GAME FISH OF THE NORTH.—One of the best books on fish and fishing ever published. Entertaining as well as instructive, and full of illustrations. . 12mo. cloth, $1.50

Balzac's Novels.

CESAR BIROTTEAU.—From the French. 12mo. cloth, $1.25
THE ALCHEMIST.— do.   do. $1.25
EUGENIE GRANDET.— do.   do. $1.2⁻
PETTY ANNOYANCES OF MARRIED LIFE.— do. $1.2

Thomas Bailey Aldrich.

BABIE BELL, AND OTHER POEMS.—Blue and gold binding, $1.00
OUT OF HIS HEAD.—A new romance. 12mo. cloth, $1.00

Richard H. Stoddard.

THE KING'S BELL.—A new poem. . 12mo. cloth, 75 cts.
THE MORGESONS.—A novel. By Mrs. R. H. Stoddard. $1.00

Edmund C. Stedman.

ALICE OF MONMOUTH.—A new poem. 12mo. cloth, $1.00
LYRICS AND IDYLS.— . . . . do. 75 cts.

M. T. Walworth.

LULU.—A new novel. . . . 12mo. cloth, $1.50
HOTSPUR.— do. . . do. $1.50

Author of " Olie."

NEPENTHE.—A new novel. . . 12mo. cloth, $1.50
TOGETHER.— do. . do.

Quest.

A NEW ROMANCE.— . . . 12mo. cloth, $1.50

Victoire.

A NEW NOVEL.— . . . 12mo. cloth, $1.75

Red-Tape

AND PIGEON-HOLE GENERALS, as seen by a citizen-soldier in the
 Army of the Potomac. . . 12mo. cloth, $1.25

Author " Green Mountain Boys."

CENTEOLA.—A new work, . 12mo. cloth, $1.5c

C. French Richards.

JOHN GUILDERSTRING'S SIN.—A nove 12mo. cloth, $1.5c

J. R. Beckwith.

THE WINTHROPS.—A novel, 12mo. cloth, $1.75

Jas. H. Hackett.

NOTES AND COMMENTS ON SHAKSPEARE.— 12mo. cloth, $1.50

Miscellaneous Works.

ALEXANDER VON HUMBOLDT.—Life and travels. 12mo. cl. $1.50
LIFE OF HUGH MILLER, the Geologist.   .   .   do. $1.50
ADAM GUROWSKI.—Diary for 1863.   .   .   do. $1.25
DOESTICKS.—The Elephant Club, illustrated. .   do. $2.00
HUSBAND AND WIFE, or human development.   do. $1.25
ROCKFORD.—A novel by Mrs. L. D. Umsted.   do. $1.00
THE PRISONER OF STATE.—By D. A. Mahony.   do. $1.25
THE PARTISAN LEADER.—By Beverly Tucker. .   do. $1.25
SPREES AND SPLASHES.—By Henry Morford. .   do. $1.00
AROUND THE PYRAMIDS.—By Gen. Aaron Ward.   do. $1.50
CHINA AND THE CHINESE.—By W. L. G. Smith.   do. $1.00
WANDERINGS OF A BEAUTY.—Mrs. Edwin James.   do. $1.00
THE U. S. TAX LAW.—"Government Edition."   do.   75 cts.
TREATISE ON DEAFNESS.—By Dr. E. B. Lighthill.   do. $1.00
LYRICS OF A DAY—or newspaper poetry.   .   do. $1.00
GARRET VAN HORN.—A novel by J. S. Sauzade.   do. $1.25
THE NATIONAL SCHOOL FOR THE SOLDIER.—   do.   50 cts.
FORT LAFAYETTE.—A novel by Benjamin Wood.   do. $1.00
THE YACHTMANS PRIMER.—By T. R. Warren.   do.   50 cts.
GEN. NATHANIEL LYON.—Life and Writings. .   do. $1.00
PHILIP THAXTER.—A novel.   .   .   .   do. $1.00
LITERARY ESSAYS.—By George Brimley. .   .   do. $1.50
HAYING TIME TO HOPPING.—A novel.   .   .   do. $1.25
THE VAGABOND.— Essays by Adam Badeau.   .   do. $1.00
EDGAR POE AND HIS CRITICS.—By Mrs. Whitman. do.   75 cts.
TACTICS; or, Cupid in Shoulder-Straps.   .   do. $1.00
JOHN DOE AND RICHARD ROE.—A novel.   .   do. $1.25
LOLA MONTEZ.—Her life and lectures.   .   .   do. $1.50
DEBT AND GRACE.—By Rev. C. F. Hudson.   .   do. $1.50
HUSBAND vs. WIFE.—A comic illustrated poem.   do.   50 cts.
TRANSITION.—Edited by Rev. H. S. Carpenter.   do. $1.00
ROUMANIA.—By Dr. Jas. O. Noyes, illustrated.   do. $1.50
VERNON GROVE.—A novel. .   .   .   .   do. $1.25
ANSWER TO HUGH MILLER.—By T. A. Davies.   do. $1.25
COSMOGONY.—By Thomas A. Davies.   .   8vo. cl., $1.50
NATIONAL HYMNS.—By Richard Grant White.   do. $1.50
TWENTY YEARS Around the World. J. Guy Vassar. do. $3.50
SPIRIT OF HEBREW POETRY.—By Isaac Taylor.   do. $2.50